Books by Gene Wolfe

The Book of the New Sun
   Volume One–The Shadow of the Torturer
   Volume Two–The Claw of the Conciliator
   Volume Three–The Sword of the Lictor

Published by TIMESCAPE BOOKS

Most Timescape Books are available at special quantity discounts for bulk purchases for sales promotions, premiums or fund raising. Special books or book excerpts can also be created to fit specific needs.

For details write or telephone the office of the Vice President of Special Markets, Pocket Books, 1230 Avenue of the Americas, New York, New York 10020. (212) 245-6400, ext. 1760.

THE
SWORD
OF THE
LICTOR

Volume Three of
The Book of the New Sun

GENE WOLFE

A TIMESCAPE BOOK
PUBLISHED BY POCKET BOOKS NEW YORK

Another *Original* publication of TIMESCAPE BOOKS

A Timescape Book published by
POCKET BOOKS, a Simon & Schuster division of
GULF & WESTERN CORPORATION
1230 Avenue of the Americas, New York, N.Y. 10020

Copyright © 1981 by Gene Wolfe

Library of Congress Catalog Card Number: 81-9427

ISBN: 0-671-45450-1

First Timescape Books paperback printing December, 1982

10 9 8 7 6 5 4 3 2 1

POCKET and colophon are registered trademarks of Simon & Schuster.

Use of the trademark TIMESCAPE is by exclusive license from Gregory Benford, the trademark owner.

Printed in the U.S.A.

Into the distance disappear the mounds of human heads.
I dwindle—go unnoticed now.
But in affectionate books, in children's games,
I will rise from the dead to say: the sun!

—Osip Mandelstam

Contents

THE
SWORD
OF THE
LICTOR

I

Master of the House of Chains

"IT WAS IN my hair, Severian," Dorcas said. "So I stood under the waterfall in the hot stone room—I don't know if the men's side is arranged in the same way. And every time I stepped out, I could hear them talking about me. They called you the black butcher, and other things I don't want to tell you about."

"That's natural enough," I said. "You were probably the first stranger to enter the place in a month, so it's only to be expected that they would chatter about you, and that the few women who knew who you were would be proud of it and perhaps tell some tales. As for me, I'm used to it, and you must have heard such expressions on the way here many times; I know I did."

"Yes," she admitted, and sat down on the sill of the embrasure. In the city below, the lamps of the swarming shops were beginning to fill the valley of the Acis with a yellow radiance like the petals of a jonquil, but she did not seem to see them.

"Now you understand why the regulations of the guild forbid me from taking a wife—although I will break them for you, as I have told you many times, whenever you want me to."

"You mean that it would be better for me to live somewhere else, and only come to see you once or twice a week, or wait till you came to see me."

"That's the way it's usually done. And eventually the women who talked about us today will realize that sometime they, or their sons or husbands, may find themselves beneath my hand."

"But don't you see, this is all beside the point. The thing is . . ." Here Dorcas fell silent, and then, when neither of us had spoken for some time, she rose and began to pace the room, one arm clasping the other. It was something I had never seen her do before, and I found it disturbing.

"What is the point, then?" I asked.

"That it wasn't true then. That it is now."

"I practiced the Art whenever there was work to be had. Hired myself out to towns and country justices. Several times you watched me from a window, though you never liked to stand in the crowd—for which I hardly blame you."

"I didn't watch," she said.

"I recall seeing you."

"I didn't. Not when it was actually going on. You were intent on what you were doing, and didn't see me when I went inside or covered my eyes. I used to watch, and wave to you, when you first vaulted onto the scaffold. You were so proud then, and stood just as straight as your sword, and looked so fine. You were honest. I remember watching once when there was an official of some sort up there with you, and the condemned man and a hieromonach. And yours was the only honest face."

"You couldn't possibly have seen it. I must surely have been wearing my mask."

"Severian, I didn't have to see it. I know what you look like."

"Don't I look the same now?"

"Yes," she said reluctantly. "But I have been down below. I've seen the people chained in the tunnels. When we sleep tonight, you and I in our soft bed, we will be sleeping on top of them. How many did you say there were when you took me down?"

"About sixteen hundred. Do you honestly believe those sixteen hundred would be free if I were no longer present to guard them? They were here, remember, when we came."

Dorcas would not look at me. "It's like a mass grave," she said. I could see her shoulders shake.

"It should be," I told her. "The archon could release them,

but who could resurrect those they've killed? You've never lost anyone, have you?"

She did not reply.

"Ask the wives and the mothers and the sisters of the men our prisoners have left rotting in the high country whether Abdiesus should let them go."

"Only myself," Dorcas said, and blew out the candle.

Thrax is a crooked dagger entering the heart of the mountains. It lies in a narrow defile of the valley of the Acis, and extends up it to Acies Castle. The harena, the pantheon, and the other public buildings occupy all the level land between the castle and the wall (called the Capulus) that closes the lower end of the narrow section of the valley. The private buildings of the city climb the cliffs to either side, and many are in large measure dug into the rock itself, from which practice Thrax gains one of its sobriquets—the City of Windowless Rooms.

Its prosperity it owes to its position at the head of the navigable part of the river. At Thrax, all goods shipped north on the Acis (many of which have traversed nine tenths of the length of Gyoll before entering the mouth of the smaller river, which may indeed be Gyoll's true source) must be unloaded and carried on the backs of animals if they are to travel farther. Conversely, the hetmans of the mountain tribes and the landowners of the region who wish to ship their wool and corn to the southern towns bring them to take boat at Thrax, below the cataract that roars through the arched spillway of Acies Castle.

As must always be the case when a stronghold imposes the rule of law over a turbulent region, the administration of justice was the chief concern of the archon of the city. To impose his will on those without the walls who might otherwise have opposed it, he could call upon seven squadrons of dimarchi, each under its own commander. Court convened each month, from the first appearance of the new moon to the full, beginning with the second morning watch and continuing as long as necessary to clear the day's docket. As chief executor of the archon's sentences, I was required to attend these sessions, so that he might be assured that the punishments he decreed should be made neither softer nor more severe by those who might otherwise have been charged with transmitting them to me; and to oversee the operation of the Vincula, in which the prisoners were detained, in all its details. It was a responsibility equivalent on a lesser scale to that of Master Gurloes in our Citadel, and during the first few weeks I spent in Thrax it weighed heavily upon me.

It was a maxim of Master Gurloes's that no prison is ideally situated. Like most of the wise tags put forward for the edification of young men, it was inarguable and unhelpful. All escapes fall into three categories—that is, they are achieved by stealth, by violence, or by the treachery of those set as guards. A remote place does most to render escapes by stealth difficult, and for that reason has been favored by the majority of those who have thought long upon the subject.

Unfortunately, deserts, mountaintops, and lone isles offer the most fertile fields for violent escape—if they are besieged by the prisoners' friends, it is difficult to learn of the fact before it is too late, and next to impossible to reinforce their garrisons; and similarly, if the prisoners rise in rebellion, it is highly unlikely that troops can be rushed to the spot before the issue is decided.

A facility in a well-populated and well-defended district avoids these difficulties, but incurs even more severe ones. In such places a prisoner needs, not a thousand friends, but one or two; and these need not be fighting men—a scrubwoman and a street vendor will do, if they possess intelligence and resolution. Furthermore, once the prisoner has escaped the walls, he mingles immediately with the faceless mob, so that his reapprehension is not a matter for huntsmen and dogs but for agents and informers.

In our own case, a detached prison in a remote location would have been out of the question. Even if it had been provided with a sufficient number of troops, in addition to its clavigers, to fend off the attacks of the autochthons, zoanthrops, and cultellarii who roamed the countryside, not to mention the armed retinues of the petty exultants (who could never be relied upon), it would still have been impossible to provision without the services of an army to escort the supply trains. The Vincula of Thrax is therefore located by necessity within the city—specifically, about halfway up the cliffside on the west bank, and a half league or so from the Capulus.

It is of ancient design, and always appeared to me to have been intended as a prison from the beginning, though there is a legend to the effect that it was originally a tomb, and was only a few hundred years ago enlarged and converted to its new purpose. To an observer on the more commodious east bank, it appears to be a rectangular bartizan jutting from the rock, a bartizan four stories high at the side he sees, whose flat, merloned roof terminates against the cliff. This visible portion of the structure—which many visitors to the city must take for the whole of it—is in fact the smallest and least important part. At the time I was lictor, it held no more than our administrative offices, a barracks for the clavigers, and my own living quarters.

The prisoners were lodged in a slanted shaft bored into the rock. The arrangement used was neither one of individual cells such as we had for our clients in the oubliette at home, nor the common room I had encountered while I was myself confined in the House Absolute. Instead, the prisoners were chained along the walls of the shaft, each with a stout iron collar about his neck, in such a way as to leave a path down the center wide enough that two clavigers could walk it abreast without danger that their keys might be snatched away.

This shaft was about five hundred paces long, and had over a thousand positions for prisoners. Its water supply came from a cistern sunk into the stone at the top of the cliff, and sanitary wastes were disposed of by flushing the shaft whenever this cistern threatened to overflow. A sewer drilled at the lower end of the shaft conveyed the wastewater to a conduit at the cliff base that ran through the wall of the Capulus to empty into the Acis below the city.

The rectangular bartizan clinging to the cliff, and the shaft itself, must originally have constituted the whole of the Vincula. It had subsequently been complicated by a confusion of branching galleries and parallel shafts resulting from past attempts to free prisoners by tunneling from one or another of the private residences in the cliff face, and from countermines excavated to frustrate such attempts—all now pressed into service to provide additional accommodations.

The existence of these unplanned or poorly planned additions rendered my task much more difficult than it would otherwise have been, and one of my first acts was to begin a program of closing unwanted and unnecessary passages by filling them with a mixture of river stones, sand, water, burned lime, and gravel, and to start widening and uniting those passages that remained in such a way as to eventually achieve a rational structure. Necessary though it was, this work could be carried forward only very slowly, since no more than a few hundred prisoners could be freed to work at a time, and they were for the most part in poor condition.

For the first few weeks after Dorcas and I arrived in the city, my duties left me time for nothing else. She explored it for us both, and I charged her strictly to inquire about the Pelerines for me. On the long journey from Nessus the knowledge that I carried the Claw of the Conciliator had been a heavy burden. Now, when I was no longer traveling and could no longer attempt to trace the Pelerines along the way or even reassure myself that I was walking in a direction that might eventually bring me in contact with them, it became an almost unbearable weight. While we were traveling I had slept under the stars with the gem in the top of my boot, and with it concealed in the toe on those few occasions when we were able to stop beneath a roof. Now I found that I could not sleep at all unless I had it with me, so I could assure myself, whenever I woke in the night, that I retained possession of it. Dorcas sewed a little sack of doeskin for me to hold it, and I wore it about my neck day and night. A dozen times during those first weeks I dreamed I saw the gem aflame, hanging in the air above me like its own burning cathedral, and woke to find it blazing so brightly that a faint radiance showed through the thin leather. And once or twice each night I awakened to discover that I was lying on my back with the sack on my chest seemingly grown so heavy (though I could lift it with my hand without effort) that it was crushing out my life.

Dorcas did everything in her power to comfort and assist me; yet I could see she was conscious of the abrupt change in our relationship and disturbed by it even more than I. Such changes are always, in my experience, unpleasant—if only because they imply the likelihood of further change. While we had been journeying together (and we had been traveling with greater or lesser expedition from the moment in the Garden of Endless Sleep when Dorcas helped me clamber, half-drowned, onto the floating walkway of sedge) it had been as equals and companions, each of us walking every league we covered on our own feet or riding our own mount. If I had supplied a measure of physical protection to Dorcas, she had equally supplied a certain moral shelter to me, in that few could pretend for long to despise her innocent beauty, or profess horror at my office when in looking at me they could not help but see her as well. She had been my counselor in perplexity and my comrade in a hundred desert places.

When we at last entered Thrax and I presented Master Palaemon's letter to the archon, all that was by necessity ended. In my fuligin habit I no longer had to fear the crowd—rather, they feared me as the highest official of the most dreaded arm of the state. Dorcas lived now, not as an equal but as the paramour the Cumaean had once called her, in the quarters in the Vincula set aside for me. Her counsel had become useless or nearly so because the difficulties that oppressed me were the legal and administrative ones I had been trained for years to wrestle with and about which she knew nothing; and moreover because I seldom had the time or the energy to explain them to her so that we might discuss them.

Thus, while I stood for watch after watch in the archon's court, Dorcas fell into the habit of wandering the city, and we, who had been incessantly together throughout the latter part of the spring, came now in summer to see each other hardly at all, sharing a meal in the evening and climbing exhausted into a bed where we seldom did more than fall asleep in each other's arms.

At last the full moon shone. With what joy I beheld it from the roof of the bartizan, green as an emerald in its mantle of forest and round as the lip of a cup! I was not yet free, since all the details of excruciations and administration that had been accumulating during my attendance on the archon remained to be dealt with; but I was now at least free to devote my full attention to them, which seemed then nearly as good a thing as freedom itself. I had invited Dorcas to go with me on the next day, when I made an inspection of the subterranean parts of the Vincula.

It was an error. She grew ill in the foul air, surrounded by the misery of the prisoners. That night, as I have already recounted, she told me she had gone to the public baths (a rare thing for her, whose fear of water was so great that she washed herself bit by bit with a sponge dipped in a bowl no deeper than a dish of soup) to free her hair and skin from the odor of the shaft, and that she had heard the bath attendants pointing her out to the other patrons.

II

Upon the Cataract

THE FOLLOWING MORNING, before she left the bartizan, Dorcas cut her hair until she almost seemed a boy, and thrust a white peony through the circulet that confined it. I labored over documents until afternoon, then borrowed a layman's jelab from the sergeant of my clavigers and went out hoping to encounter her.

The brown book I carry says there is nothing stranger than to explore a city wholly different from all those one knows, since to do so is to explore a second and unsuspected self. I have found a thing stranger: to explore such a city only after one has lived in it for some time without learning anything of it.

I did not know where the baths Dorcas had mentioned stood, though I had surmised from talk I had heard in court that they existed. I did not know where the bazaar where she bought her cloth and cosmetics was located, or even if there were more than one. I knew nothing, in short, beyond what I could see from the embrasure, and the brief route from the Vincula to the archon's palace. I had, perhaps, a too-ready confidence in my own ability to find my way about in a city so much smaller than Nessus; even so I took the precaution of making certain from time to time, as I trod the crooked streets that straggled down the cliff between cave-houses excavated from the rock and swallow-houses jutting out from it, that I could still see the familiar shape of the bartizan, with its barricaded gate and black gonfalon.

In Nessus the rich live toward the north where the waters of Gyoll are purer, and the poor to the south where they are foul. Here in Thrax that custom no longer held, both because the Acis flowed so swiftly that the excrement of those upstream (who were, of course, but a thousandth part as numerous as those who lived about the northern reaches of Gyoll) hardly affected its flood, and because water taken from above the cataract was conveyed to the public fountains and the homes of the wealthy by aqueducts, so that no reliance had to be put upon the river save when the largest quantities of water—as for manufacturing or wholesale washing—were required.

Thus in Thrax the separation was by elevation. The wealthiest lived on the lowest slopes near the river, within easy reach of the shops and public offices, where a brief walk brought them to piers from which they could travel the length of the city in slave-rowed caïques. Those somewhat less well off had their houses higher, the middle class in general had theirs higher still, and so on until the very poorest dwelt just below the fortifications at the cliff tops, often in jacals of mud and reeds that could be reached only by long ladders.

I was to see something of those miserable hovels, but for the present I remained in the commercial quarter near the water. There the narrow streets were so thronged with people that I at first thought a festival was in progress, or perhaps that the war—which had seemed so remote while I remained in Nessus but had become progressively more immediate as Dorcas and I journeyed north—was now near enough to fill the city with those who fled before it.

Nessus is so extensive that it has, as I have heard said, five buildings for each living inhabitant. In Thrax that ratio is surely reversed, and on that day it seemed to me at times that there must have been fifty for each roof. Too, Nessus is a cosmopolitan city, so that although one saw many foreigners there, and occasionally even cacogens come by ship from other worlds, one was always conscious that they *were* foreigners, far from their homes. Here the streets swarmed with diverse humanity, but they merely reflected the diverse nature of the mountain setting, so that when I saw, for example, a man whose hat was made from a bird's pelt with the wings used for ear flaps, or a man in a shaggy coat of kaberu skin, or a man with a tattooed face, I might see a hundred more such tribesmen around the next corner.

These men were eclectics, the descendants of settlers from the south who had mixed their blood with that of the squat, dark autochthons, adopted certain of their customs, and mingled these with still others acquired from the amphitryons farther north and those, in some instances, of even less-known peoples, traders and parochial races.

Many of these eclectics favor knives that are curved—or as they are sometimes called, bent—having two relatively straight sections, with an elbow a little toward the point. This shape is said to make it easier to pierce the heart by stabbing beneath the breastbone; the blades are stiffened with a central rib, are sharpened on both sides, and are kept very sharp; there is no guard, and their hafts are commonly of bone. (I have described these knives in detail because they are as characteristic of the region as anything can be said to be, and because it is from them that Thrax takes another of its names: the City of Crooked Knives. There is also the resemblance of the plan of the city to the blade of such a knife, the curve of the defile corresponding to the curve of the blade, the River Acis to the central rib, Acies Castle to the point, and the Capulus to the line at which the steel vanishes into the haft.)

One of the keepers of the Bear Tower once told me that there is no animal so dangerous or so savage and unmanageable as the hybrid resulting when a fighting dog mounts a she-wolf. We are accustomed to think of the beasts of the forest and mountain as wild, and to think of the men who spring up, as it seems, from their soil as savage. But the truth is that there is a wildness more vicious (as we would know better if we were not so habituated to it) in certain domestic animals, despite their understanding so much human speech and sometimes even speaking a few words; and there is a more profound savagery in men and women whose ancestors have lived in cities and towns since the dawn of humanity. Vodalus, in whose veins flowed the undefiled blood of a thousand exultants—exarchs, ethnarchs, and starosts—was capable of violence unimaginable to the autochthons that stalked the streets of Thrax, naked beneath their huanaco cloaks.

Like the dog-wolves (which I never saw, because they were too vicious to be useful), these eclectics took all that was most cruel and ungovernable from their mixed parentage; as friends or followers they were sullen, disloyal, and contentious; as enemies, fierce, deceitful, and vindictive. So at least I had heard from my subordinates at the Vincula, for eclectics made up more than half the prisoners there.

I have never encountered men whose language, costume, or customs are foreign without speculating on the nature of the women of their race. There is always a connection, since the two are the growths of a single culture, just as the leaves of a tree, which one sees, and the fruit, which one does not see because it is hidden by the leaves, are the growths of a single organism. But the observer who would venture to predict the appearance and flavor of the fruit from the outline of a few leafy boughs seen (as it were) from a distance, must know a great deal about leaves and fruit if he is not to make himself ridiculous.

Warlike men may be born of languishing women, or they may have sisters nearly as strong as themselves and more resolute. And so I, walking among crowds composed largely of these eclectics and the townsmen (who seemed to me not much different from the citizens of Nessus, save that their clothing and their manners were somewhat rougher) found myself speculating on dark-eyed, dark-skinned women, women with glossy black hair as thick as the tails of the skewbald mounts of their brothers, women whose faces I imagined as strong yet delicate, women given to ferocious resistance and swift surrender, women who could be won but not bought—if such women exist in this world.

From their arms I traveled in imagination to the places where they might be found, the lonely huts crouched by mountain springs, the hide yurts standing alone in the high pastures. Soon I was as intoxicated with the thought of the mountains as I had been once, before Master Palaemon had told me the correct location of Thrax, with the idea of the sea. How glorious are they, the immovable idols of Urth, carved with unaccountable tools in a time inconceivably ancient, still lifting above the rim of the world grim heads crowned with mitres, tiaras, and diadems spangled with snow, heads whose eyes are as large as towns, figures whose shoulders are wrapped in forests.

Thus, disguised in the dull jelab of a townsman, I elbowed my way down streets packed with humanity and reeking with the odors of ordure and cookery, with my imagination filled with visions of hanging stone, and crystal streams like carcanets.

Thecla must, I think, have been taken at least into the foothills of these heights, no doubt to escape the heat of some particularly torrid summer; for many of the scenes that rose in my mind (as it seemed, of their own accord) were noticeably childlike. I saw rock-loving plants whose virginal flowers I beheld with an immediacy of vision no adult achieves without kneeling; abysses that seemed not only frightening but shocking, as though their existence were an affront to the laws of nature; peaks so high they appeared to be literally without summit, as though the whole world had been falling forever from some unimaginable Heaven, which yet retained its hold on these mountains.

Eventually I reached Acies Castle, having walked almost the entire length of the city. I made my identity known to the postern guards there and was permitted to enter and climb to the top of the donjon, as I had once climbed our Matachin Tower before taking my leave of Master Palaemon.

When I had gone there to make my farewell to the only place I had known, I had stood at one of the loftiest points of the Citadel, which was itself poised atop one of the highest elevations in the whole area of Nessus. The city had been spread before me to the limits of vision, with Gyoll traced across it like the green slime of a slug across a map; even the Wall had been visible on the horizon at some points, and nowhere was I beneath the shadow of a summit much superior to my own.

Here the impression was far different. I bestrode the Acis, which leaped toward me down a succession of rocky steps each twice or three times the height of a tall tree. Beaten to a foaming whiteness that glittered in the sunlight, it disappeared beneath me and reappeared as a ribbon of silver racing through a city as neatly contained in its declivity as one of those toy villages in a box that I (but it was Thecla) recalled receiving on a birthday.

Yet I stood, as it were, at the bottom of a bowl. On every side the walls of stone ascended, so that to look at any one of them was to believe, for a moment at least, that gravity had been twisted until it stood at right angles to its proper self by some sorcerer's multiplication with imaginary numbers, and the height I saw was properly the level surface of the world.

For a watch or more, I think, I stared up at those walls, and traced the spidery lines of the waterfalls that dashed down them in thunder and clean romance to join the Acis, and watched the clouds trapped among them that seemed to press softly against their unyielding sides like sheep bewildered and dismayed among pens of stone.

Then I grew weary at last of the magnificence of the mountains and my mountain dreams—or rather, not weary, but dizzied by them until my head reeled with vertigo, and I seemed to see those merciless heights even when I closed my eyes, and felt that in my dreams, that night and for many nights, I would fall from their precipices, or cling with bloody fingers to their hopeless walls.

Then I turned in earnest to the city and reassured myself with the sight of the bartizan of the Vincula, a very modest little cube now, cemented to a cliff that was hardly more than a ripple among the incalculable waves of stone around it. I plotted the courses of the principal streets, seeking (as in a game, to sober myself from my long gazing on the mountains) to identify those I had walked in reaching the castle, and to observe from this new perspective the buildings and market squares I had seen on the way. By eye I looted the bazaars, finding that there were two, one on either side of the river; and I marked afresh the familiar landmarks I had learned to know from the embrasure of the Vincula—the harena, the pantheon, and the archon's palace. Then, when everything I had seen from the ground had been confirmed from my new vantage point, and I felt I understood the spatial relationship of the place at which I stood to what I had known earlier of the plan of the city, I began to explore the lesser streets, peering along the twisted paths that climbed the upper cliffs and probing narrow alleys that often seemed no more than mere bands of darkness between buildings.

In seeking them out, my gaze came at last to the margins of the river again, and I began to study the landings there, and the storehouses, and even the pyramids of barrels and boxes and bales that waited there to be carried aboard some vessel. Now the water no longer foamed, save when it was obstructed by the piers. Its color was nearly indigo, and like the indigo shadows seen at evening on a snowy day, it seemed to slip silently along, sinuous and freezing; but the motion of the hurrying caiques and laden feluccas showed how much turbulence lay concealed beneath that smooth surface, for the larger craft swung their long bowsprits like fencers, and both yawed crabwise at times while their oars threshed the racing eddies.

When I had exhausted all that lay farther downstream, I leaned from the parapet to observe the closest reach of the river and a wharf that was no more than a hundred strides from the postern gate. Looking down at the stevedores there who toiled to unburden one of the narrow river boats, I saw near them, unmoving, a tiny figure with bright hair. At first I thought her a child because she seemed so small beside the burly, nearly naked laborers; but it was Dorcas, sitting at the very edge of the water with her face in her hands.

III

Outside the Jacal

WHEN I REACHED Dorcas I could not make her speak. It was not simply that she was angry with me, although I thought so at the time. Silence had come upon her like a disease, not injuring her tongue and lips but disabling her will to use them and perhaps even her desire to, just as certain infections destroy our desire for pleasure and even our comprehension of joy in others. If I did not lift her face to mine, she would look at nothing, staring at the ground beneath her feet without, I think, seeing even that, or covering her face with her hands, as she had been covering it when I found her.

I wanted to talk to her, believing—then—that I could say something, though I was not certain what, that would restore her to herself. But I could not do so there on the wharf, with stevedores staring at us, and for a time I could find no place to which I could lead her. On a little street nearby that had begun to climb the slope east of the river, I saw the board of an inn. There were patrons eating in its narrow common room, but for a few aes I was able to rent a chamber on the floor above it, a place with no furniture but a bed and little space for any, with a ceiling so low that at one end I could not stand erect. The hostess thought we were renting her chamber for a tryst, naturally enough under the circumstances—but thought too, because of Dorcas's despairing expression, that I had some hold on her or had bought her from a procurer, and so gave her a look of melting sympathy that I do not believe she noticed in the least, and me one of recrimination.

I shut and bolted the door and made Dorcas lie on the bed; then I sat beside her and tried to cajole her into conversation, asking her what was wrong, and what I might do to right whatever it was that troubled her, and so on. When I found that had no effect, I began to talk about myself, supposing that it was only her horror of the conditions in the Vincula that had moved her to sever herself from discourse with me.

"We are despised by everyone," I said. "And so there is no reason why I should not be despised by you. The surprising thing is not that you should have come to hate me now, but that you could go this long before coming to feel as the rest do. But because I love you, I am going to try to state the case for our guild, and thus for myself, hoping that perhaps afterward you won't feel so badly about having loved a torturer, even though you don't love me any longer.

"We are not cruel. We take no delight in what we do, except in doing it well, which means doing it quickly and doing neither more nor less than the law instructs us. We obey the judges, who hold their offices because the people consent to it. Some individuals tell us we should do nothing of what we do, and that no one should do it. They say that punishment inflicted with cold blood is a greater crime than any crime our clients could have committed.

"There may be justice in that, but it is a justice that would destroy the whole Commonwealth. No one could feel safe and no one could be safe, and in the end the people would rise up—at first against the thieves and the murderers, and then against anyone who offended the popular ideas of propriety, and at last against mere strangers and outcasts. Then they would be back to the old horrors of stoning and burning, in which every man seeks to outdo his neighbor for fear he will be thought tomorrow to hold some sympathy for the wretch dying today.

"There are others who tell us that certain clients are deserving of the most severe punishment, but that others are not, and that we should refuse to perform our office upon those others. It certainly must be that some are more guilty than the rest, and it may even be that some of these who are handed over to us have done no wrong at all, neither in the matter in which they are accused, nor in any other.

"But the people who urge these arguments are doing no more than setting themselves up as judges over the judges appointed by the Autarch, judges with less training in the law and without the authority to call witnesses. They demand that we disobey the real judges and listen to them, but they cannot show that they are more deserving of our obedience.

"Others yet hold that our clients should not be tortured or executed, but should be made to labor for the Commonwealth, digging canals, building watchtowers, and the like. But with the cost of their guards and chains, honest workers might be hired, who otherwise would want for bread. Why should these loyal workers starve so that murderers shall not die, nor thieves feel any pain? Furthermore, these murderers and thieves, being without loyalty to the law and without hope of reward, would not work save under the lash. What is that lash but torture again, going under a new name?

"Still others say that all those judged guilty should be confined, in comfort and without pain, for many years—and often for as long as they will live. But those who have comfort and no pain live long, and every orichalk spent to maintain them so would have to be taken from better purposes. I know little of the war, but I know enough to understand how much money is needed to buy weapons and pay soldiers. The fighting is in the mountains to the north now, so that we fight as if behind a hundred walls. But what if it should reach the pampas? Would it be possible to hold back the Ascians when there was so much room to maneuver? And how would Nessus be fed if the herds there were to fall into their hands?

"If the guilty are not to be locked away in comfort, and are not to be tortured, what remains? If they are all killed, and all killed alike, then a poor woman who steals will be thought as bad as a mother who poisons her own child, as Morwenna of Saltus did. Would you wish that? In time of peace, many might be banished. But to banish them now would only be to deliver a corps of spies to the Ascians, to be trained and supplied with funds and sent back among us. Soon no one could be trusted, though he spoke our own tongue. Would you wish that?"

Dorcas lay so silent upon the bed that I thought for a moment she had fallen asleep. But her eyes, those enormous eyes of perfect blue, were open; and when I leaned over to look at her, they moved, and seemed for a time to watch me as they might have watched the spreading ripples in a pond.

"All right, we are devils," I said. "If you would have it so. But we are necessary. Even the powers of Heaven find it necessary to employ devils."

Tears came into her eyes, though I could not tell whether she wept because she had hurt me or because she found that I was still present. In the hope of winning her back to her old affection for me, I began to talk of the times when we were still on the way to Thrax, reminding her of how we had met in the clearing after we had fled the grounds of the House Absolute, and of how we had talked in those great gardens before Dr. Talos's play, walking through the blossoming orchard to sit on an old bench beside a broken fountain, and of all she had said to me there, and of all that I had said to her.

And it seemed to me that she became a trifle less sorrowful until I mentioned the fountain, whose waters had run from its cracked basin to form a little stream that some gardener had sent wandering among the trees to refresh them, and there to end by soaking the ground; but then a darkness that was nowhere in the room but on Dorcas's face came to settle there like one of those strange things that had pursued Jonas and me through the cedars. Then she would no longer look at me, and after a time she truly slept.

I got up as silently as I could, unbolted the door, and went down the crooked stair. The hostess was still working in the common room below, but the patrons who had been there were gone. I explained to her that the woman I had brought was ill, paid the rent of the room for several days, and promising to return and take care of any other expenses, asked her to look in on her from time to time, and to feed her if she would eat.

"Ah, it will be a blessing to us to have someone sleeping in the room," the hostess said. "But if your darling's sick, is the Duck's Nest the best place you can find for her? Can't you take her home?"

"I'm afraid living in my house is what has made her ill. At least, I don't want to risk the chance that returning there will make her worse."

"Poor darling!" The hostess shook her head. "So pretty too, and doesn't look more than a child. How old is she?"

I told her I did not know.

"Well, I'll have a visit with her and give her some soup when she's ready for it." She looked at me as if to say that the time would come soon enough once I was away. "But I want you to know that I won't hold her a prisoner for you. If she wants to leave, she'll be free to go."

When I stepped out of the little inn, I wished to return to the Vincula by the most direct route; but I made the mistake of supposing that since the narrow street on which the Duck's Nest stood ran almost due south, it would be quicker to continue along it and cross the Acis lower down than to retrace the steps Dorcas and I had already taken and go back to the foot of the postern wall of Acies Castle.

The narrow street betrayed me, as I would have expected if I had been more familiar with the ways of Thrax. For all those crooked streets that snake along the slopes, though they may cross one another, on the whole run up and down; so that to reach one cliff-hugging house from another (unless they are quite close together or one above the other) it is necessary to walk down to the central strip near the river, and then back up again. Thus before long I found myself as high up the eastern cliff as the Vincula was on the western one, with less prospect of reaching it than I had when I left the inn.

To be truthful, it was not a wholly unpleasant discovery. I had work to do there, and no particular desire to do it, my mind being still full of thoughts of Dorcas. It felt better to wear out my frustrations by the use of my legs, and so I resolved to follow the capering street to the top if need be and see the Vincula and Acies Castle from that height, and then to show my badge of office to the guards at the fortifications there and walk along them to the Capulus and so cross the river by the lowest way.

But after half a watch of strenuous effort, I found I could go no farther. The street ended against a precipice three or four chains high, and perhaps had properly ended sooner, for the last few score paces I had walked had been on what was probably no more than a private path to the miserable jacal of mud and sticks before which I stood.

After making certain there was no way around it, and no way to the top for some distance from where I stood, I was about to turn away in disgust when a child slipped out of the jacal, and sidling toward me in a half bold, half fearful way, watching me with its right eye only, extended a small and very dirty hand in the universal gesture of beggars. Perhaps I would have laughed at the poor little creature, so timid and so importunate, if I had felt in a better mood; as it was, I dropped a few aes into the soiled palm.

Encouraged, the child ventured to say, "My sister is sick. Very sick, sieur." From the timbre of its voice I decided it was a boy; and because he turned his head almost toward me when he spoke, I could see that his left eye was swollen shut by some infection. Tears of pus had run from it to dry on the cheek below. "Very, very sick."

"I see," I told him.

"Oh, no, sieur. You cannot, not from here. But if you wish you can look in through the door—you will not bother her."

Just then a man wearing the scuffed leather apron of a mason called, "What is it, Jader? What does he want?" He was toiling up the path in our direction.

As anyone might have anticipated, the boy was only frightened into silence by the question. I said, "I was asking the best way to the lower city."

The mason answered nothing, but stopped about four strides from me and folded arms that looked harder than the stones they broke. He seemed angry and distrustful, though I could not be sure why. Perhaps my accent had betrayed that I came from the south; perhaps it was only because of the way I was dressed, which though it was by no means rich or fantastic, indicated that I belonged to a social class higher than his own.

"Am I trespassing?" I asked. "Do you own this place?"

There was no reply. Whatever he felt about me, it was plain that in his opinion there could be no communication between us. When I spoke to him, it could only be as a man speaks to a beast, and not even to intelligent beasts at that, but only as a drover shouts at kine. And on his side, when I spoke it was only as beasts speak to a man, a sound made in the throat.

I have noticed that in books this sort of stalemate never seems to occur; the authors are so anxious to move their stories forward (however wooden they may be, advancing like market carts with squeaking wheels that are never still, though they go only to dusty villages where the charm of the country is lost and the pleasures of the city will never be found) that there are no such misunderstandings, no refusals to negotiate. The assassin who holds a dagger to his victim's neck is eager to discuss the whole matter, and at any length the victim or the author may wish. The passionate pair in love's embrace are at least equally willing to postpone the stabbing, if not more so.

In life it is not the same. I stared at the mason, and he at me. I felt I could have killed him, but I could not be sure of it, both because he looked unusually strong and because I could not be certain he did not have some concealed weapon, or friends in the miserable dwellings close by. I felt he was about to spit onto the path between us, and if he had I would have flung my jelab over his head and pinned him. But he did not, and when we had stared at each other for several moments, the boy, who perhaps had no idea of what was taking place said again, "You can look through the door, sieur. You won't bother my sister." He even dared to tug a little at my sleeve in his eagerness to show he had not lied, not seeming to realize that his own appearance justified any amount of begging.

"I believe you," I said. But then I understood that to say I believed him was to insult him by showing that I did not have faith enough in what he said to put it to the test. I bent and peered, though at first I could see little, looking as I was from the bright sunshine into the shadowy interior of the jacal.

The light was almost squarely behind me. I felt its pressure on the nape of my neck, and I was conscious that the mason could attack me with impunity now that my back was toward him.

Tiny as it was, the room inside was not cluttered. Some straw had been heaped against the wall farthest from the door, and the girl lay upon it. She was in that state of disease in which we no longer feel pity for the sick person, who has instead become an object of horror. Her face was a death's head over which was stretched skin as thin and translucent as the head of a drum. Her lips could no longer cover her teeth even in sleep, and under the scythe of fever, her hair had fallen away until only wisps remained.

I braced my hands on the mud and wattle wall beside the door and straightened up. The boy said, "You see she is very sick, sieur. My sister." He held out his hand again.

I saw it—I see it before me now—but it made no immediate impression on my mind. I could think only of the Claw; and it seemed to me that it was pressing against my breastbone, not so much like a weight as like the knuckles of an invisible fist. I remembered the uhlan who had appeared dead until I touched his lips with the Claw, and who now seemed to me to belong to the remote past; and I remembered the man-ape, with his stump of arm, and the way Jonas's burns had faded when I ran the Claw along their length. I had not used it or even considered using it since it had failed to save Jolenta.

Now I had kept its secret so long that I was afraid to try it again. I would have touched the dying girl with it, perhaps, if it had not been for her brother looking on; I would have touched the brother's diseased eye with it if it had not been for the surly mason. As it was, I only labored to breathe against the force that strained my ribs, and did nothing, walking away downhill without noticing in what direction I walked. I heard the mason's saliva fly from his mouth and smack the eroded stone of the path behind me; but I did not know what the sound was until I was almost back at the Vincula and had more or less returned to myself.

IV

In the Bartizan of the Vincula

"YOU HAVE COMPANY, Lictor," the sentry told me, and when I only nodded to acknowledge the information, he added, "It might be best for you to change first, Lictor." I did not need then to ask who my guest was; only the presence of the archon would have drawn that tone from him.

It was not difficult to reach my private quarters without passing through the study where I conducted the business of the Vincula and kept its accounts. I spent the time it took to divest myself of my borrowed jelab and put on my fuligin cloak in speculating as to why the archon, who had never come to me before, and whom, for that matter, I had seldom even seen outside his court, should find it necessary to visit the Vincula—so far as I could see, without an entourage.

The speculation was welcome because it kept certain other thoughts at a distance. There was a large silvered glass in our bedroom, a much more effective mirror than the small plates of polished metal to which I was accustomed; and on it, as I saw for the first time when I stood before it to examine my appearance, Dorcas had scrawled in soap four lines from a song she had once sung for me:

> Horns of Urth, you fling notes to the sky,
> Green and good, green and good.
> Sing at my step; a sweeter glade have I.
> Lift, oh, lift me to the fallen wood!

There were several large chairs in the study, and I had anticipated finding the archon in one of them (though it had also
crossed my mind that he might be availing himself of the
opportunity to go through my papers—something he had
every right to do if he chose). He was standing at the embrasure instead, looking out over his city much as I myself had
looked out at it from the ramparts of Acies Castle earlier that
afternoon. His hands were clasped behind him, and as I
watched I saw them move as if each possessed a life of its
own, engendered by his thoughts. It was some time before he
turned and caught sight of me.

"You are here, Master Torturer. I did not hear you come
in."

"I am only a journeyman, Archon."

He smiled and seated himself on the sill, his back to the
drop. His face was coarse, with a hook nose and large eyes
rimmed with dark flesh, but it was not a masculine face; it
might almost have been the face of an ugly woman. "Charged
by me with the responsibility for this place, you remain a
mere journeyman?"

"I can be elevated only by the masters of our guild,
Archon."

"But you are the best of their journeymen, judging from the
letter you carried, from their choosing you to send here, and
from the work you've done since you arrived. Anyway, no one
here would know the difference if you chose to put on airs.
How many masters are there?"

"I would know, Archon. Only two, unless someone has
been elevated since I've been gone."

"I'll write them and ask them to elevate you *in absentia.*"

"I thank you, Archon."

"It's nothing," he said, and turned to stare out the embrasure as though the situation embarrassed him. "You should
have word of it, I suppose, in a month."

"They will not elevate me, Archon. But it will make Master
Palaemon happy to hear you think so well of me."

He swung around again to look at me. "We need not be so
formal, surely. My name is Abdiesus, and there is no reason
you should not use it when we're alone. You're Severian, I
believe?"

I nodded.

He turned away again. "This is a very low opening. I was
examining it before you came in, and the wall hardly reaches

above my knees. It would be easy, I'm afraid, for someone to fall out of it."

"Only for someone as tall as yourself, Abdiesus."

"In the past, were not executions performed, occasionally, by casting the victim from a high window or from the edge of a precipice?"

"Yes, both those methods have been employed."

"Not by you, I suppose." Once more he faced me.

"Not within living memory, so far as I know, Abdiesus. I have performed decollations—both with the block and with the chair—but that is all."

"But you would have no objection to the use of other means? If you were instructed to employ them?"

"I am here to carry out the archon's sentences."

"There are times, Severian, when public executions serve the public good. There are others when they would only do harm by inciting public unrest."

"That is understood, Abdiesus," I said. As sometimes I have seen in the eyes of a boy the worry of the man he will be, I could see the future guilt that had already come (perhaps without his being aware of it) to settle on the archon's face.

"There will be a few guests at the palace tonight. I hope that you will be among them, Severian."

I bowed. "Among the divisions of administration, Abdiesus, it has long been customary to exclude one—my own—from the society of the others."

"And you feel that is unjust, which is wholly natural. Tonight, if you wish to think of it in that way, we will be making some restitution."

"We of the guild have never complained of injustice. Indeed, we have gloried in our unique isolation. Tonight, however, the others may feel they have reason to protest to you."

A smile twitched at his mouth. "I'm not concerned about that. Here, this will get you onto the grounds." He extended his hand, holding delicately, as though he feared it would flutter from his fingers, one of those disks of stiff paper, no bigger than a chrisos and lettered in gold leaf with ornate characters, of which I had often heard Thecla speak (she stirred in my mind at the touch of it), but which I had never before seen.

"Thank you, Archon. Tonight, you said? I will try to find suitable clothing."

"Come dressed as you are. It's to be a ridotto—your habit

will be your costume." He stood and stretched himself with the air, I thought, of one who nears the completion of a long and disagreeable task. "A moment ago we spoke of some of the less elaborate ways that you might perform your function. It might be well for you to bring whatever equipment you will require tonight."

I understood. I would need nothing beyond my hands, and told him so; then, feeling I had already been remiss in my duties as his host, I invited him to take what refreshment we had.

"No," he said. "If you knew how much I am forced to eat and drink for courtesy's sake, you'd know how much I relish the company of someone whose hospitable offers I can refuse. I don't suppose your fraternity has ever considered using food as a torment, instead of starvation?"

"It is called planteration, Archon."

"You must tell me about it sometime. I can see your guild is far ahead of my imagination—no doubt by a dozen centuries. After hunting, yours must be the oldest science of them all. But I cannot stay longer. We will see you at evening?"

"It is nearly evening now, Archon."

"At the end of the next watch then."

He went out; it was not until the door closed behind him that I detected the faint odor of the musk that had perfumed his robe.

I looked at the little circle of paper I held, turning it over in my hand. Pictured on the back were a falsity of masks, in which I recognized one of the horrors—a face that was no more than a mouth ringed with fangs—I had seen in the Autarch's garden when the cacogens tore away their disguises, and a man-ape's face from the abandoned mine near Saltus.

I was tired from my long walk as well as from the work (almost a full day's, for I had risen early) that had preceded it; and so before going out again I undressed and washed myself, ate some fruit and cold meat, and sipped a glass of the spicy northern tea. When a problem troubles me deeply, it remains in my mind even when I am unaware of it. So it was with me then; though I was not conscious of them, the thought of Dorcas lying in her narrow, slant-ceilinged room in the inn and the memory of the dying girl on her straw bound my eyes and stopped my ears. It was because of them, I think, that I did not hear my sergeant, and did not know, until he entered, that I had been taking up kindling from its box beside the fireplace and breaking the sticks with my hands. He asked if I were going out again, and since he was responsible for the operation of the Vincula in my absence I told him I was, and that I could not say when I would return. Then I thanked him for the loan of his jelab, which I said I would not need again.

"You are welcome to it anytime, Lictor. But that was not what concerned me. I wanted to suggest that you take a couple of our clavigers when you go down to the city."

"Thank you," I said. "But it is well policed, and I will be in no danger."

He cleared his throat. "It's a matter of the prestige of the Vincula, Lictor. As our commander, you should have an escort."

I could see he was lying, but I could also see that he was lying for what he believed to be my good, and so I said, "I will consider it, assuming you have two presentable men you can spare."

He brightened at once.

"However," I continued, "I don't want them to carry weapons. I'm going to the palace, and it would be insulting to our master the archon if I were to arrive with an armed guard."

At that he began to stammer, and I turned on him as though I were furious, throwing down the splintered wood so that it crashed against the floor. "Out with it! You think I am threatened. What is it?"

"Nothing, Lictor. Nothing that concerns you, particularly. It is just . . ."

"Just what?" Knowing he was going to speak now, I went to the sideboard and poured us two cups of rosolio.

"There have been several murders in the city, Lictor. Three last night, two the night before. Thank you, Lictor. To your health."

"To yours. But murders are nothing unusual, are they? The eclectics are forever stabbing one another."

"These men were burned to death, Lictor. I really don't know much about it—no one seems to. Possibly you know more yourself." The sergeant's face was as expressionless as a carving of coarse, brown stone; but I saw him look quickly at the cold fireplace as he spoke, and I knew he attributed my breaking of the sticks (the sticks that had been so hard and dry in my hands but that I had not felt there until long after he entered, just as Abdiesus had not, perhaps, realized he was contemplating his own death until long after I had come to watch him) to something, some dark secret, the archon had imparted to me, when in fact it was nothing more than the memory of Dorcas and her despair, and of the beggar girl, whom I confused with her. He said, "I have two good fellows waiting outside, Lictor. They're ready to go whenever you are, and they will wait for you until you're ready to come back."

I told him that was very good, and he turned away at once so I would not guess he knew, or believed he knew, more than he had reported to me; but his stiff shoulders and corded neck, and the quick steps he took toward the door, conveyed more information than his stony eyes ever could.

My escorts were beefy men chosen for their strength. Flourishing their big, iron claves, they accompanied me as I shouldered *Terminus Est* down the winding streets, walking to either side when the way was wide enough, before and behind me when it was not. At the edge of the Acis I dismissed them, making them the more eager to leave me by telling them they had my permission to spend the remainder of the evening as they saw fit, and hired a narrow little caique (with a gaily painted canopy I had no need of now that the day's last watch was over) to carry me upriver to the palace.

It was the first time I had actually ridden on the Acis. As I sat in the stern, between the steersman-owner and his four oarsmen, with the clear, icy river rushing by so near that I could have trailed both hands in it if I wished, it seemed impossible that this frail wooden shell, which from the embrasure of our bartizan must have appeared no more than a dancing insect, could hope to gain a span against the current. Then the steersman spoke and we were off—hugging the bank to be sure, but seeming almost to skip over the river like a thrown stone, so rapid and perfectly timed were the strokes of our eight oars and so light and narrow and smooth were we, traveling more in the air above the water than in the water itself. A pentagonal lantern set with panes of amethyst glass hung from the sternpost; just at the moment when I, in my ignorance, thought we were at the point of being caught amidships by the current, capsized, and swept sinking down to the Capulus, the steersman let the tiller hang by its lashings while he lit the wick.

He was right, of course, and I wrong. As the little door of the lantern shut upon the butter-yellow flame within and the violet beams leaped forth, an eddy caught us, spun us about, whirled us upstream a hundred strides or more while the rowers shipped their oars, and left us in a miniature bay as quiet as a millpond and half-filled with gaudy pleasure boats. Water stairs, very similar to the steps from which I had swum in Gyoll as a boy though much cleaner, marched out of the depths of the river and up to the brilliant torches and elaborate gates of the palace grounds.

I had often seen this palace from the Vincula, and thus I knew that it was not the subterranean structure modeled on the House Absolute that I might otherwise have expected. No more was it any such grim fortress as our Citadel—apparently the archon and his predecessors had considered the strongpoints of Acies Castle and the Capulus, doubly linked as they were by the walls and forts strung along the crests of the cliffs, sufficient security for the safety of the city. Here the ramparts were mere box hedges intended to exclude the gaze of the curious and perhaps to give a check to casual thieves. Buildings with gilded domes were scattered over a pleasance that seemed intimate and colorful; from my embrasure they had looked much like peridots broken from their string and dropped upon a figured carpet.

There were sentries at the filigree gates, dismounted troopers in steel corselets and helmets, with blazing lances and long-bladed cavalry spathae; but they had the air of minor and amateur actors, good-natured, hard-bitten men enjoying a respite from running fights and wind-swept patrols. The pair to whom I showed my circle of painted paper no more than glanced at it before waving me inside.

V

Cyriaca

I WAS ONE of the first guests to arrive. There were more bustling servants still than masquers, servants who seemed to have begun their work only a moment before, and to be determined to complete it at once. They lit candelabra with crystal lenses and coronas lucis suspended from the upper limbs of the trees, carried out trays of food and drink, positioned them, shifted them, then carried them back to one of the domed buildings again—the three acts being performed by three servants, but occasionally (no doubt because the others were busy elsewhere) by one.

For a time I wandered about the grounds, admiring the flowers by the fast fading twilight. Then, glimpsing people in costume between the pillars of a pavilion, I strolled inside to join them.

What such a gathering could be in the House Absolute, I have already described. Here, where the society was entirely provincial, it had, rather, the atmosphere of children playing dress-up in their parents' old clothing; I saw men and women costumed as autochthons, with their faces stained russet and dabbed with white, and even one man who was an autochthon and yet was dressed like one, in a costume no more and no less authentic than the others, so that I was inclined to laugh at him until I realized that though he and I might be the only ones who knew it, he was in fact costumed more originally than any of the rest, as a citizen of Thrax in costume. Around all these autochthons, real and self-imagined, were a score of other figures not less absurd—officers dressed as women and women dressed as soldiers, eclectics as fraudulent as the autochthons, gymnosophists, ablegates and their acolytes, eremites, eidolons, zoanthrops half beast and half human, and deodands and remontados in picturesque rags, with eyes painted wild.

I found myself thinking how strange it would be if the New Sun, the Daystar himself, were to appear now as suddenly as he had appeared so long ago when he was called the Conciliator, appearing here because it was an inappropriate place and he had always preferred the least appropriate places, seeing these people through fresher eyes than we ever could; and if he, thus appearing here, were to decree by theurgy that all of them (none of whom I knew and none of whom knew me) should forever after live the roles they had taken up tonight, the autochthons hunching over smoky fires in mountain huts of stone, the real autochthon forever a townsman at a ridotto, the women spurring toward the enemies of the Commonwealth with sword in hand, the officers doing needlepoint at north windows and looking up to sigh over empty roads, the deodands mourning their unspeakable abominations in the wilderness, the remontados burning their own homes and setting their eyes upon the mountains; and only I unchanged, as it is said the velocity of light is unchanged by mathematical transformations.

Then, while I was grinning to myself behind my mask, it seemed that the Claw, in its soft leathern sack, drove against my breastbone to remind me that the Conciliator had been no jest, and that I bore some fragment of his power with me. At that moment, as I looked across the room over all the feathered and helmeted and wild-haired heads, I saw a Pelerine.

I made my way across to her as quickly as I could, pushing aside those who did not stand aside for me. (They were but few, for though not one of them thought I was what I seemed, my height made them take me for an exultant, with no true exultants near.)

The Pelerine was neither young nor old; beneath her narrow domino her face seemed a smooth oval, refined and remote like the face of the chief priestess who had permitted me to pass in the tent cathedral after Agia and I had destroyed the altar. She held a little glass of wine as if to toy with it, and when I knelt at her feet she set it on a table so she could give me her fingers to kiss.

"Shrive me, Domnicellae," I begged her. "I have done you and all your sisters the greatest harm."

"Death does us all harm," she answered.

"I am not he." I looked up at her then, and the first doubt struck me.

Over the chatter of the crowd I heard the hiss of her in-drawn breath. "You are not?"

"No, Domnicellae." And though I doubted her already, I feared she would flee from me, and I reached out to catch the cincture that dangled from her waist. "Domnicellae, forgive me, but are you a true member of the order?"

Without speaking she shook her head, then fell to the floor.

It is not uncommon for a client in our oubliette to feign unconsciousness, but the imposture is easily detected. The false fainter deliberately closes his eyes and keeps them closed. In a true faint, the victim, who is almost as likely to be a man as a woman, first loses control of his eyes, so that for an instant they no longer look in precisely the same direction; sometimes they tend to roll up under their lids. These lids, in turn, seldom entirely close, since their closing is not a deliber-ate action but a mere relaxation of their muscles. One can usually see a slender crescent of the sclera between the upper and lower lids, as I did when this woman fell.

Several men helped me carry her to an alcove, and there was a good deal of foolish talk about heat and excitement, neither of which had been present. For a time it was impossi-ble to drive the onlookers away—then the novelty was gone, and it would have been almost equally impossible for me to have kept them there had I desired to do so. By then the woman in scarlet was beginning to stir, and I had learned from a woman of about the same age who was dressed as a child that she was the wife of an armiger whose villa stood at no great distance from Thrax, but who had gone to Nessus on some business or other. I went back to the table then and fetched her little glass and touched her lips with the red liquid it contained.

"No," she said weakly. "I don't want it . . . It's sangaree and I hate it—I—I only chose it because the color matches my costume."

"Why did you faint? Was it because I thought you were a real conventual?"

"No, because I guessed who you are," she said, and we were silent for a moment, she still half-reclining on the divan to which I had helped carry her, I sitting at her feet.

I brought the moment when I had knelt before her to life again in my mind; I have, as I have said, the power to so reconstruct every instant of my life. And at last I had to say, "How did you know?"

"Anyone else in those clothes, asked if he were Death, would have said he was . . . because he would be in costume. I sat in the archon's court a week ago, when my husband charged one of our peons with theft. That day I saw you standing to one side, with your arms folded on the guard of the sword you carry now, and when I heard you say what you did, when you had just kissed my fingers, I recognized you, and I thought . . . Oh, I don't know what I thought! I suppose I thought you had knelt to me because you intended to kill me. Just from the way you stood, you always looked, when I saw you in court, like someone who would be gallant to the poor people whose heads he was going to lop off, and particularly to women."

"I only knelt to you because I am anxious to locate the Pelerines, and your costume, like my own, did not seem to be a costume."

"It isn't. That is to say, I'm not entitled to wear it, but it isn't just something I had my maids run up for me. It's a real investiture." She paused. "Do you know I don't even know your name?"

"Severian. Yours is Cyriaca—one of the women mentioned it while we were taking care of you. May I ask how you came to have those clothes, and if you know where the Pelerines are now?"

"This isn't a part of your duty, is it?" For a moment she stared into my eyes, then she shook her head. "Something private. I was nurtured by them. I was a postulant, you know. We traveled up and down the continent, and I used to have wonderful botany lessons just looking at the trees and flowers as we passed. Sometimes when I think back on it, it feels as if we went from palms to pines in a week, though I know that can't be true.

"I was going to take final vows, and the year before you're to be invested they make the investiture so you can try it on and get the fit right, and then so that you'll see it among your ordinary clothes each time you unpack. It's like a girl's looking at her mother's wedding dress, when it was her grand-mother's too and she knows she'll be married in it, if she is ever married. Only I never wore my investiture, and when I went home, after a long time of waiting until we passed close by since there would be no one to escort me, I took it with me.

"I hadn't thought of it for a long time. Then when I got the archon's invitation I got it out again and decided to wear it tonight. I'm proud of my figure, and we only had to let it out a little here and there. It becomes me, I think, and I have the face for a Pelerine, though I don't have their eyes. Actually I never had the eyes, though I used to think I'd get them when I took my vows, or afterward. Our director of postulants had that look. She could sit sewing, and to look at her eyes you would believe they were seeing to the ends of Urth where the perischii live, staring right through the old, torn skirt and the walls of the tent, staring through everything. No, I don't know where the Pelerines are now—I doubt if they do themselves, though perhaps the Mother does."

I said, "You must have had some friends among them. Didn't some of your fellow postulants stay?"

Cyriaca shrugged. "None of them ever wrote to me. I really don't know."

"Do you feel well enough to go back to the dance?" Music was beginning to filter into our alcove.

Her head did not move, but I saw her eyes, which had been tracing the corridors of the years when she talked of the Pelerines, swing around to look at me sidelong. "Is that what you want to do?"

"I suppose not. I'm never completely at ease among crowds, unless the people are my friends."

"You have some, then?" She seemed genuinely astonished.

"Not here—well, one friend here. In Nessus I used to have the brothers of our guild."

"I understand." She hesitated. "There's no reason we have to go. This affair will wear out the night, and at dawn, if the archon is still enjoying himself, they'll let down the curtains to exclude the light, and perhaps even raise the celure over the garden. We can sit here as long as we wish, and every time one of the servers comes around we'll get what we like to eat and drink. When someone we want to talk with goes by, we'll make him stop and entertain us."

"I'm afraid I would begin to bore you before the night was much worn," I said.

"Not at all, because I have no intention of allowing you to talk much. I'm going to talk myself, and make you listen to me. To begin—do you know you are very handsome?"

"I know that I am not. But since you've never seen me without this mask, you can't possibly know what I look like."

"On the contrary."

She leaned forward as though to examine my face through the eyeholes. Her own mask, which was the color of her gown, was so small that it was hardly more than a convention, two almond-shaped loops of fabric about her eyes; yet it lent her an exotic air she would not otherwise have possessed, and lent her too, I think, a feeling of mystery, of a concealment that lifted from her the weight of responsibility.

"You are a very intelligent man I am sure, but you haven't been to as many of these things as I have, or you would have learned the art of judging faces without seeing them. It's hardest, of course, when the person you're looking at has on a wooden vizard that doesn't conform to the face, but even then you can tell a great deal. You have a sharp chin, don't you? With a little cleft."

"Yes to the sharp chin," I said. "No to the cleft."

"You're lying to throw me off, or else you've never noticed it. I can judge chins by looking at waists, particularly in men, which is where my chief interest lies. A narrow waist means a sharp chin, and that leather mask leaves just enough showing to confirm it. Even though your eyes are deeply set, they're large and mobile, and that means a cleft chin in a man, particularly when the face is thin. You have high cheekbones—their outlines show a trifle through the mask, and your flat cheeks will make them look higher. Black hair, because I can see it on the backs of your hands, and thin lips that show through the mouth of the mask. Since I can't see all of them, they curve and curl about, which is a most desirable thing in a man's lips."

I did not know what to say, and to tell the truth I would have given a great deal to leave her just then; at last I asked, "Do you want me to take my mask off so you can check the accuracy of your assessments?"

"Oh, no, you mustn't. Not until they play the aubade. Besides, you should consider my feelings. If you did and I found you weren't handsome after all, I should be deprived of an interesting night." She had been sitting up. Now she smiled and leaned back on the divan again, her hair spreading about her in a dark aureole. "No, Severian, instead of unmasking your face, you must unmask your spirit. Later you will do that by showing me everything you would do were you free to do whatever you wished, and now by telling me everything I want to know about you. You come from Nessus—I've learned that much. Why are you so eager to find the Pelerines?"

VI

The Library of the Citadel

AS I WAS about to answer her question, a couple strolled by our alcove, the man robed in a sanbenito, the woman dressed as a midinette. They only glanced at us as they passed, but something—the inclination, perhaps, of the two heads together, or some expression of the eyes—told me that they knew, or at least suspected, I was not in masquerade. I pretended I had noticed nothing, however, and said, "Something that belongs to the Pelerines came into my hands by accident. I want to return it to them."

"You're not going to do them harm then?" Cyriaca asked. "Can you tell me what it is?"

I did not dare to tell the truth, and I knew I would be asked to produce whatever object I named, and so I said, "A book— an old book, beautifully illustrated. I don't pretend to know anything about books, but I feel sure it's of religious importance and quite valuable," and from my sabretache I drew the brown book from Master Ultan's library that I had carried away when I left Thecla's cell.

"Old, yes," Cyriaca said. "And more than a little water-stained, I see. May I look at it?"

I handed it to her and she fanned the pages, then stopped at a picture of the sikinnis, holding it up until it caught the gleam of a lamp burning in a niche above our divan. The

horned men seemed to leap in the flickering light, the sylphs
to writhe.

"I don't know anything about books either," she said, hand-
ing it back. "But I have an uncle who does, and I think he
might give a great deal for this one. I wish he were here tonight so he could see it—though perhaps it's all for the best,
because I'd probably try to get it from you in some way. In
every pentad he travels as far as I ever did when I was with
the Pelerines, just to seek out old books. He's even gone to the
lost archives. Have you heard about those?"

I shook my head.

"All I know is what he told me once when he had drunk a
little more of our estate cuvee than he usually takes, and it
may be that he didn't tell me everything, because as I talked
to him I had the feeling he was a bit afraid I might try to go
myself. I never have, though I've regretted it sometimes. Anyway, in Nessus, a long way south of the city most people visit,
so far down the great river in fact that most people think the
city would have ended long before, there stands an ancient
fortress. Everyone save perhaps for the Autarch himself—may
his spirit live in a thousand successors—has forgotten it long
ago, and it's supposed to be haunted. It stands upon a hill
overlooking Gyoll, my uncle told me, staring out over a field
of ruined sepulchers, guarding nothing."

She paused and moved her hands, shaping the hill and its
stronghold in the air before her. I had the feeling that she had
told the story many times, perhaps to her children. It made
me conscious that she was indeed old enough to have them,
children old enough themselves to have listened to this and
other tales many times. No years had marked her smooth,
sensuous face; but the candle of youth that burned so brightly
still in Dorcas and had shed its clear, unworldly light even
about Jolenta, that had shone so hard and bright behind
Thecla's strength and had lit the mist-shrouded paths of the
necropolis when her sister Thea took Vodalus's pistol at the
grave side, had in her been extinguished so long that not even
the perfume of its flame remained. I pitied her.

"You must know the story of how the race of ancient days
reached the stars, and how they bargained away all the wild
half of themselves to do so, so that they no longer cared for
the taste of the pale wind, nor for love or lust, nor to make
new songs nor to sing old ones, nor for any of the other animal things they believed they had brought with them out of

the rain forests at the bottom of time—though in fact, so my uncle told me, those things brought them. And you know, or you should know, that those to whom they sold those things, who were the creations of their own hands, hated them in their hearts. And truly they had hearts, though the men who had made them never reckoned with that. Anyway, they resolved to ruin their makers, and they did it by returning, when mankind had spread to a thousand suns, all that had been left with them long before.

"So much, at least, you should know. My uncle once told it to me as I have told it to you, and he found all that and more recorded in a book in his collection. It was a book no one had opened, as he believed, for a chiliad.

"But how they did what they did is less well known. I remember that when I was a child, I imagined the bad machines digging—digging by night until they had cleared away the twisted roots of old trees and laid bare an iron chest they had buried when the world was very young, and that when they struck off the lock of that chest, all the things we've spoken of came flying out like a swarm of golden bees. That's foolish, but even now I can hardly imagine what the reality of those thinking engines can have been like."

I recalled Jonas, with the light, bright metal where the skin of his loins ought to have been, but I could not picture Jonas setting free a plague to trouble mankind, and shook my head.

"But my uncle's book, he said, made clear what it was they did, and the things they let go free were no swarm of insects but a flood of artifacts of every kind, calculated by them to revive all those thoughts that people had put behind them because they could not be written in numbers. The building of everything from cities to cream pitchers was in the hands of the machines, and after a thousand lifetimes of building cities that were like great mechanisms, they turned to building cities that were like banks of cloud before a storm, and others like the skeletons of dragons."

"When was this?" I asked.

"A very long time ago—long before the first stones of Nessus were laid."

I had put an arm about her shoulders, and now she let her hand creep into my lap; I felt its heat and slow search.

"And they followed the same principle in all they did. In the shaping of furniture, for example, and the cutting of clothing. And because the leaders who had decided so long before that all the thoughts symbolized by the clothes and furniture, and by the cities, should be put behind mankind forever were long dead, and the people had forgotten their faces and their maxims, they were delighted with the new things. Thus all that empire, which had been built only upon order, passed away.

"But though the empire dissolved, the worlds were a long time dying. At first, so that the things they were returning to humans would not be rejected again, the machines conceived of pageants and phantasmagoria, whose performances inspired those who watched them to think on fortune or revenge or the invisible world. Later they gave each man and woman a companion, unseen by all other eyes, as an advisor. The children had such companions long before.

"When the powers of the machines had weakened further—as the machines themselves wished—they could no longer maintain these phantoms in the minds of their owners, nor could they build more cities, because the cities that remained were already nearly empty.

"They had reached, so my uncle told me, that point at which they had hoped mankind would turn on them and destroy them, yet no such thing had occurred, because by this time they who had been despised as slaves or worshiped as devils before were greatly loved.

"And so they called all who loved them best around them, and for long years taught them all the things their race had put away, and in time they died.

"Then all those whom they had loved, and who had loved them, took counsel together as to how their teachings could be preserved, for they well knew their kind would not come again upon Urth. But bitter quarrels broke out among them. They had not learned together, but rather each of them, man or woman, had listened to one of the machines as if there were no one in the world but those two. And because there was so much knowledge and only a few to learn it, the machines had taught each differently.

"Thus they divided into parties, and each party into two, and each of those two into two again, until at last every individual stood alone, misunderstood and reviled by all the others and reviling them. Then each went away, out of the cities that had held the machines or deeper into them, save for a very few who by habit remained in the palaces of the machines to watch beside their bodies."

A sommelier brought us cups of wine almost as clear as water, and as still as water until some motion of the cup woke it. It perfumed the air like those flowers no man can see, the flowers that can be found only by the blind; and to drink it was like drinking strength from the heart of a bull. Cyriaca took her cup eagerly, and draining it cast it ringing into a corner.

"Tell me more," I said to her, "of this story of the lost archives."

"When the last machine was cold and still and each of those who had learned from them the forbidden lore mankind had cast aside was separated from all the rest, there came dread into the heart of each. For each knew himself to be only mortal, and most, no longer young. And each saw that with his own death the knowledge he loved best would die. Then each of them—each supposing himself the only one to do so—began to write down what he had learned in the long years when he had harkened to the teachings of the machines that spilled forth all the hidden knowledge of wild things. Much perished but much more survived, sometimes falling into the hands of those who copied it enlivened by their own additions or weakened by omissions . . . Kiss me, Severian."

Though my mask hampered us, our lips met. As she drew away, the shadow memories of Thecla's old bantering love affairs, played out among the pseudothyrums and catachtonian boudoirs of the House Absolute welled up within me, and I said, "Don't you know this kind of thing requires a man's undivided attention?"

Cyriaca smiled. "That's why I did it—I wanted to see if you were listening.

"Anyway, for a long time—no one knows quite how long, I suppose, and anyway the world was not as near the sun's failing then and its years were longer—these writings circulated or else lay moldering in cenotaphs where their authors had concealed them for safekeeping. They were fragmentary, contradictory, and eisegesistic. Then when some autarch (though they were not called autarchs then) hoped to recapture the dominion exercised by the first empire, they were gathered up by his servants, white-robed men who ransacked cocklofts and threw down the androsphinxes erected to memorialize the machines and entered the cubicula of moiraic women long dead. Their spoil was gathered into a great heap in the city of Nessus, which was then newly built, to be burned.

"But on the night before the burning was to begin, the autarch of that time, who had never dreamed before the wild dreams of sleep but only waking dreams of dominion, dreamed at last. And in his dream he saw all the untamed worlds of life and death, stone and river, beast and tree slipping away from his hands forever.

"When morning came, he ordered that the torches not be kindled, but that there should be a great vault built to house all the volumes and scrolls the white-robed men had gathered. For he thought that if the new empire he planned should fail him at last, he would retire to that vault and enter the worlds that, in imitation of the ancients, he was determined to cast aside.

"His empire did fail him, as it had to. The past cannot be found in the future where it is not—not until the metaphysical world, which is so much larger and so much slower than the physical world, completes its revolution and the New Sun comes. But he did not retire as he had planned into that vault and the curtain wall he had caused to be built about it, for when once the wild things have been put behind a man for good and all, they are trap-wise and cannot be recaptured.

"Nevertheless, it is said that before all he gathered was sealed away, he set a guardian over it. And when that guardian's time on Urth was done, he found another, and he another, so that they continue ever faithful to the commands of that autarch, for they are saturated in the wild thoughts sprung from the lore saved by the machines, and such faith is one of those wild things."

I had been disrobing her as she spoke, and kissing her breasts; but I said, "Did all those thoughts of which you spoke go out of the world when the autarch locked them away? Haven't I ever heard of them?"

"No, because they had been passed from hand to hand for a long time, and had entered into the blood of all the peoples. Besides, it is said that the guardian sometimes sends them out, and though they always return to him at last, they are read, whether by one or many, before they sink once more into his dark."

"It is a wonderful story," I said. "I think that perhaps I know more of it than you, but I had never heard it before." I found that her legs were long, and smoothly tapered from thighs like cushions of silk to slender ankles; all her body, indeed, was shaped for delight.

Her fingers touched the clasp that held my cloak about my shoulders. "Need you take this off?" she asked. "Can't it cover us?"

"It can," I said.

VII

Attractions

ALMOST I DROWNED in the delight she gave me, for though I did not love her as I had once loved Thecla, nor as I loved Dorcas even then, and she was not beautiful as Jolenta had once been beautiful, I felt a tenderness for her that was no more than in part born of the unquiet wine, and she was such a woman as I had dreamed of as a ragged boy in the Matachin Tower, before I had ever beheld Thea's heart-shaped face by the side of the opened grave; and she knew far more of the arts of love than any of the three.

When we rose we went to a flowing basin of silver to wash. There were two women there who had been lovers as we had been, and they stared at us and laughed; but when they saw I would not spare them because they were women, they fled shrieking.

Then we cleansed each other. I know Cyriaca believed that I would leave her then, as I believed that she would leave me; but we did not separate (though it would, perhaps, have been better if we had), but went out into the silent little garden, which was full of night, and stood beside a lonely fountain.

She held my hand, and I held hers as children do. "Have you ever visited the House Absolute?" she asked. She was watching our reflections in the moon-drenched water, and her voice was so low I could scarcely hear her.

I told her that I had, and at the words her hand tightened on mine.

"Did you visit the Well of Orchids there?"

I shook my head.

"I have been to the House Absolute also, but I have never seen the Well of Orchids. It is said that when the Autarch has a consort—as ours does not—she holds her court there, in the most beautiful place in the world. Even now, only the loveliest are permitted to walk in that spot. When I was there we stayed, my lord and I, in a certain small room appropriate to our armigerial rank. One evening when my lord was gone and I did not know where, I went out into the corridor, and as I stood there looking up and down, a high functionary of the court passed by. I did not know his name or his office, but I stopped him and asked if I might go to the Well of Orchids."

She paused. For the space of three or four breaths there was no sound but the music from the pavilions and the tinkling of the fountain.

"And he stopped and looked at me, I think in some surprise. You cannot know how it feels to be a little armigette from the north, in a gown sewn by your own maids, and provincial jewels, and be looked at so by someone who has spent all his life among the exultants of the House Absolute. Then he smiled."

She gripped my hand very tightly now.

"And he told me. Down such and such a corridor and turn at such a statue, up certain steps and along the ivory path. Oh, Severian, my lover!"

Her face was radiant as the moon itself. I knew the moment she had described had been the crown of her life, and that she now treasured the love I had given her partially, and perhaps largely, because it had recalled to her that moment, when her beauty had been weighed by one she felt fit to rule upon it, and had not been found wanting. My reason told me I should take offense at that, but I could find no resentment in me.

"He went away, and I began to walk as he had said—a score of strides, perhaps two score. Then I met my lord, and he ordered me to return to our little room."

"I see," I said, and shifted my sword.

"I think you do. Is it wrong then for me to betray him like this? What do you think?"

"I am no magistrate."

"Everyone judges me . . . all my friends . . . all my lovers, of whom you are neither the first nor the last; even those women in the caldarium just now."

"We are trained from childhood not to judge, but only to carry out the sentences handed down by the courts of the Commonwealth. I will not judge you or him."

"I judge," she said, and turned her face toward the bright, hard light of the stars. For the first time since I had glimpsed her across the crowded ballroom I understood how I could have mistaken her for a monial of the order whose habit she wore. "Or at least, I tell myself I judge. And I find myself guilty, but I can't stop. I think I draw men like you to myself. Were you drawn? There were women there lovelier than I am now, I know."

"I'm not certain," I said. "While we were coming here to Thrax . . ."

"You have a story too, don't you? Tell me, Severian. I've already told you almost the only interesting thing that has ever happened to me."

"On the way here, we—I'll explain some other time who I was traveling with—fell in with a witch and her famula and her client, who had come to a certain place to reinspirit the body of a man long dead."

"Really?" Cyriaca's eyes sparkled. "How wonderful! I've heard of such things but I've never seen them. Tell me all about it, but make sure you tell me the truth."

"There really isn't anything much to tell. Our path lay through a deserted city, and when we saw their fire, we went to it because we had someone with us who was ill. When the witch brought back the man she had come to revive, I thought at first that she was restoring the whole city. It wasn't until several days afterward that I understood . . ."

I found I could not say what it was I understood; that it was in fact on the level of meaning above language, a level we like to believe scarcely exists, though if it were not for the constant discipline we have learned to exercise upon our thoughts, they would always be climbing to it unaware.

"Go on."

"I didn't really understand, of course. I still think about it, and I still don't. But I know somehow that she was bringing him back, and *he* was bringing the stone town back with him, as a setting for himself. Sometimes I have thought that perhaps it had never had any reality apart from him, so that when we rode over its pavements and the rubble of its walls, we were actually riding among his bones."

"And did he come?" she asked. "Tell me!"

"Yes, he returned. And then the client was dead, and the sick woman who had been with us also. And Apu-Punchau—that was the dead man's name—was gone again. The witches ran away, I think, though perhaps they flew. But what I wanted to say was that we went on the next day on foot, and stayed the next night in the hut of a poor family. And that night while the woman who was with me slept, I talked to the man, who seemed to know a great deal about the stone town, though he did not know its original name. And I spoke with his mother, who I think knew something more than he, though she would not tell me as much."

I hesitated, finding it hard to speak of such things to this woman. "At first I supposed their ancestors might have come from that town, but they said it had been destroyed long before the coming of their race. Still, they knew much lore of it, because the man had sought for treasures there since he had been a boy, though he had never found anything, he said, save for broken stones and broken pots, and the tracks of other searchers who had been there long before him.

"'In ancient days,' his mother told me, 'they believed that you could draw buried gold by putting a few coins of your own in the ground, with this spell or that. Many a one did it, and some forgot the place, or were kept from digging their own up again. That's what my son finds. That is the bread we eat.'"

I remembered her as she had been that night, old and stooped as she warmed her hands at a little fire of turf. Perhaps she resembled one of Thecla's old nurses, for something about her brought Thecla closer to the surface of my mind than she had been since Jonas and I had been imprisoned in the House Absolute, so that once or twice when I caught sight of my hands, I was startled to see the thickness of the fingers, and their brown color, and to see them bare of rings.

"Go on, Severian," Cyriaca said again.

"Then the old woman told me there was something in the stone town that truly drew its like to it. 'You have heard tales of necromancers,' she said, 'who fish for the spirits of the dead. Do you know there are vivimancers among the dead, who call to them those who can make them live again? There is such a one in the stone town, and once or twice in each saros one of those he has called to him will sup with us.' And then she said to her son, 'You will recall the silent man who slept beside his staff. You were only a child, but you will remember him, I think. He was the last until now.' Then I knew that I, too, had been drawn by the vivimancer Apu-Punchau, though I had felt nothing."

Cyriaca gave me a sidelong look. "Am I dead then? Is that what you're saying? You told me there was a witch who was the necromancer, and that you only stumbled upon her fire. I think that you yourself were the witch you spoke of, and no doubt the sick person you mentioned was your client, and the woman your servant."

"That's because I have neglected to tell you all the parts of the story that have any importance," I said. I would have laughed at being thought a witch; but the Claw pressed against my breastbone, telling me that by its stolen power I was a witch indeed in everything except knowledge; and I understood—in the same sense that I had "understood" before—that though Apu-Punchau had brought it to his hand, he could not (or would not?) take it from me. "Most importantly," I went on, "when the revenant vanished, one of the scarlet capes of the Pelerines, like the one you're wearing now, was left behind in the mud. I have it in my sabretache. Do the Pelerines dabble in necromancy?"

I never heard the answer to my question, for just as I spoke, the tall figure of the archon came up the narrow path that led to the fountain. He was masked, and costumed as a barghest, so that I would not have known him if I had seen him in a good light; but the dimness of the garden stripped his disguise from him as effectively as human hands could have, so that as soon as I saw the loom of his height, and his walk, I knew him at once.

"Ah," he said. "You have found her. I ought to have anticipated that."

"I thought so," I told him, "but I wasn't sure."

VIII

Upon the Cliff

I LEFT THE palace grounds by one of the landward gates. There were six troopers on guard there, with nothing of the air of relaxation that had characterized the two at the river stairs a few watches before. One, politely but unmistakably barring the way, asked me if I had to leave so early. I identified myself and said that I was afraid I must—that I still had work to do that night (as indeed I did) and would have a hard day facing me the next morning as well (as indeed I would).

"You're a hero then." The soldier sounded slightly more friendly. "Don't you have an escort, Lictor?"

"I had two clavigers, but I dismissed them. There's no reason I can't find my way back to the Vincula alone."

Another trooper, who had not spoken previously, said, "You can stay inside until morning. They'll find you a quiet place to bunk down."

"Yes, but my work wouldn't get done. I'm afraid I must leave now."

The soldier who had been blocking my way stood aside. "I'd like to send a couple of men with you. If you'll wait a moment, I'll do it. I have to get permission from the officer of the guard."

"That won't be necessary," I told him, and left before they could say more. Something—presumably the committer of the murders my sergeant had told me of—was clearly stirring in the city; it seemed almost certain that another death had occurred while I was in the archon's palace. The thought filled me with a pleasant excitement—not because I was such a fool as to imagine myself superior to any attack, but because the idea of being attacked, of risking death that night in the dark streets of Thrax, lifted some part of the depression I would otherwise have felt. This unfocused terror, this faceless menace of the night, was the earliest of all my childhood fears; and as such, now that childhood was behind me, it had the homey quality of all childhood things when we are fully grown.

I was already on the same side of the river as the jacal I had visited that afternoon, and had no need to take boat again; but the streets were strange to me and in the dark seemed almost a labyrinth built to confound me. I made several false starts before I found the narrow way I wanted, leading up the cliff.

The dwellings to either side of it, which had stood silent while they waited for the mighty wall of stone opposite them to rise and cover the sun, were murmurous with voices now, and a few windows glowed with the light of grease lamps. While Abdiesus reveled in his palace below, the humble folk of the high cliff celebrated too, with a gaiety that differed from his chiefly in that it was less riotous. I heard the sounds of love as I passed, just as I had heard them in his garden after leaving Cyriaca for the last time, and the voices of men and women in quiet talk, and bantering too, here as there. The palace garden had been scented by its flowers, and its air was washed by its own fountains and by the great fountain of cold Acis, which rushed by just outside. Here those odors were no more; but a breeze stirred among the jacals and the caves with their stoppered mouths, bringing sometimes the stench of ordure, and sometimes the aroma of brewing tea or some humble stew, and sometimes only the clean air of the mountains.

When I was high up the cliff face, where no one dwelt who was rich enough to afford more light than a cooking fire would give, I turned and looked back at the city much as I had looked down upon it—though with an entirely different spirit—from the ramparts of Acies Castle that afternoon. It is said that there are crevices in the mountains so deep that one can see stars at their bottoms—crevices that pass, then, entirely through the world. Now I felt I had found one. It was like looking into a constellation, as though all of Urth had fallen away, and I was staring into the starry gulf.

It seemed likely that by this time they were searching for me. I thought of the archon's dimarchi cantering down the silent streets, perhaps carrying flambeaux snatched up in the garden. Far worse was the thought of the clavigers I had until now commanded fanning out from the Vincula. Yet I saw no moving lights and heard no faint, hoarse cries, and if the Vincula was disturbed, it was not a disturbance that affected the dim streets webbing the cliff across the river. There should have been a winking gleam too where the great gate opened to let out the freshly roused men, closed, then opened again; but there was none. I turned at last and began to climb once more. The alarm had not yet been given. Still, it would soon sound.

There was no light in the jacal and no noise of speech. I took the Claw from its little bag before I entered, for fear I would lack the nerve to do so once I was inside. Sometimes it blazed like a firework, as it had in the inn at Saltus. Sometimes it possessed no more light than a bit of glass. That night in the jacal it was not brilliant, but it glowed with so deep a blue that the light itself seemed almost a clearer darkness. Of all the names of the Conciliator, the one that is, I believe, least used, and which has always seemed the most puzzling to me, is that of Black Sun. Since that night, I have felt myself almost to comprehend it. I could not hold the gem in my fingers as I had done often before and was yet to do afterward; I laid it flat on the palm of my right hand so that my touch would commit no more sacrilege than was strictly necessary. With it held thus before me, I stooped and entered the jacal.

The girl lay where she had lain that afternoon. If she still breathed I could not hear her, and she did not move. The boy with the infected eye slept on the bare earth at her feet. He must have bought food with the money I had given him; corn husks and fruit peels were scattered over the floor. For a moment I dared to hope that neither of them would wake.

The deep light of the Claw showed the girl's face to be a weaker and more horrible thing than I had seen it by day, accentuating the hollows under her eyes, and her sunken cheeks. I felt I should say something, invoke the Increate and his messengers by some formula, but my mouth was dry and more empty of words than any beast's. Slowly I lowered my hand toward her until the shadow of it cut off all the light that had bathed her. When I lifted my hand again there had been no change, and remembering that the Claw had not helped Jolenta, I wondered if it were possible that it could have no good effect on women, or if it were necessary that a woman hold it. Then I touched the girl's forehead with it, so that for a moment it seemed a third eye in that deathlike face.

Of all the uses I made of it, that was the most astounding, and perhaps the only one in which it was not possible that any self-deception on my part, or any coincidence no matter how farfetched, could account for what occurred. It may have been that the man-ape's bleeding was staunched by his own belief, that the uhlan on the road by the House Absolute was merely stunned and would have revived in any event, that the apparent healing of Jonas's wounds had been no more than a trick of the light.

But now it was as though some unimaginable power had acted in the interval between one chronon and the next to wrench the universe from its track. The girl's real eyes, dark as pools, opened. Her face was no longer the skull mask it had been, but only the worn face of a young woman. "Who are you in those bright clothes?" she asked. And then, "Oh, I am dreaming."

I told her I was a friend, and that there was no reason for her to be afraid.

"I am not afraid," she said. "I would be if I were awake, but I am not now. You look as if you have fallen from the sky, but I know you are only the wing of some poor bird. Did Jader catch you? Sing for me . . ."

Her eyes closed again; this time I could hear the slow sighing of her breath. Her face remained as it had been while they were open—thin and drawn, but with the stamp of death rubbed away.

I took the gem from her forehead and touched the boy's eye with it as I had touched his sister's face, but I am not sure it was necessary that I do so. It appeared normal before it ever felt the kiss of the Claw, and it may be that the infection was already vanquished. He stirred in his sleep and cried out as though in some dream he were running ahead of slower boys and urging them to follow him.

I put the Claw back into its little bag and sat on the earthen floor among the husks and peels, listening to him. After a time he grew quiet again. Starlight made a dim pattern near the door; other than that, the jacal was utterly dark. I could hear the sister's regular breathing, and the boy's own.

She had said that I, who had worn fuligin since my elevation to journeyman, and gray rags before that, was dressed in bright clothing. I knew she had been dazzled by the light at her forehead—anything, any clothing, would have appeared bright to her then. And yet, I felt that in some sense she was correct. It was not that (as I have been tempted to write) I came to hate my cloak and trousers and boots after that moment; but rather that I came in some sense to feel they were indeed the disguise they had been taken to be when I was at the archon's palace, or the costume they had appeared to be when I took part in Dr. Talos's play. Even a torturer is a man, and it is not natural for a man to dress always and exclusively in that hue that is darker than black. I had despised my own hypocrisy when I had worn the brown mantle from Agilus's shop; perhaps the fuligin beneath it was a hypocrisy as great or greater.

Then the truth began to force itself upon my mind. If I had ever truly been a torturer, a torturer in the sense that Master Gurloes and even Master Palaemon were torturers, I was one no longer. I had been given a second chance here in Thrax. I had failed in that second chance as well, and there would be no third. I might gain employment by my skills and my clothing, but that was all; and no doubt it would be better for me to destroy them when I could, and try to make a place for myself among the soldiers who fought the northern war, once I had succeeded—if I ever succeeded—in returning the Claw.

The boy stirred and called a name that must have been his sister's. She murmured something still in sleep. I stood and watched them for a moment more, then slipped out, fearful that the sight of my hard face and long sword would frighten them.

IX

The Salamander

OUTSIDE, THE STARS seemed brighter, and for the first time in many weeks the Claw had ceased to drive itself against my chest.

When I descended the narrow path, it was no longer necessary to turn and halt to see the city. It spread itself before me in ten thousand twinkling lights, from the watchfire of Acies Castle to the reflection of the guard-room windows in the water that rushed through the Capulus.

By now all the gates would be closed against me. If the dimarchi had not already ridden forth, they would do so before I reached the level land beside the river; but I was determined to see Dorcas once more before I left the city, and, somehow, I had no doubt of my ability to do so. I was just beginning to turn over plans for escaping the walls afterward when a new light flared out far below.

It was small at that distance, no more than a pinprick like all the others; yet it was not like them at all, and perhaps my mind only registered it as light because I knew nothing else to liken it to. I had seen a pistol fired at full potential that night in the necropolis when Vodalus resurrected the dead woman—a coherent beam of energy that had split the mists like lightning. This fire was not like that, but it was more nearly like that than like anything else I could call to mind. It flared briefly and died, and a heartbeat afterward I felt the wash of heat upon my face.

Somehow I missed the little inn called the Duck's Nest in the dark. I have never known if I took a wrong turning or merely walked past the shuttered windows without glimpsing the sign hanging overhead. However it happened, I soon found myself farther from the river than I should have been, striding along a street that ran for a time at least parallel to the cliff, with the smell of scorched flesh in my nostrils as at a branding. I was about to retrace my steps when I collided in the dark with a woman. So hard and unexpectedly did we strike each other that I nearly fell, and as I went reeling back, I heard the thud of her body on the stone.

"I didn't see you," I said as I reached down for her.

"Run! Run!" she gasped. And then, "Oh, help me up." Her voice was faintly familiar.

"Why should I run?" I pulled her to her feet. In the faint light I could see the blur of her face, and even, I thought, something of the fear there.

"It killed Jurmin. He burned alive. His staff was still on fire when we found him. He . . ." Whatever she had begun to say after that trailed off into sobs.

"What burned Jurmin?" When she did not answer, I shook her, but that only made her weep the harder. "Don't I know you? Talk, woman! You're the mistress of the Duck's Nest. Take me there!"

"I can't," she said. "I'm afraid. Give me your arm, please, sieur. We ought to get inside."

"Fine. We'll go to the Duck's Nest. It can't be far—now what is this?"

"Too far!" She wept. "Too far!"

There was something in the street with us. I do not know whether I had failed to detect its approach, or it had been undetectable until then; but it was suddenly present. I have heard people who have a horror of rats say they are aware of them the moment they enter a house, even if the animals are not visible. It was so now. There was a feeling of heat without warmth; and though the air held no odor, I sensed that its power to support life was being drained away.

The woman seemed still unaware of it. She said, "It burned

three last night near the harena, and one tonight, they said, close by the Vincula. And now Jurmin. It's looking for some-body—that's what they say."

I recalled the notules and the thing that had snuffled along the walls of the antechamber of the House Absolute, and I said, "I think it has found him."

I let her go and turned, then turned again, trying to discover where it was. The heat grew, but no light showed. I was tempted to take out the Claw so as to see by its glow; then I recalled how it had waked whatever slept beneath the mine of the man-apes, and I feared the light would only permit this thing—whatever it might be—to locate me. I was not sure my sword would be more effective against it than it had been against the notules when Jonas and I had fled them through the cedar wood; nevertheless, I drew it.

Almost at once there was a clatter of hooves and a yell as two dimarchi thundered round a corner no more than a hun-dred strides away. Had there been more time I would have smiled to see how closely they corresponded to the figures I had imagined. As it was, the firework glare of their lances outlined something dark and crooked and stooped that stood between us.

It turned toward the light, whatever it was, and seemed to open as a flower might, growing tall more swiftly, almost, than the eye could follow it, thinning until it had become a crea-ture of glowing gauze, hot yet somehow reptilian, as those many-colored serpents we see brought from the jungles of the north are reptilian still, though they seem works of colored enamel. The mounts of the soldiers reared and screamed, but one of the men, with more presence of mind than I would have shown, fired his lance into the heart of the thing that faced him. There was a flare of light.

The hostess of the Duck's Nest slumped against me, and I, not wishing to lose her, supported her with my free arm. "I think it's seeking living heat," I told her. "It should go for the destriers. We'll get away."

Just as I spoke, it turned toward us.

I have already said that from behind, when it opened itself toward the dimarchi, it seemed a reptilian flower. That im-pression persisted now when we saw it in its full terror and glory, but it was joined by two others. The first was the sensa-tion of intense and otherworldly heat; it seemed a reptile still, but a reptile that burned in a way never known on Urth, as though some desert asp had dropped into a sphere of snow. The second was of raggedness fluttering in a wind that was not of air. It seemed a blossom still, but it was a blossom whose petals of white and pale yellow and flame had been tattered by some monstrous tempest born in its own heart.

In all these impressions, surrounding them and infusing them, was a horror I cannot describe. It drew all resolution and strength from me, so that for that moment I could neither flee nor attack it. The creature and I seemed fixed in a matrix of time that had nothing to do with anything that had gone before or since, and that, since it held us who were its only occupants immobile, could be altered by nothing.

A shout broke the spell. A second party of dimarchi had galloped into the street behind us, and seeing the creature were lashing their mounts to the charge. In less than the space of a breath they were boiling around us, and it was only by the intercession of Holy Katharine that we were not ridden down. If I had ever doubted the courage of the Autarch's soldiery I lost those doubts then, for both parties hurled themselves upon the monster like hounds upon a stag.

It was useless. There came a blinding flash and the sensation of fearful heat. Still holding the half-unconscious woman, I sprinted down the street.

I meant to turn where the dimarchi had entered it, but in my panic (and it was panic, not only my own, but that of Thecla screaming in my mind) I rounded the corner too late or too soon. Instead of the steep descent to the lower city I expected, I found myself in a little, stub-end court built on a spur of rock jutting from the cliff. By the time I realized what was wrong, the creature, now again a twisted, dwarfish thing but radiating a terrible and invisible energy, was at the mouth of the court.

In the starlight it might have been only an old, hunched man in a black coat, but I have never felt more terror than I did at the sight of it. There was a jacal at the back of the court: a larger structure than the hovel in which the sick girl and her brother had suffered, but built of sticks and mud in the same fashion. I kicked its door in and ran into a little warren of odious rooms, bolting through the first and into another, through that into a third where a half dozen men and women lay sleeping, through that into a fourth—only to see a window that looked out over the city much as my own embrasure in the Vincula did. It was the end, the farthest room of the house, hanging like a swallow's nest over a drop that seemed at that moment to go down forever.

From the room we had just left I could hear the angry voices of the people I had wakened. The door flew open, but whoever had come to expel the intruder must have seen the gleam of *Terminus Est;* he stopped short, swore, and turned away. A moment later someone screamed and I knew the creature of fire was in the jacal.

I tried to set the woman upright, but she fell in a heap at my feet. Outside the window there was nothing—the wattled wall ended a few cubits down, and the supports of the floor did not extend beyond it. Above, an overhanging roof of rotten thatch offered no more purchase to my hand than gossamer. As I struggled to grasp it, there came a flood of light that destroyed all color and cast shadows as dark as fuligin itself, shadows like fissures in the cosmos. I knew then that I must fight and die as the dimarchi had, or jump, and I swung about to face the thing that had come to kill me.

It was still in the room beyond, but I could see it through the doorway, opened again now as it had been in the street. The half-consumed corpse of some wretched crone lay before it on the stone floor, and while I watched, it seemed to bend over her in what was, I would almost swear, an attitude of inquiry. Her flesh blistered and cracked like the fat of a roast, then fell away. In a moment even her bones were no more than pale ashes the creature scattered as it advanced.

Terminus Est I believe to have been the best blade ever forged, but I knew she could accomplish nothing against the power that had routed so many cavalrymen; I cast her to one side in the vague hope that she might be found and eventually returned to Master Palaemon, and took the Claw from its little bag at my throat.

It was my last, faint chance, and I saw at once that it had failed me. However the creature sensed the world about it (and I had guessed from its movements that it was nearly blind on our Urth), it could make out the gem clearly, and it did not fear it. Its slow advance became a rapid and purposeful flowing forward. It reached the doorway—there was a burst of smoke, a crash, and it was gone. Light from below flashed through the hole it had burned in the flimsy floor that began where the stone of the outcrop ended; at first it was the color-less light of the creature, then a rapid alternation of chatoyant pastels—peacock blue, lilac, and rose. Then only the faint, reddish light of leaping flames.

X

Lead

THERE WAS A moment when I thought I would fall into the gaping hole in the center of the little room before I could regain *Terminus Est* and carry the mistress of the Duck's Nest to safety, and another when I was certain everything was going to fall—the trembling structure of the room itself and us together.

Yet in the end we escaped. When we reached the street, it was clear of dimarchi and townsfolk alike, the soldiers no doubt having been drawn to the fire below, and the people frightened indoors. I propped the woman with my arm, and though she was still too terrified to answer my questions intelligibly, I let her choose our way; as I had supposed she would, she led us unerringly to her inn.

Dorcas was asleep. I did not wake her, but sat down in the dark on a stool near the bed where there was now also a little table sufficient to hold the glass and bottle I had taken from the common room below. Whatever the wine was, it seemed strong in my mouth and yet no more than water after I had swallowed it; by the time Dorcas woke, I had drunk half the bottle and felt no more effect from it than I would have if I had swallowed so much sherbet.

She started up, then let her head fall upon the pillow again. "Severian. I should have known it was you."

"I'm sorry if I frightened you," I said. "I came to see how you were."

"That's very kind. It always seems, though, that when I wake up you're bending over me." For a moment she closed her eyes again. "You walk so very quietly in those thick-soled boots of yours, do you know that? It's one reason people are afraid of you."

"You said I reminded you of a vampire once, because I had been eating a pomegranate and my lips were stained with red. We laughed about it. Do you remember?" (It had been in a field within the Wall of Nessus, when we had slept beside Dr. Talos's theater and awakened to feast on fruit dropped the night before by our fleeing audience.)

"Yes," Dorcas said. "You want me to laugh again, don't you? But I'm afraid I can't ever laugh anymore."

"Would you like some wine? It was free, and it's not as bad as I expected."

"To cheer me? No. One ought to drink, I think, when one is cheerful already. Otherwise nothing but more sorrow is poured into the cup."

"At least have a swallow. The hostess here says you've been ill and haven't eaten all day."

I saw Dorcas's golden head move on the pillow then as she turned it to look at me; and since she seemed fully awake, I ventured to light the candle.

She said, "You're wearing your habit. You must have frightened her out of her wits."

"No, she wasn't afraid of me. She's pouring into her cup whatever she finds in the bottle."

"She's been good to me—she's very kind. Don't be hard on her if she chooses to drink so late at night."

"I wasn't being hard on her. But won't you have something? There must be food in the kitchen here, and I'll bring you up whatever you want."

My choice of phrase made Dorcas smile faintly. "I've been bringing up my own food all day. That was what she meant when she told you I'd been ill. Or did she tell you? Spewing. I should think you could smell it yet, though the poor woman did what she could to clean up after me."

Dorcas paused and sniffed. "What is it I do smell? Scorched cloth? It must be the candle, but I don't suppose you can trim the wick with that great blade of yours."

I said, "It's my cloak, I think. I've been standing too near a fire."

"I'd ask you to open the window, but I see it's open already. I'm afraid it's bothering you. It does blow the candle about. Do the flickering shadows make you dizzy?"

"No," I said. "It's all right as long as I don't actually look at the flame."

"From your expression, you feel the way I always do around water."

"This afternoon I found you sitting at the very edge of the river."

"I know," Dorcas said, and fell silent. It was a silence that lasted so long that I was afraid she was not going to speak again at all, that the pathological silence (as I now was sure it had been) that had seized her then had returned.

At last I said, "I was surprised to see you there—I remember that I looked several times before I was sure it was you, although I had been searching for you."

"I spewed, Severian. I told you that, didn't I?"

"Yes, you told me."

"Do you know what I brought up?"

She was staring at the low ceiling, and I had the feeling that there was another Severian there, the kind and even noble Severian who existed only in Dorcas's mind. All of us, I suppose, when we think we are talking most intimately to someone else, are actually addressing an image we have of the person to whom we believe we speak. But this seemed more than that; I felt that Dorcas would go on talking if I left the room. "No," I answered. "Water, perhaps?"

"Sling-stones."

I thought she was speaking metaphorically, and only ventured, "That must have been very unpleasant."

Her head rolled on the pillow again, and now I could see her blue eyes with their wide pupils. In their emptiness they might have been two little ghosts. "Sling-stones, Severian my darling. Heavy little slugs of metal, each about as big around as a nut and not quite so long as my thumb and stamped with the word *strike*. They came rattling out of my throat into the bucket, and I reached down—put my hand down into the filth that came up with them and pulled them up to see. The woman who owns this inn came and took the bucket away, but I had wiped them off and saved them. There are two, and they're in the drawer of that table now. She brought it to put my dinner on. Do you want to see them? Open it."

I could not imagine what she was talking about, and asked if she thought someone was trying to poison her.

"No, not at all. Aren't you going to open the drawer? You're so brave. Don't you want to look?"

"I trust you. If you say there are sling-stones in the table, I'm sure they're there."

"But you don't believe I coughed them up. I don't blame you. Isn't there a story about a hunter's daughter who was blessed by a pardal, so that beads of jet fell from her mouth when she spoke? And then her brother's wife stole the blessing, and when she spoke toads hopped from her lips? I remember hearing it, but I never believed it."

"How could anyone cough up lead?"

Dorcas laughed, but there was no mirth in it. "Easily. So very easily. Do you know what I saw today? Do you know why I couldn't talk to you when you found me? And I couldn't, Severian, I swear it. I know you thought I was just angry and being stubborn. But I wasn't—I had become like a stone, wordless, because nothing seemed to matter, and I'm still not sure anything does. I'm sorry, though, for what I said about your not being brave. You are brave, I know that. It's only that it seems not brave when you're doing things to the poor prisoners here. You were so brave when you fought Agilus, and later when you would have fought with Baldanders because we thought he was going to kill Jolenta . . ."

She fell silent again, then sighed. "Oh, Severian, I'm so tired."

"I wanted to talk to you about that," I said. "About the prisoners. I want you to understand, even if you can't forgive me. It was my profession, the thing I was trained to do from boyhood." I leaned forward and took her hand; it seemed as frail as a songbird.

"You've said something like this before. Truly, I understand."

"And I could do it well. Dorcas, that's what you *don't* understand. Excruciation and execution are arts, and I have the feel, the gift, the blessing. This sword—all the tools we use live when they're in my hands. If I had remained at the Citadel, I might have been a master. Dorcas, are you listening? Does this mean anything at all to you?"

"Yes," she said. "A bit, yes. I'm thirsty, though. If you're through drinking, pour me a little of that wine now, please."

I did as she asked, filling the glass no more than a quarter full because I was afraid she might spill it on her bedclothes.

She sat up to drink, something I had not been certain until then that she was capable of, and when she had swallowed the last scarlet drop hurled the glass out the window. I heard it shatter on the street below.

"I don't want you to drink after me," she told me. "And I knew that if I didn't do that you would."

"You think whatever is wrong with you is contagious, then?"

She laughed again. "Yes, but you have it already. You caught it from your mother. Death. Severian, you never asked me what it was I saw today."

XI

The Hand of the Past

AS SOON AS Dorcas said, "You never asked me what I saw today," I realized that I had been trying to steer the conversation away from it. I had a premonition that it would be something quite meaningless to me, to which Dorcas would attach great meaning, as madmen do who believe the tracks of worms beneath the bark of fallen trees to be a supernatural script. I said, "I thought it might be better to keep your mind off it, whatever it was."

"No doubt it would, if only we could do it. It was a chair."

"A chair?"

"An old chair. And a table, and several other things. It seems that there is a shop in the Turners' Street that sells old furniture to the eclectics, and to those among the autochthons who have absorbed enough of our culture to want it. There is no source here to supply the demand, and so two or three times a year the owner and his sons go to Nessus—to the abandoned quarters of the south—and fill their boat. I talked to him, you see; I know all about it. There are tens of thousands of empty houses there. Some have fallen in long ago, but some are still standing as their owners left them. Most have been looted, yet they still find silver and bits of jewelry now and then. And though most have lost most of their furniture, the owners who moved almost always left some things behind."

I felt that she was about to weep, and I leaned forward to stroke her forehead. She showed me by a glance that she did not wish me to, and laid herself on the bed again as she had been before.

"In some of those houses, all the furnishings are still there. Those are the best, he said. He thinks that a few families, or perhaps only a few people living alone, remained behind when the quarter died. They were too old to move, or too stubborn. I've thought about it, and I'm sure some of them must have had something there they could not bear to leave. A grave, perhaps. They boarded their windows against the marauders, and they kept dogs, and worse things, to protect them. Eventually they left—or they came to the end of life, and their animals devoured their bodies and broke free; but by that time there was no one there, not even looters or scavengers, not until this man and his sons."

"There must be a great many old chairs," I said.

"Not like that one. I knew everything about it—the carving on the legs and even the pattern in the grain of the arms. So much came back then. And then here, when I vomited those pieces of lead, things like hard, heavy seeds, then I knew. Do you remember, Severian, how it was when we left the Botanic Garden? You, Agia, and I came out of that great, glass vivarium, and you hired a boat to take us from the island to the shore, and the river was full of nenuphars with blue flowers and shining green leaves. Their seeds are like that, hard and heavy and dark, and I have heard that they sink to the bottom of Gyoll and remain there for whole ages of the world. But when chance brings them near the surface they sprout no matter how old they may be, so that the flowers of a chiliad past are seen to bloom again."

"I have heard that too," I said. "But it means nothing to you or me."

Dorcas lay still, but her voice trembled. "What is the power that calls them back? Can you explain it?"

"The sunshine, I suppose—but no, I cannot explain it."

"And is there no source of sunlight except the sun?"

I knew then what it was she meant, though something in me could not accept it.

"When that man—Hildegrin, the man we met a second time on top of the tomb in the ruined stone town—was ferrying us across the Lake of Birds, he talked of millions of dead people, people whose bodies had been sunk in that water. How were they made to sink, Severian? Bodies float. How do they weight them? I don't know. Do you?"

I did. "They force lead shot down the throats."

"I thought so." Her voice was so weak now that I could scarcely hear her, even in that silent little room. "No, I knew so. I knew it when I saw them."

"You think that the Claw brought you back."

Dorcas nodded.

"It has acted, sometimes, I'll admit that. But only when I took it out, and not always then. When you pulled me out of the water in the Garden of Endless Sleep, it was in my sabretache and I didn't even know I had it."

"Severian, you allowed me to hold it once before. Could I see it again now?"

I pulled it from its soft pouch and held it up. The blue fires seemed sleepy, but I could see the cruel-looking hook at the center of the gem that had given it its name. Dorcas extended her hand, but I shook my head, remembering the wineglass.

"You think I will do it some harm, don't you? I won't. It would be a sacrilege."

"If you believe what you say, and I think you do, then you must hate it for drawing you back . . ."

"From death." She was watching the ceiling again, now smiling as if she shared some deep and ludicrous secret with it. "Go ahead and say it. It won't hurt you."

"From sleep," I said. "Since if one can be recalled from it, it is not death—not death as we have always understood it, the death that is in our minds when we say *death*. Although I have to confess it is still almost impossible for me to believe that the Conciliator, dead now for so many thousands of years, should act through this stone to raise others."

Dorcas made no reply. I could not even be sure she was listening.

"You mentioned Hildegrin," I said, "and the time he rowed us across the lake in his boat, to pick the avern. Do you remember what he said of death? It was that she was a good friend to the birds. Perhaps we ought to have known then that such a death could not be death as we imagine it."

"If I say I believe all that, will you let me hold the Claw?"

I shook my head again.

Dorcas was not looking at me, but she must have seen the motion of my shadow; or perhaps it was only that her mental Severian on the ceiling shook his head as well. "You are right, then—I was going to destroy it if I could. Shall I tell you what I really believe? I believe I have been dead—not sleeping, but dead. That all my life took place a long, long time ago when I lived with my husband above a little shop, and took care of our child. That this Conciliator of yours who came so long ago was an adventurer from one of the ancient races who outlived the universal death." Her hands clutched the blanket. "I ask you, Severian, when he comes again, isn't he to be called the New Sun? Doesn't that sound like it? And I believe that when he came he brought with him something that had the same power over time that Father Inire's mirrors are said to have over distance. It is that gem of yours."

She stopped and turned her head to look at me defiantly; when I said nothing, she continued. "Severian, when you brought the uhlan back to life it was because the Claw twisted time for him to the point at which he still lived. When you half healed your friend's wounds, it was because it bent the moment to one when they would be nearly healed. And when you fell into the fen in the Garden of Endless Sleep, it must have touched me or nearly touched me, and for me it became the time in which I had lived, so that I lived again. But I have been dead. For a long, long time I was dead, a shrunken corpse preserved in the brown water. And there is something in me that is dead still."

"There is something in all of us that has always been dead," I said. "If only because we know that eventually we will die. All of us except the smallest children."

"I'm going to go back, Severian. I know that now, and that's what I've been trying to tell you. I have to go back and find out who I was and where I lived and what happened to me. I know you can't go with me . . ."

I nodded.

"And I'm not asking you to. I don't even want you to. I love you, but you are another death, a death that has stayed with me and befriended me as the old death in the lake did, but death all the same. I don't want to take death with me when I go to look for my life."

"I understand," I said.

"My child may still be alive—an old man, perhaps, but still alive. I have to know."

"Yes," I said. But I could not help adding, "There was a time when you told me I was not death. That I must not let others persuade me to think of myself in that way. It was behind the orchard on the grounds of the House Absolute. Do you remember?"

"You have been death to me," she said. "I have succumbed to the trap I warned you of, if you like. Perhaps you are not death, but you will remain what you are, a torturer and a carnifex, and your hands will run with blood. Since you remember that time at the House Absolute so well, perhaps you ... I can't say it. The Conciliator, or the Claw, or the Increate, has done this to me. Not you."

"What is it?" I asked.

"Dr. Talos gave us both money afterward, in the clearing. The money he had got from some court official for our play. When we were traveling, I gave everything to you. May I have it back? I'll need it. If not all of it, at least some of it."

I emptied the money in my sabretache onto the table. It was as much as I had received from her, or a trifle more.

"Thank you," she said. "You won't need it?"

"Not as badly as you will. Besides, it is yours."

"I'm going to leave tomorrow, if I feel strong enough. The day after tomorrow whether I feel strong or not. I don't suppose you know how often the boats put out, going downriver?"

"As often as you want them to. You push them in, and the river does the rest."

"That's not like you, Severian, or at least not much. More the sort of thing your friend Jonas would have said, from what you've told me. Which reminds me that you're not the first visitor I've had today. Our friend—your friend, at least—Hethor was here. That's not funny to you, is it? I'm sorry, I just wanted to change the subject."

"He enjoys it. Enjoys watching me."

"Thousands of people do when you perform in public, and you enjoy doing it yourself."

"They come to be horrified, so they can congratulate themselves later on being alive. And because they like the excitement, and the suspense of not knowing whether the condemned will break down, or if some macabre accident will occur. I enjoy exercising my skill, the only real skill I have—enjoy making things go perfectly. Hethor wants something else."

"The pain?"

"Yes, the pain, but something more too."

Dorcas said, "He worships you, you know. He talked with

me for some time, and I think he would walk into a fire if you told him to." I must have winced at that, because she continued, "All this about Hethor is making you ill, isn't it? One sick person is enough. Let's speak of something else."

"Not ill as you are, no. But I can't think of Hethor except as I saw him once from the scaffold, with his mouth open and his eyes . . ."

She stirred uncomfortably. "Yes, those eyes—I saw them tonight. Dead eyes, though I suppose I shouldn't be the one to say that. A corpse's eyes. You have the feeling that if you touched them they would be as dry as stones, and never move under your finger."

"That isn't it at all. When I was on the scaffold in Saltus and looked down and saw him, his eyes danced. You said, though, that the dull eyes he has at most times reminded you of a corpse's. Haven't you ever looked into the glass? Your own eyes are not the eyes of a dead woman."

"Perhaps not." Dorcas paused. "You used to say they were beautiful."

"Aren't you glad to live? Even if your husband is dead, and your child is dead, and the house you once lived in is a ruin— if all those things are true—aren't you full of joy because you are here again? You're not a ghost, not a revenant like those we saw in the ruined town. Look in the glass as I told you. Or if you won't, look into my face or any man's and see what you are."

Dorcas sat up even more slowly and painfully than she had risen to drink the wine, but this time she swung her legs over the edge of the bed, and I saw that she was naked under the thin blanket. Before her illness Jolenta's skin had been perfect, with the smoothness and softness of confectionery. Dorcas's was flecked with little golden freckles, and she was so slender that I was always aware of her bones; yet she was more desirable in her imperfection than Jolenta had ever been in the lushness of her flesh. Conscious of how culpable it would be to force myself on her or even to persuade her to open to me now, when she was ill and I was on the point of leaving her, I still felt desire for her stir in me. However much I love a woman—or however little—I find I want her most when I can no longer have her. But what I felt for Dorcas was stronger than that, and more complex. She had been, though only for so brief a time, the closest friend I had known, and our possession of each other, from the frantic desire in our converted storeroom in Nessus to the long and lazy playing in the bedchamber of the Vincula, was the characteristic act of our friendship as well as our love.

"You're crying," I said. "Do you want me to leave?"

She shook her head, and then, as though she could no longer contain the words that seemed to force themselves out, she whispered, "Oh, won't you go too, Severian? I didn't mean it. Won't you come? Won't you come with me?"

"I can't."

She sank back into the narrow bed, smaller now and more childlike. "I know. You have your duty to your guild. You can't betray it again and face yourself, and I won't ask you. It's only that I never quite gave up hoping you might."

I shook my head as I had before. "I have to flee the city—"

"Severian!"

"And to the north. You'll be going south, and if I were with you, we would have courier boats full of soldiers after us."

"Severian, what happened?" Dorcas's face was very calm, but her eyes were wide.

"I freed a woman. I was supposed to strangle her and throw her body into the Acis, and I could have done it—I didn't feel anything for her, not really, and it should have been easy. But when I was alone with her, I thought of Thecla. We were in a little summerhouse screened with shrubbery, that stood at the edge of the water. I had my hands around her neck, and I thought of Thecla and how I had wanted to free her. I couldn't find a way to do it. Have I ever told you?"

Almost imperceptibly, Dorcas shook her head.

"There were brothers everywhere, five to pass by the shortest route, and all of them knew me and knew of her." (Thecla was shrieking now in some corner of my mind.) "All I really would have had to do would have been to tell them Master Gurloes had ordered me to bring her to him. But I would have had to go with her then, and I was still trying to devise some way by which I could stay in the guild. I did not love her enough."

"It's past now," Dorcas said. "And, Severian, death is not the terrible thing you think it." We had reversed our roles, like lost children who comfort each other alternately.

I shrugged. The ghost I had eaten at Vodalus's banquet was nearly calm again; I could feel her long, cool fingers on my brain, and though I could not turn inside my own skull to see her, I knew her deep and violet eyes were behind my own. It required an effort not to speak with her voice. "At any rate, I was there with the woman, in the summerhouse, and we were alone. Her name was Cyriaca. I knew or at least suspected that she knew where the Pelerines were—she had been one of them for a time. There are silent means of excruciation that require no equipment, and although they are not spectacular, they are quite effective. One reaches into the body, as it were, and manipulates the client's nerves directly. I was going to use what we call Humbaba's Stick, but before I had touched her she told me. The Pelerines are near the pass of Orithyia caring for the wounded. This woman had a letter, she said, only a week ago, from someone she had known in the order . . ."

XII

Following the Flood

THE SUMMERHOUSE HAD boasted a solid roof, but the sides were mere latticework, closed more by the tall forest ferns planted against them than by their slender laths. Moonbeams leaked through. More came in at the doorway, reflected from the rushing water outside. I could see the fear in Cyriaca's face, and the knowledge that her only hope was that I retained some love for her; and I knew that she was thus without hope, for I felt nothing.

"At the Autarch's camp," she repeated. "That was what Einhildis wrote. In Orithyia, near the springs of Gyoll. But you must be careful if you go there to return the book—she said too that cacogens had landed somewhere in the north."

I stared at her, trying to determine whether she were lying.

"That's what Einhildis told me. I suppose they must have wished to avoid the mirrors at the House Absolute so they could escape the eyes of the Autarch. He's supposed to be their servitor, but sometimes he acts as if they were his."

I shook her. "Are you joking with me? The Autarch serves them?"

"Please! Oh, please . . ."

I dropped her.

"Everyone . . . Erebus! Pardon me." She sobbed, and though she lay in shadow I sensed that she was wiping her eyes and nose with the hem of her scarlet habit. "Everyone knows it except the peons, and the goodmen and the good women. All the armigers and even most of the optimates, and of course the exultants have always known. I've never seen the Autarch, but I'm told that he, the Viceroy of the New Sun, is scarcely taller than I am. Do you think our proud exultants would permit someone like that to rule if there weren't a thousand cannon behind him?"

"I've seen him," I said, "and I wondered about that." I sought among Thecla's memories for confirmation of what Cyriaca said, but I found only rumor.

"Would you tell me about him? Please, Severian, before—"

"No, not now. But why should the cacogens be a danger to me?"

"Because the Autarch will surely send scouts to locate them, and I suppose the archon here will too. Anyone found near them will be assumed to have been spying for them, or what's worse, seeking them out in the hope of enlisting them in some plot against the Phoenix Throne."

"I understand."

"Severian, don't kill me. I beg you. I'm not a good woman— I've never been a good woman, never since I left the Pelerines, and I can't face dying now."

I asked her, "What have you done, anyway? Why does Abdiesus want you killed? Do you know?" It is simplicity itself to strangle an individual whose neck muscles are not strong, and I was already flexing my hands for the task; yet at the same time I wished it had been permissible for me to use *Terminus Est* instead.

"Only loved too many men, men other than my husband."

As if moved by the memory of those embraces, she rose and came toward me. Again the moonlight fell upon her face; her eyes were bright with unshed tears.

"He was cruel to me, so cruel, after our marriage . . . and so I took a lover, to spite him, and afterwards, another . . ."

(Her voice dropped until I could hardly hear the words.)

"And at last taking a new lover becomes a habit, a way of pushing back the days and showing yourself that all your life has not run between your fingers already, showing yourself that you are still young enough for men to bring gifts, young enough that men still want to stroke your hair. That was what I had left the Pelerines for, after all." She paused and seemed to gather her strength. "Do you know how old I am? Did I tell you?"

"No," I said.

"I won't, then. But I might almost be your mother. If I had conceived within a year or two of the time it became possible for me. We were far in the south, where the great ice, all blue and white, sails on black seas. There was a little hill where I used to stand and watch, and I dreamed of putting on warm clothes and paddling out to the ice with food and a trained bird I never really had but only wanted to have, and so riding my own ice island north to an isle of palms, where I would discover the ruins of a castle built in the morning of the world. You would have been born then, perhaps, while I was alone on the ice. Why shouldn't an imaginary child be born on an imaginary trip? You would have grown up fishing and swimming in water warmer than milk."

"No woman is killed for being unfaithful, except by her husband," I said.

Cyriaca sighed, and her dream fell from her. "Among the landed armigers hereabout, he is one of the few who support the archon. The others hope that by disobeying him as much as they dare and fomenting trouble among the eclectics they can persuade the Autarch to replace him. I have made my husband a laughing stock—and by extension his friends and the archon."

Because Thecla was within me, I saw the country villa—half manor and half fort, full of rooms that had scarcely changed in two hundred years. I heard the tittering ladies and the stamping hunters, and the sound of the horn outside the windows, and the deep barking of the boarhounds. It was the world to which Thecla had hoped to retreat; and I felt pity for this woman, who had been forced into that retreat when she had never known any wider sphere.

Just as the room of the Inquisitor in Dr. Talos's play, with its high judicial bench, lurked somewhere at the lowest level of the House Absolute, so we have each of us in the dustiest cellars of our minds a counter at which we strive to repay the debts of the past with the debased currency of the present. At that counter I tendered Cyriaca's life in payment for Thecla's.

When I led her from the summerhouse, she supposed, I know, that I intended to kill her at the edge of the water. Instead, I pointed to the river.

"This flows swiftly south until it meets the flood of Gyoll, which then runs more slowly to Nessus, and at last to the southern sea. No fugitive can be found in the maze of Nessus who does not wish it, for there are streets and courts and tenements there without number, and all the faces of all lands are seen a hundred times over. If you could go there, dressed as you are now, without friends or money, would you do so?"

She nodded, one pale hand at her throat.

"There is no barrier to boats yet at the Capulus; Abdiesus knows he need not fear any attack made against the current there until midsummer. But you will have to shoot the arches, and you may drown. Even if you reach Nessus, you will have to work for your bread—wash for others, perhaps, or cook."

"I can dress hair and sew. Severian, I have heard that sometimes, as the last and most terrible torture, you tell your prisoner she will be freed. If that is what you're doing to me now, I beg you to stop. You've gone far enough."

"A caloyer does that, or some other religious functionary. No client would believe us. But I want to be certain there will be no foolishness of returning to your home or seeking a pardon from the archon."

"I am a fool," Cyriaca said. "But no. Not even such a fool as I am would do that, I swear."

We skirted the water's edge until we came to the stairs where the sentries stood to admit the archon's guests, and the little, brightly hued pleasure boats were moored. I told one of the soldiers we were going to try the river, and asked if we would have any difficulty hiring rowers to take us back upstream. He said we might leave the boat at the Capulus if we wished, and return in a fiacre. When he turned away to resume his conversation with his comrade, I pretended to inspect the boats, and slipped the painter of the one farthest from the torches of the guard post.

Dorcas said, "And so now you are going north as a fugitive, and I have taken your money."

"I won't need much, and I will get more." I stood up.

"Take back half at least." When I shook my head, she said, "Then take back two chrisos. I can whore, if worst comes to worst, or steal."

"If you steal, your hand will be struck off. And it is better that I strike off hands for my dinner than that you give your hands for yours."

I started to go, but she sprang out of bed and held my cloak. "Be careful, Severian. There is something—Hethor called it a salamander—loose in the city. Whatever it is, it burns its victims."

I told her I had much more to fear from the archon's soldiers than from the salamander, and left before she could say more. But as I toiled up a narrow street on the western bank that my boatmen had assured me would lead to the cliff top, I wondered if I would not have more to fear from the cold of the mountains, and their wild beasts, than from either. I wondered too about Hethor, and how he had followed me so far into the north, and why. But more than I thought on any of those things, I thought about Dorcas, and what she had been to me, and I to her. It was to be a long time before I would so much as glimpse her again, and I believe that in some way I sensed that. Just as when I had first left the Citadel I had pulled up my hood so that the passersby might not observe my smiles, so now I hid my face to conceal the tears running down my cheeks.

I had seen the reservoir that supplied the Vincula twice before by day, but never by night. It had appeared small then, a rectangular pond no larger than the foundation of a house and no deeper than a grave. Under the waning moon it seemed almost a lake, and might have been as deep as the cistern below the Bell Tower.

It lay no more than a hundred paces from the wall that defended the western margin of Thrax. There were towers on that wall—one quite near the reservoir—and no doubt the garrisons had by that time been ordered to apprehend me if I tried to escape from the city. At intervals, as I had walked along the cliff, I had glimpsed the sentries who patrolled the wall; their lances were unkindled, but their crested helms showed against the stars, and sometimes faintly caught the light.

Now I crouched, looking out over the city and relying on my fuligin cloak and hood to deceive their eyes. The barred iron portcullises of the arches of the Capulus had been lowered—I could detect the roiling of the Acis where it battered against them. That removed all doubt: Cyriaca had been stopped—or more probably, simply seen and reported. Abdiesus might or might not make strenuous efforts to capture her; it seemed most probable to me that he would allow her to vanish, and so avoid drawing attention to her. But he would surely apprehend me if he could, and execute me as the traitor to his rule that I was.

From the water I looked to water again, from the rushing Acis to the still reservoir. I had the word for the sluice gate, and I used it. The ancient mechanism ground up as though moved by phantom slaves, and then the still waters rushed too, rushed faster than the raging Acis at the Capulus. Far below, the prisoners would hear their roar, and those nearest the entrance would see the white foam of the flood. In a moment those who stood would be up to their ankles in water, and those who had slept would be scrambling to their feet. In another moment, all would be waist deep; but they were chained in their places, and the weaker would be supported by the stronger—none, I hoped, would drown. The clavigers at the entrance would leave their posts and hurry up the steep trail to the cliff top to see who had tampered with the reservoir there.

And as the last water drained away, I heard the stones dislodged by their feet rattling down the slope. I closed the sluice gate again and lowered myself into the slimy and nearly vertical passage that the water had just traversed. Here my progress would have been far easier if I had not been carrying *Terminus Est*. To brace my back against one side of that crooked, chimneylike pipe, I had to unsling her; yet I could not spare a hand to hold her. I put her baldric around my neck, let her blade and sheath hang down, and managed her weight as well as I could. Twice I slipped, but each time I was saved by a turn of the narrowing sluice; and at last, after so long a time that I was certain the clavigers would have returned, I saw the gleam of red torchlight and drew forth the Claw.

I was never to see it flame so bright again. It was blinding, and I carrying it upraised down the long tunnel of the Vincula, could only wonder that my hand was not reduced to ashes. No prisoner, I think, saw *me*. The Claw fascinated them as a lantern by night does the deer of the forest; they stood motionless, their mouths open, their raddled, bearded faces uplifted, their shadows behind them as sharp as silhouettes cut in metal and dark as fuligin.

At the very end of the tunnel, where the water ran out into the long, sloping sewer that carried it below the Capulus, were the weakest and most diseased prisoners; and it was there that I saw most clearly the strength the Claw lent them all. Men and women who had not stood straight in the memory of the oldest claviger now seemed tall and strong. I waved in salute to them, though I am sure none of them observed it. Then I put the Claw of the Conciliator back into its little pouch, and we were plunged into a night beside which the night of the surface of Urth would be day.

The rush of water had swept the sewer clean, and it was easier to descend than the sluice had been, for though it was narrower, it was less steep, and I could crawl rapidly down headforemost. There was a grill at the bottom; but as I had noted on one of my inspection tours, it was nearly rusted through.

XIII

Into the Mountains

SPRING HAD ENDED and summer begun when I crept away from the Capulus in the gray light, but even so it was never warm in the high lands except when the sun was near the zenith. Yet I did not dare to go into the valleys where the villages huddled, and all day I walked up, into the mountains, with my cloak furled across one shoulder to make it look as nearly as possible like the garment of an eclectic. I also dismounted the blade of *Terminus Est* and reassembled it without the guard, so that the sheathed sword seen from a distance would have the appearance of a staff.

By noon the ground was all of stone, and so uneven that I did as much climbing as walking. Twice I saw the glint of armor far below me, and looking down beheld little parties of dimarchi cantering down trails most men could scarcely have persuaded themselves to walk, their scarlet military capes billowing behind them. I found no edible plants and sighted no game other than high soaring birds of prey. Had I seen any, I would have had no chance of taking it with my sword, and I possessed no other weapon.

All that sounds desperate enough, but the truth was that I was thrilled by the mountain views, the vast panorama of the empire of air. As children we have no appreciation of scenery because, having not yet stored similar scenes in our imagination, with their attendant emotions and circumstances, we perceive it without psychic depth. I now looked at the cloud-crowned summits with my view of Nessus from the nose cone of our Matachin Tower and my view of Thrax from the battlements of Acies Castle before me as well, and miserable though I was, I was ready to faint with pleasure.

That night I spent huddled in the lee of a naked rock. I had not eaten since I had changed clothes in the Vincula, which now seemed weeks, if not years, before. In actuality, it had been only months since I had smuggled a worn kitchen knife to poor Thecla, and seen her blood seeping, a groping worm of crimson, from beneath her cell door.

I had chosen my stone well, at least. It blocked the wind, so that as long as I remained behind it I might almost have rested in the quiet, frigid air of some ice cave. A step or two to either side brought me into the full blast, so that I was chilled to the bone in a single frosty moment.

I slept for about a watch, I think, without any dreams that outlived my sleep, then woke with the impression—which was not a dream, but the sort of foundationless knowledge or pseudoknowledge that comes to us at times when we are weary and fearful—that Hethor was leaning over me. I seemed to feel his breath, stinking and icy cold, upon my face; his eyes, no longer dull, blazed into mine. When I was fully awake, I saw that the points of light I had taken for their pupils were in fact two stars, large and very bright in the thin, clean air.

I tried to sleep again, closing my eyes and forcing myself to remember the warmest and most comfortable places I had known: the journeyman's quarters I had been given in our tower, which had then seemed so palatial with their privacy and soft blankets after the apprentices' dormitory; the bed I had once shared with Baldanders, into which his broad back had projected heat like a stove's; Thecla's apartments in the House Absolute; the snug room in Saltus where I had lodged with Jonas.

Nothing helped. I could not sleep again, and yet I dared not to try to walk farther for fear that I would fall over some precipice in the dark. I spent the remainder of the night staring at the stars; it was the first time I had ever really experienced the majesty of the constellations, of which Master Malrubius had taught us when I was the smallest of the apprentices. How strange it is that the sky, which by day is a stationary ground on which the clouds are seen to move, by night becomes the backdrop for Urth's own motion, so that we feel her rolling beneath us as a sailor feels the running of the tide. That night the sense of this slow turning was so strong that I was almost giddy with its long, continued sweep.

Strong too was the feeling that the sky was a bottomless pit into which the universe might drop forever. I had heard people say that when they looked at the stars too long they grew terrified by the sensation of being drawn away. My own fear— and I felt fear—was not centered on the remote suns, but rather on the yawning void; and at times I grew so frightened that I gripped the rock with my freezing fingers, for it seemed to me that I must fall off Urth. No doubt everyone feels some touch of this, since it is said that there exists no climate so mild that people will consent to sleep in unroofed houses.

I have already described how I woke thinking that Hethor's face (I suppose because Hethor had been much in my mind since I talked to Dorcas) was staring into mine, yet discovered when I opened my eyes that the face retained no detail except the two bright stars that had been its own. So it was with me at first when I tried to pick out the constellations, whose names I had often read, though I had only the most imperfect idea of the part of the sky in which each might be found. At first all the stars seemed a featureless mass of lights, however beautiful, like the sparks that fly upward from a fire. Soon, of course, I began to see that some were brighter than others, and that their colors were by no means uniform. Then, quite unexpectedly, when I had been staring at them for a long time, the shape of a peryton seemed to spring out as distinctly as if the bird's whole body had been powdered with the dust ground from diamonds. In a moment it was gone again, but it soon returned, and with it other shapes, some corresponding to constellations of which I had heard, others that were, I am afraid, entirely of my own imagining. An amphisbaena, or snake with a head at either end, was particularly distinct.

When these celestial animals burst into view, I was awed by their beauty. But when they became so strongly evident (as they quickly did) that I could no longer dismiss them by an act of will, I began to feel as frightened of them as I was of falling into that midnight abyss over which they writhed; yet this was not a simple physical and instinctive fear like the other, but rather a sort of philosophical horror at the thought of a cosmos in which rude pictures of beasts and monsters had been painted with flaming suns.

After I covered my head with my cloak, which I was forced to do lest I go mad, I fell to thinking of the worlds that circled those suns. All of us know they exist, many being mere endless plains of rock, others spheres of ice or of cindery hills where lava rivers flow, as is alleged of Abaddon; but many others being worlds more or less fair, and inhabited by creatures either descended from the human stock or at least not wholly different from ourselves. At first I thought of green skies, blue grass, and all the rest of the childish exotica apt to inflict the mind that conceives of other than Urthly worlds. But in time I tired of those puerile ideas, and began in their place to think of societies and ways of thought wholly different from our own, worlds in which all the people, knowing themselves descended from a single pair of colonists, treated one another as brothers and sisters, worlds where there was no currency but honor, so that everyone worked in order that he might be entitled to associate himself with some man or woman who had saved the community, worlds in which the long war between mankind and the beasts was pursued no more. With these thoughts came a hundred or more new ones—how justice might be meted out when all loved all, for example; how a beggar who retained nothing but his humanity might beg for honor, and the ways in which people who would kill no sentient animal might be shod and fed.

When I had first come to realize, as a boy, that the green circle of the moon was in fact a sort of island hung in the sky, whose color derived from forests, now immemorially old, planted in the earliest days of the race of Man, I had formed an intention of going there, and had added to it all the other worlds of the universe as I came in time to realize their existence. I had abandoned that wish as a part (I thought) of growing up, when I learned that only people whose positions in society appeared to me unattainably high ever succeeded in leaving Urth.

Now that old longing was rekindled again, and though it seemed to have grown more absurd still with the passage of the years (for surely the little apprentice I had been had more chance of flashing between the stars at last than the hunted outcast I had become) it was immensely firmer and stronger because I had learned in the intervening time the folly of limiting desire to the possible. I would go, I was resolved. For the remainder of my life I would be sleeplessly alert for any opportunity, however slight. Already I had found myself once alone with the mirrors of Father Inire; then Jonas, wiser by far than I, had without hesitation cast himself on the tide of photons. Who could say that I would never find myself before those mirrors again?

With that thought, I snatched my cloak away from my head, resolved to look upon the stars once more, and found that the sunlight had come lancing over the crowns of the mountains to dim them almost to insignificance. The titan faces that loomed above me now were only those of the long-dead rulers of Urth, haggard by time, their cheeks fallen away in avalanches.

I stood and stretched. It was clear that I could not spend the day without food, as I had spent the day before; and clearer still that I could not spend the next night as I had spent this, with no shelter but my cloak. Thus, though I did not dare yet go down into the peopled valleys, I shaped my path to take me to the high forest I could see marching over the slopes below me.

It took most of the morning to reach it. When at last I scrambled down to stand among the scrub birches that were its outriders, I saw that although it was more steeply pitched than I had supposed, it contained, toward its center where the ground was somewhat more level and the sparse soil thus a trifle richer, trees of very considerable height, so closely spaced that the apertures between their trunks were hardly wider than the trunks themselves. They were not, of course, the glossy-leaved hardwoods of the tropical forest we had left behind on the south bank of the Cephissus. These were shaggy-barked conifers for the most part, tall, straight trees that leaned, even in their height and strength, away from the shadow of the mountain, and showed plainly in at least a quarter of their number the wounds of their wars with wind and lightning.

I had come hoping to find woodcutters or hunters from whom I might claim the hospitality that everyone (as city people fondly believe) offers to strangers in the wilds. For a long time, however, I was disappointed in that hope. Again and again I paused to listen for the ringing of an ax or the baying of hounds. There was only silence, and indeed, though the trees would have provided a great quantity of lumber, I saw no signs that any had ever been cut.

At last I came across a little brook of ice-cold water that wandered among the trees, fringed with dwarfed and tender bracken and grass as fine as hair. I drank my fill, and for perhaps half a watch followed the water down the slope through a succession of miniature falls and tarns, wondering, as no doubt others have for countless chiliads, to observe it grown slowly larger, though it had recruited no others of its kind that I could see.

Eventually it was swollen until the trees themselves were no longer safe from it, and I saw ahead the trunk of one, four cubits thick at least, that had fallen across it, its roots undermined. I approached it with no great care, for there was no sound to warn me, and bracing myself on a projecting stub vaulted to the top.

Almost I tumbled into an ocean of air. The battlement of Acies Castle, from which I had seen Dorcas in her dejection, was a balustrade compared to that height. Surely the Wall of Nessus is the only work of hands that could rival it. The brook fell silently upon a gulf that blew it to spray, so that it vanished into a rainbow. The trees below might have been toys made for a boy by an indulgent father, and at the edge of them, with a little field beyond, I saw a house no bigger than a pebble, with a wisp of white smoke, the ghost of the ribbon of water that had fallen and died, curling up to disappear like it into nothingness.

To descend the cliff appeared at first only too easy, for the momentum of my vault had nearly carried me over the fallen trunk, which itself hung half over the edge. When I had regained my balance, however, it seemed close to impossible. The rock face was sheer over large areas, so far as I could see, and though perhaps if I had carried a rope I could have let myself down and so reached the house well before night, I of course had none, and in any case would have been very slow to trust a rope of such immense length as would have been required.

I spent some time exploring the top of the cliff, however, and eventually discovered a path that, though very precipitous and very narrow, showed unmistakable signs of use. I will not recount the details of the climb down, which really have little to do with my story, although they were as may be imagined deeply absorbing at the time. I soon learned to watch only the path and the face of the cliff, to my right or left as the path wound back and forth. For most of its length it was a steep descent about a cubit wide or a little less. Occasionally it became a series of descending steps cut into the living rock, and at one point there were only hand and foot holes, which I descended like a ladder. These were far easier—viewed objectively—than the crevices to which I had clung by night at the mouth of the mine of the man-apes, and at least I was spared the shock of crossbow quarrels exploding about my ears; but the height was a hundred times greater, and dizzying.

Perhaps because I was forced to labor so hard to ignore the drop on the opposite side, I became acutely conscious of the vast, sectioned sample of the world's crust down which I crawled. In ancient times—so I read once in one of the texts Master Palaemon set me—the heart of Urth herself was alive, and the shifting motions of that living core made plains erupt like fountains, and sometimes opened seas in a night between islands that had been one continent when last seen by the sun. Now it is said she is dead, and cooling and shrinking within her stony mantle like the corpse of an old woman in one of those abandoned houses Dorcas had described, mummifying in the still, dry air until her clothing falls in upon itself. So it is, it is said, with Urth; and here half a mountain had dropped away from its mating half, falling a league at least.

XIV

The Widow's House

IN SALTUS, WHERE Jonas and I stayed for a few days and where I performed the second and third public decollations of my career, the miners rape the soil of metals, building stones, and even artifacts laid down by civilizations forgotten for chiliads before the Wall of Nessus ever rose. This they do by narrow shafts bored into the hillsides until they strike some rich layer of ruins, or even (if the tunnelers are particularly fortunate) a building that has preserved some part of its structure so that it serves them as a gallery already made.

What was done with so much labor there might have been accomplished on the cliff I descended with almost none. The past stood at my shoulder, naked and defenseless as all dead things, as though it were time itself that had been laid open by the fall of the mountain. Fossil bones protruded from the surface in places, the bones of mighty animals and of men. The forest had set its own dead there as well, stumps and limbs that time had turned to stone, so that I wondered as I descended, if it might not be that Urth is not, as we assume, older than her daughters the trees, and imagined them growing in the emptiness before the face of the sun, tree clinging to tree with tangled roots and interlacing twigs until at last their accumulation became our Urth, and they only the nap of her garment.

Deeper than these lay the buildings and mechanisms of humanity. (And it may be that those of other races lay there as well, for several of the stories in the brown book I carried seemed to imply that colonies once existed here of those beings whom we call the cacogens, though they are in fact of myriad races, each as distinct as our own.) I saw metals there that were green and blue in the same sense that copper is said to be red or silver white, colored metals so curiously wrought that I could not be certain whether their shapes had been intended as works of art or as parts for strange machines, and it may be indeed that among some of those unfathomable peoples there is no distinction.

At one point, only slightly less than halfway down, the line of the fault had coincided with the tiled wall of some great building, so that the windy path I trod slashed across it. What the design was those tiles traced, I never knew; as I descended the cliff I was too near to see it, and when I reached the base at last it was too high for me to discern, lost in the shifting mists of the falling river. Yet as I walked, I saw it as an insect may be said to see the face in a portrait over whose surface it creeps. The tiles were of many shapes, though they fit together so closely, and at first I thought them representations of birds, lizards, fish and suchlike creatures, all interlocked in the grip of life. Now I feel that this was not so, that they were instead the shapes of a geometry I failed to comprehend, diagrams so complex that the living forms seemed to appear in them as the forms of actual animals appear from the intricate geometries of complex molecules.

However that might be, these forms seemed to have little connection with the picture or design. Lines of color crossed them, and though they must have been fired into the substance of the tiles in eons past, they were so willful and bright that they might have been laid on only a moment before by some titanic artist's brush. The shades most used were beryl and white, but though I stopped several times and strove to understand what might be depicted there (whether it was writing, or a face, or perhaps a mere decorative design of lines and angles, or a pattern of intertwined verdure) I could not; and perhaps it was each of those, or none, depending on the position from which it was seen and the predisposition the viewer brought to it.

Once this enigmatic wall was passed, the way down grew

easier. It was never necessary again for me to climb down a sheer drop, and though there were several more flights of steps, they were not so steep or so narrow as before. I reached the bottom before I expected it, and looked up at the path down which I had traveled with as much wonder as if I had never set foot on it—indeed, I could see several points at which it appeared to have been broken by the spalling away of sections of the cliff, so that it seemed impassable.

The house I had beheld so clearly from above was invisible now, hidden among trees; but the smoke of its chimney still showed against the sky. I made my way through a forest less precipitous than the one through which I had followed the brook. The dark trees seemed, if anything, older. The great ferns of the south were absent there, and in fact I never saw them north of the House Absolute, except for those under cultivation in the gardens of Abdiesus; but there were wild violets with glossy leaves and flowers the exact color of poor Thecla's eyes growing between the roots of the trees, and moss like the thickest green velvet, so that the ground seemed carpeted, and the trees themselves all draped in costly fabric.

Some time before I could see the house or any other sign of human presence, I heard the barking of a dog. At the sound, the silence and wonder of the trees fell back, present still but infinitely more distant. I felt that some mysterious life, old and strange, yet kindly too, had come to the very moment of revealing itself to me, then drawn away like some immensely eminent person, a master of the musicians, perhaps, whom I had struggled for years to attract to my door but who in the act of knocking had heard the voice of another guest who was unpleasing to him and had put down his hand and turned away, never to come again.

Yet how comforting it was. For almost two long days I had been utterly alone, first upon the broken fields of stone, then among the icy beauty of the stars, and then in the hushed breath of the ancient trees. Now that harsh, familiar sound made me think once more of human comfort—not only think of it, but imagine it so vividly that I seemed to feel it already. I knew that when I saw the dog himself he would be like Triskele; and so he was, with four legs instead of three, somewhat longer and narrower in the skull, and more brown than lion-colored, but with the same dancing eyes and wagging tail and lolling tongue. He began with a declaration of war, which he rescinded as soon as I spoke to him, and before I had gone twenty strides he was presenting his ears to be scratched. I came into the little clearing where the house stood with the dog romping about me.

The walls were of stone, hardly higher than my head. The thatched roof was as steep as I have ever seen, and dotted with flat stones to hold down the thatch in high winds. It was, in short, the home of one of those pioneering peasants who are the glory and despair of our Commonwealth, who in one year produce a surplus of food to support the population of Nessus, but who must themselves be fed in the next lest they starve.

When there is no paved path before a door, one can judge how often feet go out and in by the degree to which the grass encroaches on the trodden ground. Here there was only a little circle of dust the size of a kerchief before the stone step. When I saw it, I supposed that I might frighten the person who lived in that cabin (for I supposed there could only be one) if I were to appear at the door unannounced, and so since the dog had long ago ceased to bark, I paused at the edge of the clearing and shouted a greeting.

The trees and the sky swallowed it, and left only silence.

I shouted again and advanced toward the door with the dog at my heels, and had almost reached it when a woman appeared there. She had a delicate face that might easily have been beautiful had it not been for her haunted eyes, but she wore a ragged dress that differed from a beggar's only by being clean. After a moment, a round-faced little boy, larger-eyed even than his mother, peeped past her skirt.

I said, "I am sorry if I startled you, but I have been lost in these mountains."

The woman nodded, hesitated, then drew back from the door, and I stepped inside. Her house was even smaller within its thick walls than I had supposed, and it reeked with the smell of some strong vegetable boiling in a kettle suspended on a hook over the fire. The windows were few and small, and because of the depth of the walls seemed rather boxes of shadow than apertures of light. An old man sat upon a panther skin with his back to the fire; his eyes were so lacking in focus and intelligence that at first I thought him blind. There was a table at the center of the room, with five chairs about it, of which three seemed to have been made for adults. I remembered what Dorcas had told me about furniture from the abandoned houses of Nessus being brought north for eclectics who had adopted more cultivated fashions, but all the pieces showed signs of having been made on the spot.

The woman saw the direction of my glance and said, "My husband will be here soon. Before supper."

I told her, "You don't have to worry—I mean you no harm. If you'll let me share your meal and sleep here tonight out of the cold, and give me directions in the morning, I'll be glad to help with whatever work there is to be done."

The woman nodded, and quite unexpectedly the little boy piped, "Have you seen Severa?" His mother turned on him so quickly that I was reminded of Master Gurloes demonstrating the grips used to control prisoners. I heard the blow, though I hardly saw it, and the little boy shrieked. His mother moved to block the door, and he hid himself behind a chest in the corner farthest from her. I understood then, or thought I understood, that Severa was a girl or woman whom she considered more vulnerable than herself, and whom she had ordered to hide (probably in the loft, under the thatch) before letting me in. But I reasoned that any further protestation of my good intentions would be wasted on the woman, who however ignorant was clearly no fool, and that the best way to gain her confidence was to deserve it. I began by asking her for some water so that I could wash, and said that I would gladly carry it from whatever source they had if she would permit me to heat it at her fire. She gave me a pot, and told me where the spring was.

At one time or another I have been in most of the places that are conventionally considered romantic—atop high towers, deep in the bowels of the world, in palatial buildings, in jungles, and aboard a ship—yet none of these have affected me in the same way as that poor cabin of stones. It seemed to me the archetype of those caves into which, as scholars teach, humanity has crept again at the lowest point of each cycle of civilization. Whenever I have read or heard a description of an idyllic rustic retreat (and it was an idea of which Thecla was very fond) it has dwelt on cleanliness and order. There is a bed of mint beneath the window, wood stacked by the coldest wall, a gleaming flagstone floor, and so on. There was nothing of that here, no ideality; and yet the house was more perfect for all its imperfection, showing that human beings

might live and love in such a remote spot without the ability
to shape their habitat into a poem.

"Do you always shave with your sword?" the woman asked.
It was the first time she had spoken to me unguardedly.

"It is a custom, a tradition. If the sword were not sharp
enough for me to shave with, I would be ashamed to bear it.
And if it is sharp enough, what need do I have of a razor?"

"Still it must be awkward, holding such a heavy blade up
like that, and you must have to take great care not to cut
yourself."

"The exercise strengthens my arms. Besides, it's good for
me to handle my sword every chance I get, so that it becomes
as familiar as my limbs."

"You're a soldier, then. I thought so."

"I am a butcher of men."

She seemed taken aback at that, and said, "I didn't mean to
insult you."

"I'm not insulted. Everyone kills certain things—you killed
those roots in your kettle when you put them into the boiling
water. When I kill a man, I save the lives of all the living
things he would have destroyed if he had continued to live
himself, including, perhaps, many other men, and women and
children. What does your husband do?"

The woman smiled a little at that. It was the first time I had
seen her smile, and it made her look much younger. "Everything. A man has to do everything up here."

"You weren't born here then."

"No," she said. "Only Severian . . ." The smile was gone.

"Did you say Severian?"

"That's my son's name. You saw him when you came in,
and he's spying on us now. He is a thoughtless boy sometimes."

"That is my own name. I am Master Severian."

She called to the boy, "Did you hear that? The goodman's
name is the same as yours!" Then to me again, "Do you think
it's a good name? Do you like it?"

"I'm afraid I've never thought much about it, but yes, I
suppose I do. It seems to suit me." I had finished shaving, and
seated myself in one of the chairs to tend the blade.

"I was born in Thrax," the woman said. "Have you ever
been there?"

"I just came from there," I told her. If the dimarchi were to question her after I left, her description of my habit would give me away in any case.

"You didn't meet a woman called Herais? She's my mother."

I shook my head.

"Well, it's a big town, I suppose. You weren't there long?"

"No, not long at all. While you have been in these mountains, have you heard of the Pelerines? They're an order of priestesses who wear red."

"I'm afraid not. We don't get much news here."

"I'm trying to locate them, or if I can't, to join the army the Autarch is leading against the Ascians."

"My husband could give you better directions than I can. You shouldn't have come up here so high, though. Becan— that's my husband—says the patrols never bother soldiers moving north, not even when they use the old roads."

While she spoke of soldiers moving north, someone else, much nearer, was moving as well. It was a movement so stealthy as to be scarcely audible above the crackling of the fire and the harsh breathing of the old man, but it was unmistakable nonetheless. Bare feet, unable to endure any longer the utter motionlessness that silence commands, had shifted almost imperceptibly, and the planks beneath them had chirped with the new distribution of weight.

XV

He Is Ahead of You!

THE HUSBAND WHO was supposed to have come before supper did not come, and the four of us—the woman, the old man, the boy, and I—ate the evening meal without him. I had at first thought his wife's prediction a lie intended to deter me from whatever criminality I might otherwise have committed; but as the sullen afternoon wore on in that silence that presages a storm, it became apparent that she had believed what she had said, and was now sincerely worried.

Our supper was as simple, almost, as such a meal can be; but my hunger was so great that it was one of the most gratifying I recall. We had boiled vegetables without salt or butter, coarse bread, and a little meat. No wine, no fruit, nothing fresh and nothing sweet; yet I think I must have eaten more than the other three together.

When our meal was over, the woman (whose name, I had learned, was Casdoe) took a long, iron-shod staff out of a corner and set off to look for her husband, first assuring me that she required no escort and telling the old man, who seemed not to hear her, that she would not go far and would soon return. Seeing him remain as abstracted as ever before his fire, I coaxed the boy to me, and after I had won his confidence by showing him *Terminus Est* and permitting him to hold her hilt and attempt to lift her blade, I asked him whether Severa should not come down and take care of him now that his mother was away.

"She came back last night," he told me.

I thought he was referring to his mother and said, "I'm sure she'll come back tonight too, but don't you think Severa ought to take care of you now, while she's gone?"

As children who are not sufficiently confident of language to argue sometimes do, the boy shrugged and tried to turn away.

I caught him by the shoulders. "I want you to go upstairs now, little Severian, and tell her to come down. I promise I won't hurt her."

He nodded and went to the ladder, though slowly and reluctantly. "Bad woman," he said.

Then, for the first time since I had been in the house, the old man spoke. "Becan, come over here! I want to tell you about Fechin." It was a moment before I understood that he was addressing me under the impression that I was his son-in-law.

"He was the worst of us all, that Fechin. A tall, wild boy with red hair on his hands, on his arms. Like a monkey's arms, so that if you saw them reaching around the corner to take something, you'd think, except for the size, that it was a monkey taking it. He took our copper pan once, the one Mother used to make sausage in, and I saw his arm and didn't tell who had done it, because he was my friend. I never found it again, never saw it again, though I was with him a thousand times. I used to think he had made a boat of it and sailed it on the river, because that was what I had always wanted to do with it myself. I walked down the river trying to find it, and the night came before I ever knew it, before I had even turned around to go home. Maybe he polished the bottom to look in—sometimes he drew his own likeness. Maybe he filled it with water to see his reflection."

I had gone across the room to listen to him, partly because he spoke indistinctly and partly out of respect, for his aged face reminded me a little of Master Palaemon's, though he had his natural eyes. "I once met a man of your age who had posed for Fechin," I said.

The old man looked up at me; as quickly as the shadow of a bird might cross some gray rag thrown out of the house upon the grass, I saw the realization that I was not Becan come and go. He did not stop speaking, however, or in any other way acknowledge the fact. It was as if what he was saying were so urgent that it had to be told to someone, poured into any ears before it was lost forever.

"His face wasn't a monkey's face at all. Fechin was handsome—the handsomest around. He could always get food or money from a woman. He could get anything from women. I remember once when we were walking down the trail that led to where the old mill stood then. I had a piece of paper the schoolmaster had given me. Real paper, not quite white, but with a touch of brown to it, and little speckles here and there, so it looked like a trout in milk. The schoolmaster gave it to me so I could write a letter for Mother—at the school we always wrote on boards, then washed them clean with a sponge when we had to write again, and when nobody was looking we'd hit the sponge with the board and send it flying against the wall, or somebody's head. But Fechin loved to draw, and while we walked I thought about that, and how his face would look if he had paper to make a picture he could keep.

"They were the only things he kept. Everything else he lost, or gave away, or threw away, and I knew what Mother wanted to tell pretty much, and I decided if I wrote small I could get it on half the paper. Fechin didn't know I had it, but I took it out and showed it to him, then folded it and tore it in two."

Over our heads, I could hear the fluting voice of the little boy, though I could not understand what he was saying.

"That was the brightest day I've ever seen. The sun had new life to him, the way a man will when he was sick yesterday and will be sick tomorrow, but today he walks around and laughs so that if a stranger was to come he'd think there was nothing wrong, no sickness at all, that the medicines and the bed were for somebody else. They always say in prayers that the New Sun will be too bright to look at, and I always up until that day had taken it to be just the proper way of talking, the way you say a baby's beautiful, or praise whatever a good man has made for himself, that even if there were two suns in the sky you could look at both. But that day I learned it was all true, and the light of it on Fechin's face was more than I could stand. It made my eyes water. He said thank you, and we went farther along and came to a house where a girl lived.

I can't remember what her name was, but she was truly beautiful, the way the quietest are sometimes. I never knew up till then that Fechin knew her, but he asked me to wait, and I sat down on the first step in front of the gate."

Someone heavier than the boy was walking overhead, toward the ladder.

"He wasn't inside long, but when he came out, with the girl looking out the window, I knew what they had done. I looked at him, and he spread those long, thin, monkey arms. How could he share what he'd had? In the end, he made the girl give me half a loaf of bread and some fruit. He drew my picture on one side of the paper and the girl's on the other, but he kept the pictures."

The ladder creaked, and I turned to look. As I had expected, a woman was descending it. She was not tall, but full-figured and narrow-waisted; her gown was nearly as ragged as the boy's mother's, and much dirtier. Rich brown hair spilled down her back. I think I recognized her even before she turned and I saw the high cheekbones and her long, brown eyes—it was Agia. "So you knew I was here all along," she said.

"I might make the same remark to you. You seem to have been here before me."

"I only guessed that you would be coming this way. As it happened, I arrived a little before you, and I told the mistress of this house what you would do to me if she did not hide me," she said. (I supposed she wished me to know she had an ally here, if only a feeble one.)

"You've been trying to kill me ever since I glimpsed you in the crowd at Saltus."

"Is that an accusation? Yes."

"You're lying."

It was one of the few times I have ever seen Agia caught off balance. "What do you mean?"

"Only that you were trying to kill me before Saltus."

"With the avern. Yes, of course."

"And afterward. Agia, I know who Hethor is."

I waited for her to reply, but she said nothing.

"On the day we met, you told me there was an old sailor who wanted you to live with him. Old and ugly and poor, you called him, and I could not understand why you, a lovely young woman, should even consider his offer when you were not actually starving. You had your twin to protect you, and a little money coming in from the shop."

It was my turn to be surprised. She said, "I should have gone to him and mastered him. I have mastered him now."

"I thought you had only promised yourself to him, if he would kill me."

"I have promised him that and many other things, and so mastered him. He is ahead of you, Severian, waiting word from me."

"With more of his beasts? Thank you for the warning. That was it, wasn't it? He had threatened you and Agilus with the pets he had brought from other spheres."

She nodded. "He came to sell his clothes, and they were the kind worn on the old ships that sailed beyond the world's rim long ago, and they weren't costumes or forgeries or even tomb-tender old garments that had lain for centuries in the dark, but clothes not far from new. He said his ships—all those ships—became lost in the blackness between the suns, where the years do not turn. Lost so that even Time cannot find them."

"I know," I said. "Jonas told me."

"After I learned that you would kill Agilus, I went to him. He is iron-strong in some ways, weak in many others. If I had withheld my body I could have done nothing with him, but I did all the queer things he wished me to, and made him believe I love him. Now he will do anything I ask. He followed you for me after you killed Agilus; with his silver I hired the men you killed at the old mine, and the creatures he commands will kill you for me yet, if I don't do it here myself."

"You meant to wait until I slept, and then come down and murder me, I suppose."

"I would have waked you first, when I had my knife at your throat. But the child told me you knew I was here, and I thought this might be more pleasant. Tell me though—how did you guess about Hethor?"

A breath of wind stirred through the narrow windows. It made the fire smoke, and I heard the old man, who sat there in silence once more, cough, and spit onto the coals. The little boy, who had climbed down from the loft while Agia and I talked, watched us with large, uncomprehending eyes.

"I should have known it long before," I said. "My friend Jonas had been just such a sailor. You will remember him, I think—you glimpsed him at the mine mouth, and you must have known of him."

"We did."

"Perhaps they were from the same ship. Or perhaps it was only that each would have known the other by some sign, or that Hethor at least feared they would. However that may be, he seldom came near me when I was traveling with Jonas, though he had been so eager to be in my company before. I saw him in the crowd when I executed a woman and a man at Saltus, but he did not try to join me there. On the way to the House Absolute, Jonas and I saw him behind us, but he did not come running up until Jonas had ridden off, though he must have been desperate to get back his notule. When he was thrown into the antechamber of the House Absolute, he made no attempt to sit with us, even though Jonas was nearly dead; but something that left a trail of slime was searching the place when we left it."

Agia said nothing, and in her silence she might have been the young woman I had seen on the morning of the day after I left our tower unfastening the gratings that had guarded the windows of a dusty shop.

"You two must have lost my trail on the way to Thrax," I continued, "or been delayed by some accident. Even after you discovered we were in the city, you must not have known that I had charge of the Vincula, because Hethor sent his creature of fire prowling the streets to find me. Then, somehow, you found Dorcas at the Duck's Nest—"

"We were lodging there ourselves," Agia said. "We had only arrived a few days before, and we were out looking for you when you came. Afterward when I realized that the woman in the little garret room was the mad girl you had found in the Botanic Gardens, we still didn't guess it was you who had put her there, because that hag at the inn said the man had worn common clothes. But we thought she might know where you were, and that she would be more apt to talk to Hethor. His name isn't really Hethor, by the way. He says it's a much older one, that hardly anyone has heard of now."

"He told Dorcas about the fire creature," I said, "and she told me. I had heard of the thing before, but Hethor had a name for it—he called it a salamander. I didn't think anything of it when Dorcas mentioned it, but later I remembered that Jonas had a name for the black thing that flew after us outside the House Absolute. He called it a notule, and said the people on the ships had named them that because they betrayed themselves with a gust of warmth. If Hethor had a name for the fire creature, it seemed likely that it was a sailor's name too, and that he had something to do with the creature itself."

Agia smiled thinly. "So now you know all, and you have me where you want me—provided you can swing that big blade of yours in here."

"I have you without it. I had you beneath my foot at the mine mouth, for that matter."

"But I still have my knife."

At that moment the boy's mother came through the doorway, and both of us paused. She looked in astonishment from Agia to me; then, as though no surprise could pierce her sorrow or alter what she had to do, she closed the door and lifted the heavy bar into place.

Agia said, "He heard me upstairs, Casdoe, and made me come down. He intends to kill me."

"And how am I to prevent that?" the woman answered wearily. She turned to me. "I hid her because she said you meant her harm. Will you kill me too?"

"No. Nor will I kill her, as she knows."

Agia's face distorted with rage, as the face of another lovely woman, molded by Fechin himself perhaps in colored wax, might have been transformed with a gout of flame, so that it simultaneously melted and burned. "You killed Agilus, and you gloried in it! Aren't I as fit to die as he was? We were the same flesh!" I had not fully believed her when she said she was armed with a knife, but without my having seen her draw it, it was out now—one of the crooked daggers of Thrax.

For some time the air had been heavy with an impending storm. Now the thunder rolled, booming among the peaks above us. When its echoings and reechoings had almost died away, something answered them. I cannot describe that voice; it was not quite a human shout, nor was it the mere bellow of a beast.

All her weariness left the woman Casdoe, replaced by the most desperate haste. Heavy wooden shutters stood against the wall beneath each of the narrow windows; she seized the nearest, and lifting it as if it weighed no more than a pie pan sent it crashing into place. Outside, the dog barked frantically then fell silent, leaving no sound but the pattering of the first rain.

"So soon," Casdoe cried. "So soon!" To her son: "Severian, get out of the way."

Through one of the still open windows, I heard a child's voice call, *"Father, can't you help me?"*

XVI

The Alzabo

I TRIED TO assist Casdoe, and in the process turned my back on Agia and her dagger. It was an error that almost cost me my life, for she was upon me as soon as I was encumbered with a shutter. Women and tailors hold the blade beneath the hand, according to the proverb, but Agia stabbed up to open the tripes and catch the heart from below, like an accomplished assassin. I turned only just in time to block her blade with the shutter, and the point drove through the wood to show a glint of steel.

The very strength of her blow betrayed her. I wrenched the shutter to one side and threw it across the room, and her knife with it. She and Casdoe both leaped for it. I caught Agia by an arm and jerked her back, and Casdoe slammed the shutter into place with the knife out, toward the gathering storm.

"You fool," Agia said. "Don't you realize you're giving a weapon to whomever it is you're afraid of?" Her voice was calm with defeat.

"It has no need of knives," Casdoe told her.

The house was dark now except for the ruddy light of the fire. I looked around for candles or lanterns, but there were none in sight; later I learned that the few the family owned had been carried to the loft. Lightning flashed outside, outlining the edges of the shutters and making a broken line of stark light at the bottom of the door—it was a moment before I realized that it had been a broken line, when it should have been a continuous one. "There's someone outside," I said. "Standing on the step."

Casdoe nodded. "I closed the window just in time. It has never come so early before. It may be that the storm wakened it."

"You don't think it might be your husband?"

Before she could answer me, a voice higher than the little boy's called, *"Let me in, Mother."*

Even I, who did not know what it was that spoke, sensed a fearful wrongness in the simple words. It was a child's voice, perhaps, but not a human child's.

"Mother," the voice called again. *"It is beginning to rain."*

"We had better go up," Casdoe said. "If we pull the ladder after us, it cannot reach us even if it should get inside."

I had gone to the door. Without lightning, the feet of whatever it was that stood on the doorstep were invisible; but I could hear a hoarse, slow breathing above the beating of the rain, and once a scraping sound, as though the thing that waited there in the dark had shifted its footing.

"Is this your doing?" I asked Agia. "Some creature of Hethor's?"

She shook her head; the narrow, brown eyes were dancing. "They roam wild in these mountains, as you should know much better than I."

"Mother?"

There was a shuffle of feet—with that fretful question, the thing outside had turned from the door. One of the shutters was cracked, and I tried to look through the slit; I could see nothing in the blackness outside, but I heard a soft, heavy tread, precisely the sound that sometimes came through the barred ports of the Tower of the Bear at home.

"It took Severa three days ago," Casdoe said. She was trying to get the old man to rise; he did so slowly, reluctant to leave the warmth of the fire. "I never let her or Severian go among the trees, but it came into the clearing here, a watch before twilight. Since then it has returned every night. The dog wouldn't track it, but Becan went to hunt it today."

I had guessed the beast's identity by that time, though I had never beheld one of its kind. I said, "It is an alzabo, then? The creature from whose glands the analept is made?"

"It is an alzabo, yes," Casdoe answered. "I know nothing of any analept."

Agia laughed. "But Severian does. He has tasted the creature's wisdom, and carries his beloved about within himself. I understand one hears them whispering together by night, in the very heat and sweat of love."

I struck at her; but she dodged nimbly, then put the table between herself and me. "Aren't you delighted, Severian, that when the animals came to Urth to replace all those our ancestors slew, the alzabo was among them? Without the alzabo, you would have lost your dearest Thecla forever. Tell Casdoe here how happy the alzabo has made you."

To Casdoe I said, "I am truly sorry to hear of your daughter's death. I will defend this house from the animal outside, if it must be done."

My sword was standing against the wall, and to show that my will was as good as my words, I reached for it. It was fortunate I did so, for just at that instant a man's voice at the door called, *"Open, darling!"*

Agia and I sprang to stop Casdoe, but neither of us was swift enough. Before we could reach her, she had lifted the bar. The door swung back.

The beast that waited there stood upon four legs; even so, its hulking shoulders were as high as my head. Its own head was carried low, with the tips of its ears below the crest of fur that topped its back. In the firelight, its teeth gleamed white and its eyes glowed red. I have seen the eyes of many of these creatures that are supposed to have come from beyond the margin of the world—drawn, as certain philonoists allege, by the death of those whose genesis was here, even as tribes of enchors come slouching with their stone knives and fires into a countryside depopulated by war or disease; but their eyes are the eyes of beasts only. The red orbs of the alzabo were something more, holding neither the intelligence of humankind nor the innocence of the brutes. So a fiend might look, I thought, when it had at last struggled up from the pit of some dark star; then I recalled the man-apes, who were indeed called fiends, yet had the eyes of men.

For a moment it seemed the door might be shut again. I saw Casdoe, who had recoiled in horror, try to swing it to. The alzabo appeared to advance slowly and even lazily, yet it was too swift for her, and the edge of the door struck its ribs as it might have struck a stone.

"Let it stay open," I called. "We'll need whatever light there is." I had unsheathed *Terminus Est*, so that her blade caught the firelight and seemed itself a bitter fire. An arbalest like the ones Agia's henchmen had carried, whose quarrels are ignited by the friction of the atmosphere and burst when they strike like stones cast into a furnace, would have been a better weapon; but it would not have seemed an extension of my arm as *Terminus Est* did, and perhaps after all an arbalest would have permitted the alzabo to spring on me while I sought to recock it, if the first quarrel missed.

The long blade of my sword did not wholly obviate that danger. Her square, unpointed tip could not impale the beast, should it spring. I would have to slash at it in air, and though I had no doubt that I could strike the head from that thick neck while it flew toward me, I knew that to miss would be death. Furthermore, I needed space enough to make the stroke, for which that narrow room was scarcely adequate; and though the fire was dying, I needed light.

The old man, the boy Severian, and Casdoe were all gone— I was not certain if they had climbed the ladder to the loft while my attention had been fixed on the eyes of the beast, or if some of them, at least, had not fled through the doorway behind it. Only Agia remained, pressed into a corner with Casdoe's iron-tipped climbing stick to use as a weapon, as a sailor might, in desperation, try to fend off a galleass with a boat hook. I knew that to speak to her would be to call attention to her; yet it might be that if the beast so much as turned its head toward her, I would be able to sever its spine.

I said, "Agia, I must have light. It will kill me in the dark. You once told your men you would front me, if only they would kill me from behind. I will front this for you now, if you will only bring a candle."

She nodded to show she understood, and as she did the beast moved toward me. It did not spring as I had expected, however, but sidled lazily yet adroitly to the right, coming nearer while contriving to keep just beyond blade reach. After a moment of incomprehension I realized that by its position near the wall it cramped further any attack I might make, and that if it could circle me (as it nearly did) to gain a position between the fire and my own, much of the benefit I had from the firelight would be lost.

So we began a careful game, in which the alzabo sought to make what use it could of the chairs, the table, and the walls, and I tried to get as much space as I could for my sword.

Then I leaped forward. The alzabo avoided my cut, as it

seemed to me, by no more than the width of a finger, lunged at me, and drew back just in time to escape my return stroke. Its jaws, large enough to bite a man's head as a man bites an apple, had snapped before my face, drenching me in the reek of its putrid breath.

The thunder boomed again, so near that after its roar I could hear the crashing fall of the great tree whose death it had proclaimed; the lightning flash, illuminating every detail in its paralyzing glare, left me dazzled and blinded. I swung *Terminus Est* in the rush of darkness that followed, felt her bite bone, sprang to one side, and as the thunder rumbled out slashed again, this time only sending some stick of furniture flying into ruin.

Then I could see once more. While the alzabo and I had shifted ground and feinted, Agia had been moving too, and she must have made a dash for the ladder when the lightning struck. She was halfway up, and I saw Casdoe reach down to help her. The alzabo stood before me, as whole, so it seemed, as ever; but dark blood dribbled into a pool at its forefeet. Its fur looked red and ragged in the firelight, and the nails of its feet, larger and coarser than a bear's, were darkly red as well, and seemed translucent. More hideous than the speaking of a corpse could ever be, I heard the voice that had called, *"Open darling,"* at the door. It said: *"Yes, I am injured. But the pain is nothing much, and I can stand and move as before. You cannot bar me from my family forever."* From the mouth of a beast, it was the voice of a stern, stamping honest man.

I took out the Claw and laid it on the table, but it was no more than a spark of blue. "Light!" I shouted to Agia. No light came, and I heard the rattle of the ladder on the loft's floor as the women drew it up.

"Your escape is cut off, you see," the beast said, still in the man's voice.

"So is your advance. Can you jump so high, with a wounded leg?"

Abruptly the voice became the plaintive treble of the little girl. *"I can climb. Do you think I won't think to move the table over there under the hole? I, who can talk?"*

"You know yourself a beast, then."

The man's voice came again. *"We know we are within the beast, just as once we were within the cases of flesh the beast has devoured."*

"And you would consent to its devouring your wife and your son, Becan?"

"I would direct it. I do direct it. I want Casdoe and Severian to join us here, just as I joined Severa today. When the fire dies, you die too—joining us—and so shall they."

I laughed. "Have you forgotten that you got your wound when I couldn't see?" Holding *Terminus Est* at the ready, I crossed the room to the ruin of the chair, snatched up what had been its back, and threw it into the fire, making a cloud of sparks. "That was well-seasoned wood, I think, and it has been rubbed with bees' wax by some careful hand. It should burn brightly."

"Just the same, the dark will come." The beast—Becan—sounded infinitely patient. *"The dark will come, and you will join us."*

"No. When all the chair has burned and the light is failing, I will advance on you and kill you. I only wait now to let you bleed."

There was silence, the more eerie because nothing in the beast's expression hinted of thought. I knew that even as the wreck of Thecla's neural chemistry had been fixed in the nuclei of certain of my own frontal cells by a secretion distilled from the organs of just such a creature, so the man and his daughter haunted the dim thicket of the beast's brain and believed they lived; but what that ghost of life might be, what dreams and desires might enter it, I could not guess.

At last the man's voice said, *"In a watch or two, then, I will kill you or you will kill me. Or we will destroy each other. If I turn now and go out into the night and the rain, will you hunt me down when Urth turns toward the light once more? Or remain here to keep me from the woman and child that are mine?"*

"No," I said.

"On such honor as you have? Will you swear on that sword, though you cannot point it to the sun?"

I took a step backward and reversed *Terminus Est*, holding her by the blade in such a way that her tip was directed toward my own heart. "I swear by this sword, the badge of my Art, that if you do not return this night I will not hunt you tomorrow. Nor will I remain in this house."

As swiftly as a gliding snake it turned. For an instant I might, perhaps, have cut at its thick back. Then it was gone, and no trace of its presence remained save for the open door, the shattered chair, and the pool of blood (darker, I think, than the blood of the animals of this world) that soaked into the scrubbed planks of the floor.

I went to the door and barred it, returned the Claw to the little sack suspended from my neck, and then, as the beast had suggested, shifted the table until I could climb upon it and easily pull myself into the loft. Casdoe and the old man waited at the farther end with the boy called Severian, in whose eyes I saw the memories this night might hold for him twenty years hence. They were bathed in the vacillating radiance of a lamp suspended from one of the rafters.

"I have survived," I told them, "as you see. Could you hear what we said below?"

Casdoe nodded without speaking.

"If you had brought me the light I asked for, I would not have done what I did. As it was, I felt I owed you nothing. If I were you, I would leave this house as soon as it is day, and go to the lowlands. But that is up to you."

"We were afraid," Casdoe muttered.

"So was I. Where is Agia?"

To my surprise, the old man pointed, and looking at the place he indicated, I saw that the thick thatch had been parted to make an opening large enough for Agia's slender body.

That night I slept before the fire, after warning Casdoe that I would kill anyone who came down from the loft. In the morning, I walked around the house; as I had expected, Agia's knife had been pulled from the shutter.

XVII

The Sword of the Lictor

"WE ARE LEAVING," Casdoe told me. "But I will make breakfast for us before we go. You will not have to eat it with us if you do not wish to do so."

I nodded and waited outside until she brought out a wooden bowl of plain porridge and a wooden spoon; then I took them to the spring and ate. It was screened by rushes, and I did not come out; it was, I suppose, a violation of the oath I had given the alzabo, but I waited there, watching the house.

After a time Casdoe, her father, and little Severian emerged. She carried a pack and her husband's staff, and the old man and the boy had each their little sack. The dog, which must have crawled beneath the floor when the alzabo came (I cannot say I blame him, but Triskele would not have done that) was frisking about their heels. I saw Casdoe look around for me. When she failed to find me, she put down a bundle on the doorstep.

I watched them walk along the edge of their little field, which had been plowed and sown only a month or so before, and now would be reaped by birds. Neither Casdoe nor her father glanced behind them; but the boy, Severian, stopped and turned before going over the first ridge, to see once more the only home he had ever known. Its stone walls stood as

stoutly as ever, and the smoke of the breakfast fire still curled
from its chimney. His mother must have called to him then,
because he hurried after her and so disappeared from view.

I left the shelter of the rushes and went to the door. The
bundle on the step held two blankets of soft guanaco and
dried meat wrapped in a clean rug. I put the meat into my
sabretache and refolded the blankets so I could wear them
across my shoulder.

The rain had left the air fresh and clean, and it was good to
know that I would soon leave the stone cabin and its smells of
smoke and food behind me. I looked around inside, seeing the
black stain of the alzabo's blood and the broken chair. Casdoe
had moved the table back to its old place, and the Claw, that
had gleamed so feebly there, had left no mark upon its surface. There was nothing left that seemed worth the carrying; I
went out and shut the door.

Then I set off after Casdoe and her party. I did not forgive
her for having failed to give me light when I fought the alzabo—she might easily have done so by lowering her lamp
from the loft. Yet I could not greatly blame her for having
sided with Agia, a woman alone among the staring faces and
icy crowns of the mountains; and the child and the old man,
neither of whom could be said to have much guilt in the
matter, were at least as vulnerable as she.

The path was soft, so much so that I could track them in the
most literal sense, seeing Casdoe's small footprints, the boy's
even smaller ones beside them taking two strides to her one,
and the old man's, with the toes turned out. I walked slowly in
order not to overtake them, and though I knew my own danger increased with each step I took, I dared to hope that the
archon's patrols, in questioning them, would warn me. Casdoe
could not betray me, since whatever honest information she
might tender the dimarchi would lead them astray; and if the
alzabo were about, I hoped to hear or smell it before it attacked—I had not sworn, after all, to leave its prey unde-
fended, but only not to hunt it, or to remain in the house.

The path must have been no more than a game trail enlarged by Becan; it soon vanished. The scenery here was less
stark than it had been above the timberline. South-facing
slopes were often covered with small ferns and mosses, and
conifers grew from the cliffs. Falling water was seldom out of
earshot. In me Thecla recalled coming to a place much like

this to paint, accompanied by her teacher and two gruff body-guards. I began to feel that I would soon come across the easel, palette, and untidy brush case, abandoned beside some cascade when the sun no longer lingered in the spray.

Of course I did not, and for several watches there was no sign of humanity at all. Mingled with the footprints of Casdoe's party were the tracks of deer, and twice the pug marks of one of the tawny cats that prey on them. These had been made, surely, just at dawn, when the rain had stopped.

Then I saw a line of impressions left by a naked foot larger than the old man's. Each was as large, in fact, as my own booted print, and its maker's stride had been, if anything, longer. The tracks crossed at right angles to those I followed, but one imprint fell over one of the boy's, showing that their maker had passed between us.

I hurried forward.

I assumed that the footprints were those of an autochthon, though even then I wondered at his long stride—those savages of the mountains are normally rather small. If it was indeed an autochthon, he was unlikely to do Casdoe and the others any real harm, though he might pillage the goods she carried. From all I had heard of them, the autochthons were clever hunters, but not warlike.

The impressions of bare feet resumed. Two or three more individuals, at least, had joined the first.

Deserters from the army would be another matter; about a quarter of our prisoners in the Vincula had been such men and their women, and many of them had committed the most atrocious crimes. Deserters would be well armed, but I would have expected them to be well shod too, certainly not bare-foot.

A steep climb rose ahead of me. I could see the gouges made by Casdoe's staff, and the branches broken where she and the old man had used them to pull themselves up—some broken, possibly, by their pursuers as well. I reflected that the old man must be exhausted by now, that it was surprising that his daughter could still urge him on; perhaps he, perhaps all of them, knew by now that they were pursued. As I neared the crest I heard the dog bark, and then (at the same time it seemed almost an echo of the night before) a wild, wordless yell.

Yet it was not the horrible, half-human cry of the alzabo. It was a sound I had heard often before, sometimes, faintly, even while I lay in the cot next to Roche's, and often when I had carried their meals and the clients' to the journeymen on duty in our oubliette. It was precisely the shout of one of the clients on the third level, one of those who could no longer speak coherently and for that reason were never, for practical purposes, brought again to the examination room.

They were zoanthrops, such as I had seen feigned at Abdiesus's ridotto. When I reached the top I could see them, as well as Casdoe with her father and son. One cannot call them men; but they seemed men at that distance, nine naked men who circled the three, bounding and crouching. I hurried forward until I saw one strike with his club, and the old man fall.

Then I hesitated, and it was not Thecla's fear that stopped me but my own.

I had fought the man-apes of the mine bravely, perhaps, but I had to fight them. I had stood against the alzabo to stalemate, but there had been nowhere to run but the darkness outside, where it would surely have killed me.

Now there was a choice, and I hung back.

Living where she had, Casdoe must have known of them, though possibly she had never encountered them before. While the boy clung to her skirt she slashed with the staff as though it were a sabre. Her voice carried to me over the yells of the zoanthrops, shrill, unintelligible, and seemingly remote. I felt the horror one always feels when a woman is attacked, but beside it or perhaps beneath it lay the thought that she who would not fight beside me must now fight alone.

It could not last, of course. Such creatures are either frightened away at once or not frightened away at all. I saw one snatch the staff from her hand, and I drew *Terminus Est* and began to run down the long slope toward her. The naked figure had thrown her to the ground and was (as I supposed) preparing to rape her.

Then something huge plunged out of the trees to my left. It was so large and moved so swiftly that I at first thought it a red destrier, riderless and saddleless. Only when I saw the flash of its teeth and heard the scream of a zoanthrop did I realize it was the alzabo.

The others were upon it at once. Rising and falling, the heads of their ironwood bludgeons seemed for a moment grotesquely like the heads of feeding hens when corn has been scattered on the ground for them. Then a zoanthrop was thrown into the air, and he, who had been naked before, now appeared to be wrapped in a cloak of scarlet.

By the time I joined the fight, the alzabo was down, and for a moment I could give no attention to it. *Terminus Est* sang in orbit about my head. One naked figure fell, then another. A stone the size of a fist whizzed past my ear, so close that I could hear the sound; if it had struck, I would have died a moment afterward.

But these were not the man-apes of the mine, so numerous they could not, in the end, be overcome. I cut one from shoulder to waist, feeling each rib part in turn and rattle across my blade, slashed at another, split a skull.

Then there was only silence and the whimpering of the boy. Seven zoanthrops lay upon the mountain grass, four killed by *Terminus Est*, I think, and three by the alzabo. Casdoe's body was in its jaws, her head and shoulders already devoured. The old man who had known Fechin lay crumpled like a doll; that famous artist would have made something wonderful of his death, showing it from a perspective no one else could have found, and embodying the dignity and futility of all human life in the misshapen head. But Fechin was not here. The dog lay beside the old man, its jaws bloodied.

I looked about for the boy. To my horror, he was huddled against the alzabo's back. No doubt the thing had called to him in his father's voice, and he had come. Now its hindquarters trembled spasmodically and its eyes were closed. As I took him by the arm, its tongue, wider and thicker than a bull's, emerged as though to lick his hand; then its shoulders shuddered so violently that I started back. The tongue was never wholly returned to its mouth, but lay flaccid on the grass.

I drew the boy away and said, "It is over now, little Severian. Are you all right?"

He nodded and began to cry, and for a long time I held him and walked up and down.

For a moment I considered using the Claw, though it had failed me in Casdoe's house as it had failed me at times before. Yet if it had succeeded, who could say what the result might have been? I had no wish to give the zoanthrops or the alzabo new life, and what life might be granted Casdoe's headless corpse? As for the old man, he had been sitting at the doors of death already; now he had died, and swiftly. Would he have thanked me for summoning him back, to die again in a year or two? The gem flashed in the sunlight, but its flashing was mere sunshine and not the light of the Conciliator, the gegenschein of the New Sun, and I put it away again. The boy watched me with wide eyes.

Terminus Est had been bloodied to her guard and beyond. I sat upon a fallen tree and cleaned her with the rotting wood while I debated what to do, then whetted and oiled her blade. I cared nothing for the zoanthrops or the alzabo, but to leave Casdoe's body, and the old man's, to be dismembered by beasts seemed a vile thing.

Prudence warned against it as well. What if another alzabo should come, and when it had glutted itself upon Casdoe's flesh set off after the boy? I considered carrying them both back to the cabin. It was a considerable distance, however; I could not carry the two together, and it seemed sure that whichever I left behind would be violated by the time I returned for it. Drawn by the sight of so much blood, the carrion-eating teratornises were already circling overhead, each borne on wings as wide as the main yard of a caravel.

For a time I probed the ground, seeking some place soft enough that I might dig it with Casdoe's staff; in the end, I carried both bodies to a stretch of rocky ground near a watercourse, and there built a cairn over them. Under it they would lie, I hoped, for nearly a year, until the melting of the snows, at about the time of the feast of Holy Katharine, should sweep the bones of daughter and father away.

Little Severian, who had only watched at first, had himself carried small stones before the cairn was complete. When we were washing ourselves of grit and sweat in the stream, he asked, "Are you my uncle?"

I told him, "I'm your father—for now, at least. When someone's father dies, he must have a new one, if he's as young as you are. I'm the man."

He nodded, lost in thought; and quite suddenly I recalled how I had dreamed, only two nights before, of a world in which all the people knew themselves bound by ties of blood, being all descended from the same pair of colonists. I, who did not know my own mother's name, or my father's, might very well be related to this child whose name was my own, or for that matter to anyone I met. The world of which I had dreamed had been, for me, the bed on which I had lain. I wish I could describe how serious we were there by the laughing stream, how solemn and clean he looked with his wet face and the droplets sparkling in the lashes of his wide eyes.

XVIII

Severian and Severian

I DRANK AS much water as I could, and told the boy that he must do so as well, that there were many dry places in the mountains, and that we might not drink again until next morning. He had asked if we would not go home now; and though I had planned until then to retrace our route back to the house that had been Casdoe's and Becan's, I said we would not, because I knew it would be too terrible for him to see that roof again, and the field and the little garden, and then to leave them for a second time. At his age he might even suppose that his father and his mother, his sister and his grandfather were somehow still inside.

Yet we could not descend much farther—we were already well below the level at which travel was dangerous for me. The arm of the archon of Thrax stretched a hundred leagues and more, and now there was every chance that Agia would put his dimarchi on my trail.

To the northeast stood the highest peak I had yet seen. Not only its head but its shoulders too bore a shroud of snow, which descended nearly to its waist. I could not say, and perhaps no one now could, what proud face it was that stared westward over so many lesser summits; but surely he had ruled in the earliest of the greatest days of humanity, and had commanded energies that could shape granite as a carver's knife does wood. Looking at his image, it seemed to me that even the hard-bitten dimarchi, who knew the wild uplands so well, might stand in awe of him. And so we made for him, or rather for the high pass that linked the folded drapery of his robe to the mountain where Becan had once established a home. For the time being, the climbs were not severe, and we spent far more effort in walking than in climbing.

The boy Severian held my hand often when there was no need of my support. I am no great judge of the ages of children, but he seemed to me to be about of that growth when, if he had been one of our apprentices, he would first have entered Master Palaemon's schoolroom—that is to say, he was old enough to walk well, and to talk sufficiently to understand and to make himself understood.

For a watch or more he said nothing beyond what I have already related. Then, as we were descending an open, grassy slope bordered by pines, a place much like that in which his mother had died, he asked, "Severian, who were those men?"

I knew whom he meant. "They were not men, although they were once men and still resemble men. They were zoanthrops, a word that indicates those beasts that are of human shape. Do you understand what I am saying?"

The little boy nodded solemnly, then asked, "Why don't they wear clothes?"

"Because they are no longer human beings, as I told you. A dog is born a dog and a bird is born a bird, but to become a human being is an achievement—you have to think about it. You have been thinking about it for the past three or four years at least, little Severian, even though you may never have thought about the thinking."

"A dog just looks for things to eat," the boy said.

"Exactly. But that raises the question of whether a person should be forced to do such thinking, and some people decided a long time ago that he should not. We may force a dog, sometimes, to act like a man—to walk on his hind legs and wear a collar and so forth. But we shouldn't and couldn't force a man to act like a man. Did you ever want to fall asleep? When you weren't sleepy or even tired?"

He nodded.

"That was because you wanted to put down the burden of being a boy, at least for a time. Sometimes I drink too much wine, and that is because for a while I would like to stop being a man. Sometimes people take their own lives for that reason. Did you know that?"

"Or they do things that might hurt them," he said. The way he said it told me of arguments overheard; Becan had very probably been that kind of man, or he would not have taken his family to so remote and dangerous a place.

"Yes," I told him. "That can be the same thing. And sometimes certain men, and even women, come to hate the burden of thought, but without loving death. They see the animals and wish to become as they are, answering only to instinct, and not thinking. Do you know what makes you think, little Severian?"

"My head," the boy said promptly, and grasped it with his hands.

"Animals have heads too—even very stupid animals like crayfish and oxen and ticks. What makes you think is only a small part of your head, inside, just above your eyes." I touched his forehead. "Now if for some reason you wanted one of your hands taken off, there are men you can go to who are skilled in doing that. Suppose, for example, your hand had suffered some hurt from which it would never be well. They could take it away in such a fashion that there would be little chance of any harm coming to the rest of you."

The boy nodded.

"Very well. Those same men can take away that little part of your head that makes you think. They cannot put it back, you understand. And even if they could, you couldn't ask them to do it, once that part was gone. But sometimes people pay these men to take that part away. They want to stop thinking forever, and often they say they wish to turn their backs on all that humanity has done. Then it is no longer just to treat them as human beings—they have become animals, though animals who are still of human shape. You asked why they did not wear clothes. They no longer understand clothes, and so they would not put them on, even if they were very cold, although they might lie down on them or even roll themselves up in them."

"Are you like that, a little bit?" the boy asked, and pointed to my bare chest.

The thought he was suggesting had never occurred to me before, and for a moment I was taken aback. "It's the rule of my guild," I said. "I haven't had any part of my head taken away, if that's what you're asking, and I used to wear a shirt

. . . But, yes, I suppose I am a little like that, because I never thought of it, even when I was very cold."

His expression told me I had confirmed his suspicions. "Is that why you're running away?"

"No, that's not why I'm running away. If anything, I suppose you could say it is the other side of it. Perhaps that part of my head has grown too large. But you're right about the zoanthrops, that is why they are in the mountains. When a man becomes an animal, he becomes a dangerous animal, and animals like that cannot be tolerated in more settled places, where there are farms and many people. So they are driven to these mountains, or brought here by their old friends, or by someone they paid to do it before they discarded the power of human thought. They can still think a little, of course, as all animals can. Enough to find food in the wild, though many die each winter. Enough to throw stones as monkeys throw nuts, and use their clubs, and even to hunt for mates, for there are females among them as I said. Their sons and daughters seldom live long, however, and I suppose that is for the best, because they are born just as you were—and I was—with the burden of thought."

That burden lay heavily on me when we had finished speaking; so heavily indeed that for the first time I truly understood that it could be as great a curse to others as memory has sometimes been to me.

I have never been greatly sensitive to beauty, but the beauty of the sky and the mountainside were such that it seemed they colored all my musings, so that I felt I nearly grasped ungraspable things. When Master Malrubius had appeared to me after our first performance of Dr. Talos's play—something I could not then understand and still could not understand, though I grew more confident that it had occurred, and not less—he had spoken to me of the circularity of governance, though I had no concern with governance. Now it struck me that the will itself was governed, and if not by reason, then by things below or above it. Yet it was very difficult to say on what side of reason these things lay. Instinct, surely, lay below it; but might it not be above it as well? When the alzabo rushed at the zoanthrops, its instinct commanded it to preserve its prey from others; when Becan did so, his instinct, I believe, was to preserve his wife and child. Both performed the same act, and they actually performed it in the same body. Did the higher and the lower instinct join hands at the back of reason? Or is there but one instinct standing behind all reason, so that reason sees a hand to either side?

But is instinct truly that "attachment to the person of the monarch" which Master Malrubius implied was at once the highest and the lowest form of governance? For clearly, instinct itself cannot have arisen out of nothing—the hawks that soared over our heads built their nests, doubtless, by instinct; yet there must have been a time in which nests were not built, and the first hawk to build one cannot have inherited its instinct to build from its parents, since they did not possess it. Nor could such an instinct have developed slowly, a thousand generations of hawks fetching one stick before some hawk fetched two; because neither one stick nor two could be of the slightest use to the nesting hawks. Perhaps that which came before instinct was the highest as well as the lowest principle of the governance of the will. Perhaps not. The wheeling birds traced their hieroglyphics in the air, but they were not for me to read.

As we approached the saddle that joined the mountain to that other even loftier one I have described, we seemed to move across the face of all Urth, tracing a line from pole to equator; indeed the surface over which we crawled like ants might have been the globe itself turned inside out. Far behind us and far ahead of us loomed the broad, gleaming fields of snow. Below them lay stony slopes like the shore of the ice-bound southern sea. Below these were high meadows of coarse grass, now dotted with wildflowers; I remembered well those over which I had passed the day before, and beneath the blue haze that wreathed the mountain ahead I could discern their band upon the chest, like a green fourragere; beneath it the pines shone so darkly as to appear black.

The saddle to which we descended was quite different, an expanse of montane forest where glossy-leaved hardwoods lifted sickly heads three hundred cubits toward the dying sun. Among them their dead brothers remained upright, supported by the living and wrapped in winding sheets of lianas. Near the little stream where we halted for the night the vegetation had already lost most of its mountain delicacy and was acquiring something of the lushness of the lowlands; and now that we were sufficiently near the saddle for him to have a clear view of it, and his attention was no longer monopolized by the need to walk and climb, the boy pointed and asked if we were going down there.

"Tomorrow," I said. "It will be dark soon, and I would like to get through that jungle in a day."

His eyes widened at the word *jungle*. "Is it dangerous?"

"I don't really know. From what I heard in Thrax, the insects shouldn't be nearly as bad as they are in lower places, and we're not likely to be troubled by blood bats there—a friend of mine was bitten by a blood bat once, and it's not very pleasant. But that's where the big apes are, and there will be hunting cats and so on."

"And wolfs."

"And wolves, of course. Only there are wolves high up too. As high as your house was, and much higher."

The moment I mentioned his old home I regretted it, for something of the joy in living that had been returning to his face went out of it with the word. For a moment he seemed lost in thought. Then he said, "When those men—"

"Zoanthrops."

He nodded. "When the zoanthrops came and hurt Mama, did you come to help as quick as you could?"

"Yes," I said. "I came as quickly as I could make myself come." It was true, at least in some sense, but nevertheless it was painful to say.

"Good," he said. I had spread a blanket for him, and he lay down on it now. I folded it over him. "The stars got brighter, didn't they? They get brighter when the sun goes away."

I lay beside him looking up. "It doesn't go away, really. Urth just swings her face away, so that we think it does. If you don't look at me, I don't go away, even though you don't see me."

"If the sun is still there, why do the stars shine harder?"

His voice told me he was pleased with his own cleverness in argument, and I was pleased with it too; I suddenly understood why Master Palaemon had enjoyed talking with me when I was a child. I said, "A candle flame is almost invisible in bright sunshine, and the stars, which are really suns themselves, seem to fade in the same way. Pictures painted in the ancient days, when our sun was brighter, appear to show that the stars could not be seen at all until twilight. The old legends—I have a brown book in my sabretache that tells many of them—are full of magic beings who vanish slowly and reappear in the same way. No doubt those stories are based on the look of the stars then."

He pointed. "There's the hydra."

"I think you're right," I said. "Do you know any others?"

He showed me the cross and the great bull, and I pointed out my amphisbaena, and several others.

"And there's the wolf, over by the unicorn. There's a little wolf too, but I can't find him."

We discovered it together, near the horizon.

"They're like us, aren't they? The big wolf and the little wolf. We're big Severian and little Severian."

I agreed that was so, and he stared up at the stars for a long time, chewing the piece of dried meat I had given him. Then he said, "Where is the book with stories in it?"

I showed it to him.

"We had a book too, and sometimes Mama would read to Severa and me."

"She was your sister, wasn't she?"

He nodded. "We were twins. Big Severian, did you ever have a sister?"

"I don't know. My family is all dead. They've been dead since I was a baby. What kind of story would you like?"

He asked to see the book, and I gave it to him. After he had turned a few pages he returned it to me. "It's not like ours."

"I didn't think it was."

"See if you can find a story with a boy in it who has a big friend, and a twin. There should be wolfs in it."

I did the best I could, reading rapidly to outrace the fading light.

XIX

The Tale of the Boy Called Frog

Part I

Early Summer and Her Son

ON A MOUNTAINTOP beyond the shores of Urth there once lived a lovely woman named Early Summer. She was the queen of that land, but her king was a strong, unforgiving man, and because she was jealous of him he was jealous of her in turn, and killed any man he believed to be her lover.

One day Early Summer was walking in her garden when she saw a most beautiful blossom of a kind wholly new to her. It was redder than any rose and more sweetly perfumed, but its strong stalk was thornless and smooth as ivory. She plucked it and carried it to a secluded spot, and as she reclined there contemplating it, it grew to seem to her no blossom at all but such a lover as she had longed for, powerful and yet as tender as a kiss. Certain of the juices of the plant entered her and she conceived. She told the king, however, that the child was his, and since she was well guarded, he believed her.

It was a boy, and by his mother's wish he was called Spring Wind. At his birth all those who study the stars were gathered to cast his horoscope, not only those who lived upon the mountaintop, but many of the greatest of Urth's magi. Long they labored over their charts, and nine times met in solemn conclave; and at last they announced that in battle Spring Wind would be irresistible, and that no child of his would die before it had reached full growth. These prophecies pleased the king much.

As Spring Wind grew, his mother saw with secret pleasure that he delighted most in field and flower and fruit. Every green thing thrived under his hand, and it was the pruning knife he desired to hold, and not the sword. But when he was grown a young man, war came, and he took up his spear and his shield. Because he was quiet in demeanor and obedient to the king (whom he believed to be his father, and who believed himself to be the father), many supposed the prophecy would prove false. It was not so. In the heat of battle he fought coolly, his daring well judged and his caution sober; no general was more fertile of stratagems and sleights than he was, and no officer more attentive to every duty. The soldiers he led against the king's enemies were drilled until they seemed men of bronze quickened with fire, and their loyalty to him was such that they would have followed him to the World of Shadows, the realm farthest from the sun. Then men said it was the spring wind that threw down towers, and the spring wind that capsized ships, though that was not what Early Summer had intended.

Now it happened that the chances of war often brought Spring Wind to Urth, and there he came to know of two brothers who were kings. Of these, the elder had several sons, but the younger only a single daughter, a girl named Bird of the Wood. When this girl became a woman, her father was slain; and her uncle, in order that she might never breed sons who would claim their grandfather's kingdom, entered her name on the roll of the virgin priestesses. This displeased Spring Wind, because the princess was beautiful and her father had been his friend. One day it happened that he had gone alone into the world of Urth, and there he saw Bird of the Wood sleeping beside a stream, and woke her with his kisses.

Of their coupling were engendered twin sons, but though the priestesses of her order had aided Bird of the Wood in concealing their growth in her womb from the king, her uncle, they could not hide the babes. Before Bird of the Wood ever saw them, the priestesses placed them in a winnowing basket lined with blankets of featherwork and carried them to the bank of that same stream where Spring Wind had surprised her, and launching the basket in the water went away.

Part II

How Frog Found a New Mother

FAR THAT BASKET sailed, over fresh waters and salt. Other children would have died, but the sons of Spring Wind could not die, because they were not yet grown. The armored monsters of the water splashed about their basket and the apes threw sticks and nuts into it, but it drifted ever onward until at last it came to a bank whereon two poor sisters were washing clothes. These good women saw it and shouted, and when shouting availed nothing, tucked their skirts into their belts and waded into the river and brought it to shore.

Because they had been found in the water, the boys were named Fish and Frog, and when the sisters had showed them to their husbands, and it was seen that they were children of remarkable strength and handsomeness, each sister chose one. Now the sister who chose Fish was the wife of a herdsman, and the husband of the sister who chose Frog was a woodcutter.

This sister cared well for Frog and suckled him at her own breast, for it so happened that she had recently lost a child of her own. She carried him slung behind her in a shawl when her husband went into the wild lands to cut firewood, and thus it is said by the weavers of lore that she was the strongest of all women, for she carried an empire on her back.

A year passed, and at the end of it, Frog had learned to stand upright and take a few steps. One night the woodcutter and his wife were sitting beside their own little fire in a clearing in the wild lands; and while the woodcutter's wife prepared their supper, Frog walked naked to the fire and stood warming himself before the flames. Then the woodcutter, who was a gruff, kindly man, asked him, "Do you like that?" and though he had never spoken before, Frog nodded and answered, "Red flower." At that, it is said, Early Summer stirred upon her bed on the mountaintop beyond the shores of Urth.

The woodcutter and his wife were astonished, but they had no time to tell each other what had happened, or to try to persuade Frog to speak again, or even to rehearse what they would say to the herdsman and his wife when next they met them. For there came then into the clearing a dreadful sound—those who have listened say it is the most frightening on the world of Urth. So few who have heard it have lived that it has no name, but it is something like the hum of bees, and something like the sound a cat might make if a cat were larger than a cow, and something like the noise the voice-throwers learn first to make, a droning in the throat that seems to come from everywhere at once. It was the song a smilodon sings when he has crept close to his prey, the song that frightens even mastodons so much they often charge in the wrong direction and are stabbed from behind.

Surely the Pancreator knows all mysteries. He spoke the long word that is our universe, and few things happen that are not a part of that word. By his will, then, there rose a knoll not far from the fire, where there had been a great tomb in the most ancient days; and though the poor woodcutter and his wife knew nothing of it, two wolves had built their home there, a house low of roof and thick of wall, with galleries lit by green lamps descending among the ruined memorials and broken urns, a house, that is, such as wolves love. There the he-wolf sat sucking at the thighbone of a coryphodon, and the she-wolf, his wife, held her cubs to her breasts.

From near they heard the smilodon's song and cursed it in the Gray Language as wolves can curse, for no lawful beast hunts near the home of another of the hunting kind, and wolves are on good terms with the moon.

When the curse was finished, the she-wolf said, "What prey can that be, that the Butcher, that stupid killer of river-horses, has found, when you, O my husband, who wind the lizards that frisk on the rocks of the mountains that lie beyond Urth, have been content to worry a parched stick?"

"I do not devour carrion," the he-wolf answered shortly. "Nor do I pull worms from the morning grass, nor angle for frogs in the shallows."

"No more does the Butcher sing for them," said his wife.

Then the he-wolf raised his head and sniffed the air. "He hunts the son of Meschia and the daughter of Meschiane, and you know no good can come of such meat." At this the she-wolf nodded, for she knew that alone among the living creatures, the sons of Meschia kill all when one of their own is slain. That is because the Pancreator gave Urth to them, and they have rejected the gift.

His song ended, the Butcher roared so as to shake the leaves from the trees; then he screamed, for the curses of wolves are strong curses so long as the moon shines.

"How has he come to grief?" asked the she-wolf, who was licking the face of one of her daughters.

The he-wolf sniffed again. "Burnt flesh! He has leaped into their fire." He and his wife laughed as wolves do, silently, showing all their teeth; their ears stood up as tents stand in the desert, for they were listening to the Butcher as he blundered through the thickets looking for his prey.

Now the door of the wolves' house stood open, because when either of the grown wolves were at home they did not care who entered, and fewer departed than came in. It had been full of moonlight (for the moon is always a welcome guest in the houses of wolves) but it grew dark. A child stood there, somewhat fearful, it may be, of the darkness, but smelling the strong smell of milk. The he-wolf snarled, but the she-wolf called in her most motherly voice, "Come in, little son of Meschia. Here you may drink, and be warm and clean. Here are the bright-eyed, quick-footed playmates, the best in all the world."

Hearing this, the boy entered, and the she-wolf put down her milk-gorged cubs and took him to her breast.

"What good is such a creature?" said the he-wolf.

The she-wolf laughed. "You can suck at a bone of the last moon's kill and ask that? Do you not remember when war raged hereabouts, and the armies of Prince Spring Wind scoured the land? Then no son of Meschia hunted us, for they hunted one another. After their battles we came out, you and I and all the Senate of Wolves, and even the Butcher, and He Who Laughs, and the Black Killer, and we moved among the dead and dying, choosing what we wished."

"That is true," said the he-wolf. "Prince Spring Wind did great things for us. But that cub of Meschia's is not he."

The she-wolf only smiled and said, "I smell the battle smoke in the fur of his head, and upon his skin." (It was the smoke of the Red Flower.) "You and I shall be dust when the first column marches from the gate of his wall, but that first shall breed a thousand more to feed our children and their children, and their children's children."

The he-wolf nodded to this, for he knew that the she-wolf was wiser than he, and even as he could sniff out things that lay beyond the shores of Urth, so could she see the days beyond the next year's rains.

"I shall call him Frog," said the she-wolf. "For indeed the Butcher angled for frogs, as you said, O my husband." She believed that she said this in compliment to the he-wolf, because he had so readily acquiesced to her wishes; but the truth was that the blood of the people of the mountaintop beyond Urth ran in Frog, and the names of those who bear the blood cannot be concealed for long.

Outside wild laughter pealed. It was the voice of He Who Laughs, calling, "It is there, Lord! There, there, there! Here, here, here is the spoor! It went in at the door!"

"You see," the he-wolf remarked, "what comes of mentioning evil. To name is to call. That is the law." And he got down his sword and fingered the edge.

The doorway was darkened again. It was a narrow doorway, for none but fools and temples have wide doors, and wolves are no fools; Frog had filled most of it. Now the Butcher filled it all, turning his shoulders to get in, and stooping his great head. Because the wall was so thick, the doorway was like a passage.

"What seek you?" asked the he-wolf, and he licked the flat of his blade.

"What is my own, and only that," said the Butcher. Smilodons fight with a curved knife in either hand, and he was much larger than the he-wolf, but he did not wish to have to engage him in that close place.

"It was never yours," said the she-wolf. Setting Frog on the floor, she came so near the Butcher that he might have struck at her if he dared. Her eyes flashed fire. "The hunt was unlawful, for an unlawful prey. Now he has drunk of me and is a wolf forever, sacred to the moon."

"I have seen dead wolves," said the Butcher.

"Yes, and eaten their flesh, though it were too foul for the flies, I dare say. It may be you shall eat mine, if a falling tree kill me."

"You say he is a wolf. He must be brought before the Senate." The Butcher licked his lips, but with a dry tongue. He would have faced the he-wolf in the open, perhaps; but he had no heart to face the pair together, and he knew that if he gained the doorway they would snatch up Frog and retreat to the passages below ground among the tumbled ashlars of the tomb, where the she-wolf would soon be behind him.

"And what have you to do with the Senate of Wolves?" the she-wolf asked.

"Perhaps as much as he," said the Butcher, and went to look for easier meat.

Part III

The Black Killer's Gold

THE SENATE OF WOLVES meets under each full moon. All come who can, for it is assumed that any who do not come plot treachery, offering, perhaps, to guard the cattle of the sons of Meschia in return for scraps. The wolf who is absent for two Senates must stand trial when he returns, and he is killed by the she-wolves if the Senate finds him guilty.

Cubs too must come before the Senate, so that any grown wolf who wishes may inspect them to assure himself that their father was a true wolf. (Sometimes a she-wolf lies with a dog for spite, but though the sons of dogs often look much like wolf cubs, they have always a spot of white on them somewhere, for white was the color of Meschia, who remembered the pure light of the Pancreator; and his sons leave it still for a brand on all they touch.)

Thus the she-wolf stood before the Senate of Wolves at the full moon, and her cubs played before her feet, and Frog—who looked a frog indeed when the moonlight through the windows stained his skin green—stood beside her and clung to the fur of her skirt. The President of the Pack sat in the highest seat, and if he was surprised to see a son of Meschia brought before the Senate, his ears did not show it. He sang:

> "Here are the five!
> The sons and daughters born alive!
> If they be false, say how-ow-ow!
> If ye would speak, speak now-ow-ow!"

When the cubs are brought before the Senate, their parents may not defend them if they are challenged; but at any other time it is murder if any other seek to harm them.

"Speak NOW-OW-OW!" The walls echoed it back, so that in the huts in the valley the sons of Meschia barricaded their doors, and the daughters of Meschiane clutched their own children.

Then the Butcher, who had been waiting behind the last wolf, came forward. "Why do you delay?" he said. "I am not clever—I am too strong for cleverness, as you well understand. But there are four wolf cubs here, and a fifth that is not a wolf but my prey."

At this the he-wolf asked, "What right has *he* to speak here? Surely *he* is no wolf."

A dozen voices answered, "Anyone may speak, if a wolf asks his testimony. Speak, Butcher!"

Then the she-wolf loosened her sword in the scabbard and prepared for her last fight if it came to fighting. A demon she looked with her gaunt face and blazing eyes, for an angel is often only a demon who stands between us and our enemy.

"You say I am no wolf," continued the Butcher. "And you say rightly. We know how a wolf smells, and the sound and look of a wolf. That wolf has taken this son of Meschia for her cub, but we all know that having a wolf for a mother does not make a cub a wolf."

The he-wolf shouted, "Wolves are those whose mothers and fathers are wolves! I take this cub as my son!"

There was laughter at that, and when it died, one strange voice laughed on. It was He Who Laughs, come to advise the Butcher before the Senate of Wolves. He called, "Many have talked so, ho, ho! But their cubs have fed the pack."

The Butcher said, "They were killed for their white fur. The skin is under the fur. How can this live? Give it to me!"

"Two must speak," the President announced. "That is the law. Who speaks for the cub here? It is a son of Meschia, but is it also a wolf? Two who are not its parents must speak for it."

Then the Naked One, who is counted a member of the

Senate for teaching the young wolves, rose. "I have never had a son of Meschia to teach," he said. "I may learn something from it. I speak for him."

"Another," said the President. "Another must also speak."

There was only silence. Then the Black Killer strode from the back of the hall. Everyone fears the Black Killer, for though his cloak is as soft as the fur of the youngest cub, his eyes burn in the night. "Two who are no wolves have spoken here already," he said. "May I not speak also? I have gold." He held up a purse.

"Speak! Speak!" called a hundred voices.

"The law says also that a cub's life may be bought," said the Black Killer, and he poured gold into his hand, and so ransomed an empire.

Part IV

The Plowing of the Fish

IF ALL THE adventures of Frog were told—how he lived among the wolves, and learned to hunt and fight, it would fill many books. But those who bear the blood of the people of the mountaintop beyond Urth always feel its call at last; and the time came when he carried fire into the Senate of Wolves and said, "Here is the Red Flower. In his name I rule." And when no one opposed him he led forth the wolves and called them the people of his kingdom, and soon men came to him as well as wolves, and though he was still only a boy, he seemed always taller than the men about him, for he bore the blood of Early Summer.

One night when the wild roses were opening, she came to him in a dream and told him of his mother, Bird of the Wood, and of her father and her uncle, and of his brother. He found his brother, who had become a herdsman, and with the wolves and the Black Killer and many men they went to the king and demanded their heritage. He was old and his sons had died without sons, and he gave it to them, and of it Fish took the city and the farmlands, and Frog the wild hills.

But the number of the men who followed him grew. They stole women from other peoples, and bred children, and when the wolves were no longer needed and returned to the wilds, Frog judged his people should have a city to dwell in, with walls to protect them when the men were at war. He went to the herds of Fish and took a white cow and a white bull therefrom and harnessed them to a plow, and with them plowed a furrow that should mark the wall. Fish came to seek the return of his cattle while the people were preparing to build. When Frog's people showed him the furrow and told him it was to be their wall, he laughed and jumped over it; and they, knowing that small things mocked can never grow large, slew him. But he was then a man grown, so the prophecy made at the birth of Spring Wind was fulfilled.

When Frog saw the dead Fish, he buried him in the furrow to assure the fertility of the land. For so he had been taught by the Naked One, who was also called the Savage, or Squanto.

XX

The Circle of the Sorcerers

BY THE FIRST light of morning we entered the mountain jungle as one enters a house. Behind us the sunlight played on grass and bushes and stones; we passed through a curtain of tangled vines so thick I had to cut it with my sword and saw before us only shadow and the towering boles of the trees. No insect buzzed within, and no bird chirped. No wind stirred. At first the bare soil we trod was almost as stony as the mountain slopes, but before we had walked a league it grew smoother, and at last we came to a short stair that had surely been carved with the spade. "Look," said the boy, and he pointed to something red and strangely shaped that lay upon the uppermost step.

I stopped to look at it. It was a cock's head; needles of some dark metal had been run through its eyes, and it held a strip of cast snakeskin in its bill.

"What is it?" The boy's eyes were wide.

"A charm, I think."

"Left here by a witch? What does it mean?"

I tried to recall what little I knew of the false art. As a child, Thecla had been in the care of a nursemaid who tied and untied knots to speed childbirth and claimed to see the face of Thecla's future husband (was it mine, I wonder?) at midnight, reflected in a platter that had held bridal cake.

"The cock," I told the boy, "is the herald of day, and in a

magical sense his crow at dawn can be said to bring the sun. He has been blinded, perhaps, so that he will not know when dawn appears. A snake's casting of his skin means cleansing or rejuvenation. The blinded cock holds onto the old skin."

"But what does it mean?" the boy asked again.

I said I did not know; but in my heart I felt sure it was a charm against the coming of the New Sun, and it somehow pained me to find that renewal, for which I had hoped so fervently when I was a boy myself, but in which I hardly believed, should be opposed by anyone. At the same time, I was conscious that I bore the Claw. Enemies of the New Sun would surely destroy the Claw, should it fall into their hands.

Before we had gone another hundred paces, there were strips of red cloth suspended from the trees; some of these were plain, but others had been written over in black in a character I did not understand—or as seemed more likely, with symbols and ideographs of the sort those who pretend to more knowledge than they possess use in imitation of the writing of the astronomers.

"We had better go back," I said. "Or go around."

I had no sooner spoken than I heard a rustling behind me. For a moment I truly thought the figures that stepped onto the path were devils, huge-eyed and striped with black, white, and scarlet; then I saw that they were only naked men with painted bodies. Their hands were fitted with steel talons, which they held up to show me. I drew *Terminus Est*.

"We will not hinder you," one said. "Go. Leave us, if you wish." It seemed to me that beneath the paint he had the pale skin and fair hair of the south.

"You would be well advised not to. With this long blade I could kill you both before you touched me."

"Go, then," the blond man told me. "If you have no objection to leaving the child with us."

At that I looked around for little Severian. He had somehow vanished from my side.

"If you wish him returned to you, however, you will surrender your sword to me and come with us." Showing no sign of fear, the painted man walked up to me and extended his hands. The steel talons emerged from between his fingers, being fastened to a narrow bar of iron he held in his palm. "I will not ask again," he said.

I sheathed the blade, then took off the baldric that held the sheath and handed the whole to him.

He closed his eyes. Their lids had been painted with dark dots rimmed with white, like the markings of certain caterpillars that would have the birds think them snakes. "This has drunk much blood."

"Yes," I said.

His eyes opened again, and he regarded me with an unblinking stare. His painted face—like that of the other, who stood just behind him—was as expressionless as a mask. "A newly forged sword would have little power here, but this might do harm."

"I trust it will be returned to me when my son and I leave. What have you done with him?"

There was no reply. The two walked around me, one to either side, and went down the path in the direction the boy and I had been going. After a moment I followed them.

I might call the place to which they led me a village, but it was not a village in the ordinary sense, not such a village as Saltus, or even a place like the clusters of autochthon huts that are sometimes called villages. Here the trees were greater, and farther separated, than I had ever seen forest trees before, and the canopy of their leaves formed an impenetrable roof several hundred cubits overhead. So great indeed were these trees that they seemed to have been growing for whole ages; a stair led to a door in the trunk of one, which had been pierced for windows. There was a house of several stories built upon the branches of another, and a thing like a great oriole's nest swung from the limbs of a third. Open hatches showed that the ground at our feet was mined.

I was taken to one of these hatches and told to descend a crude ladder that led into darkness. For a moment (I do not know why) I feared that it might go very far, into such deep caverns as lay beneath the man-apes' nighted treasure house. It was not so. After descending what was surely not more than four times my height and clambering through what then seemed to be ruined matting, I found myself in a subterranean room.

The hatch had been shut over my head, leaving everything dark. Groping, I explored the place and found it to be about three paces by four. The floor and walls were of earth, and the ceiling of unpeeled logs; there were no furnishings whatsoever.

We had been taken at about mid morning. In seven watches

more, it would be dark. Before that time it might be that I would find myself led into the presence of someone in authority. If so, I would do what I could to persuade him that the child and I were harmless and should be let go in peace. If not, then I would climb the ladder again and see if I could not break out of the hatch. I sat down to wait.

I am certain I did not sleep; but I used the facility I have for calling forth past time, and so, at least in spirit, left that dark place. For a time I watched the animals in the necropolis beyond the Citadel wall, as I had as a boy. I saw the geese shape arrowheads against the sky, and the comings and goings of fox and rabbit. They raced across the grass for me once more, and in time left their tracks in snow. Triskele lay dead, as it seemed, on the refuse behind the Bear Tower; I went to him, saw him shudder and lift his head to lick my hand. I sat with Thecla in her narrow cell, where we read aloud to each other and stopped to argue what we had read. "The world runs down like a clock," she said. "The Increate is dead, and who will recreate him? Who could?"

"Surely clocks are supposed to stop when their owners die."

"That's superstition." She took the book from my hands so she could hold them in her own, which were long-fingered and very cold. "When the owner is on his deathbed, no one pours in fresh water. He dies, and his nurses look at the dial to note the time. Later they find it stopped, and the time is the same."

I told her, "You're saying that it stops before the owner; so if the universe is running down now, that does not mean that the Increate is dead—only that he never existed."

"But he is ill. Look around you. See this place, and the towers above you. Do you know, Severian, that you never have?"

"He could still tell someone else to fill the mechanism again," I suggested, and then, realizing what I had said, blushed.

Thecla laughed. "I haven't seen you do that since I took off my gown for you the first time. I laid your hands on my breasts, and you went red as a berry. Do you remember? Tell somebody to fill it? Where is the young atheist now?"

I put my hand upon her thigh. "Confused, as he was then, by the presence of divinity."

"You don't believe in me then? I think you're right. I must

be what you young torturers dream of—a beautiful prisoner, as yet unmutilated, who calls on you to slake her lust."

Trying to be gallant I said, "Such dreams as you lie beyond my power."

"Surely not, since I am in your power now."

Something was in the cell with us. I looked at the barred door and Thecla's lamp with its silver reflector, then into all the corners. The cell grew darker, and Thecla and even I myself vanished with the light, but the thing that had intruded upon my memory of us did not.

"Who are you," I asked, "and what do you wish with us?"

"You know well who we are, and we know who you are." The voice was cool and, I think, perhaps the most authoritative I have ever heard. The Autarch himself did not speak so.

"Who am I, then?"

"Severian of Nessus, the lictor of Thrax."

"I am Severian of Nessus," I said. "But I am no longer lictor of Thrax."

"So you would have us believe."

There was silence again, and after a time I understood that my interrogator would not question me, but rather would force me, if I desired my freedom, to explain myself to him. I wanted greatly to seize him—he could not have been more than a few cubits away—but I knew that in all likelihood he was armed with the steel talons the guards on the path had shown me. I wanted also, as I had for some time, to draw the Claw from its leathern sack, though nothing could have been more foolish. I said, "The archon of Thrax wished me to kill a certain woman. I freed her instead, and had to flee the city."

"By magic passing the posts of the soldiers."

I had always believed all self-proclaimed wonder-workers to be frauds; now something in my interrogator's voice suggested that even as they attempted to deceive others, so they might deceive themselves. There was mockery in it, but it was mockery of me, not of magic. "Perhaps," I said. "What do you know of my powers?"

"That they are insufficient to free you from this place."

"I have not attempted to free myself, and yet I have already been free."

That disturbed him. "You were not free. You merely brought the woman here in spirit!"

I let my breath out, trying to keep the sigh inaudible. In the antechamber of the House Absolute, a little girl had once mistaken me for a tall woman, when Thecla had for a time displaced my own personality. Now, it seemed, the remembered Thecla must have spoken through my mouth. I said, "Surely I am a necromancer then, who can command the spirits of the dead. For that woman is dead."

"You told us you freed her."

"Another woman, who only slightly resembled that one. What have you done to my son?"

"He does not call you his father."

"He suffers fancies," I said.

There was no reply. After a time I rose and ran my hands once more over the walls of my underground prison; they were of plain earth, as before. I had seen no light and heard no sound, but it seemed to me that it would have been possible to cover the hatch with some portable structure to exclude the day, and if the hatch were skillfully constructed, it might be lifted silently. I mounted the first rung of the ladder; it creaked beneath my weight.

I climbed a step up, and another, and it creaked at each. I tried to rise to the fourth rung, and felt my scalp and shoulders prodded as though with the points of daggers. A trickle of blood from my right ear wet my neck.

I retreated to the third rung and groped overhead. The thing that had seemed like a torn mat when I entered the underground chamber proved to be a score or more of sharp bamboo splittings, anchored somehow in the shaft with their points directed down. I had descended with ease because my body had forced them to one side; now they prevented me from ascending much as the barbs on a fish spear prevent the fish from getting away. I took hold of one and tried to break it, but though I might have done so with both hands, it was impossible with one. Given light and time I might have worked my way through them; light perhaps I might have had, but I did not dare to take the risk. I jumped to the floor again.

Another circuit of the room told me no more than I had known before, yet it seemed beyond credence that my questioner had climbed the ladder without making a sound, though he might perhaps possess some special knowledge that would permit him to pass through the bamboo. I went about the floor on my hands and knees, and learned no more than before.

I attempted to move the ladder, but it was fixed in position; so beginning at the corner nearest the shaft, I jumped and touched the wall at a point as high as I could reach, then moved half a step to one side and jumped again. When I had arrived at a place that must have been more or less opposite the spot where I had been sitting, I found it: a rectangular hole perhaps a cubit high and two across, with its lower edge slightly higher than my head. My interrogator might have climbed from it silently, perhaps with the aid of a rope, and returned the same way; but it seemed more likely that he had merely thrust his head and shoulders through, so that his voice had sounded as if he were truly in the room with me. I gripped the edge of the hole as well as I could, jumped, and pulled myself up.

XXI

The Duel of Magic

THE CHAMBER BEYOND the one in which I had been imprisoned seemed much like it, though its floor was higher. It was, of course, utterly dark; but now that I was confident I was no longer being observed, I took the Claw from its sack and looked about me by its light which was, though not bright, sufficient.

There was no ladder, but a narrow door gave access to what I assumed was a third subterranean room. Concealing the Claw again, I stepped through it, but found myself instead in a tunnel no wider than the doorway, which turned and turned again before I had taken half a dozen strides. At first I supposed it was simply a baffled passage to prevent light from betraying the opening in the wall of the room where I had been confined. But no more than three turns should have been necessary. The walls seemed to bend and divide; yet I remained in impenetrable darkness. I took out the Claw once more.

Perhaps because of the confined space in which I stood, it seemed somewhat brighter; but there was nothing to see beyond what my hands had already told me. I was alone. I stood in a maze with earthen walls and a ceiling (now just above my head) of rough poles; its narrow turnings quickly defeated the light.

I was about to thrust the Claw away again when I detected an odor at once pungent and alien. My nose is by no means the sensitive one of the he-wolf in the tale—if anything, I have rather a poorer sense of smell than most people. I thought I recognized the scent, but it was several moments before I placed it as the one I had experienced in the antechamber on the morning of our escape, when I returned for Jonas after talking to the little girl. She had said that something, some nameless seeker, had been snuffling among the prisoners there; and I had found a viscous substance on the floor and wall where Jonas lay.

I did not put the Claw back in its sack after that; but though I crossed a fetid trail several times as I wandered in the maze, I never glimpsed the creature that left it. After what must have been a watch or more of wandering, I reached a ladder that led up a short, open shaft. The square of daylight at its top was at once blinding and delightful. For a time I basked in it without even setting foot on the ladder. If I were to climb it, it seemed almost certain I would be recaptured at once; and yet I was so hungry and thirsty by then that I could hardly keep myself from doing so, and the thought of the foul thing that sought for me—it was surely one of Hethor's pets— made me want to bolt up it at once.

At last I climbed cautiously up and thrust my head above the level of the ground. I was not (as I had supposed) in the village I had seen; the windings of the maze had carried me beyond it to some secret exit. The great, silent trees stood closer here, and the light that had appeared so brilliant to me was the filtered green shade of their leaves. I emerged and found that I had left a hole between two roots, a place so obscure that I might have walked within a pace of it and yet not seen it. If I could, I would have blocked it with some weight to prevent or at least delay the escape of the creature that hunted me; but there was no stone or other object to hand that would serve such a purpose.

By the old trick of observing the slope of the ground and in so far as possible always walking downhill, I soon discovered a small stream. There was a little open sky above it, and as nearly as I could judge, the day appeared eight or nine watches over. Guessing that the village would not lie far from the source of the good water I had found, I soon found that as well. Wrapped in my fuligin cloak and standing in the deepest shade, I observed it for some time. Once a man—not painted like the two who had stopped us on the path—crossed the clearing. Once another left the suspended hut, went to the spring and drank, then returned to the hut.

It grew darker, and the strange village woke. A dozen men left the suspended hut and began to pile wood in the center of the clearing. Three more, robed and bearing forked staffs, emerged from the house of the tree. Still others, who must have been watching the jungle paths, slipped out of the shadows soon after the fire was kindled and spread a cloth before it.

One of the robed men stood with his back to the fire while the other two crouched at his feet; there was something extraordinary about them all, but I was reminded of the bearing of exultants, rather than of the Hierodules I had seen in the gardens of the House Absolute—it was the carriage that the consciousness of leadership confers, even as it severs the leader from common humanity. Painted and unpainted men sat cross-legged on the ground, facing the three. I heard the murmur of voices and the strong speech of the standing man, but I was too far to understand what was said. After a time the crouching men rose. One opened his robe like a tent, and Becan's son, whom I had made my own, stepped forth. The other produced *Terminus Est* in the same manner and drew her, displaying her bright blade and the black opal in her hilt to the crowd. Then one of the painted men rose, came some distance toward me (so that I feared he was about to see me, though I had covered my face with my mask) and lifted a door set into the ground. Soon afterward he emerged from another nearer the fire, and moving somewhat more rapidly went to the robed men to report.

There could be little doubt of what he was saying. I squared my shoulders and walked into the firelight. "I am not there," I said. "I am here."

There was an inrush of many breaths, and though I knew I might soon die, it was good to hear.

The midmost of the robed men said, "As you see, you cannot escape us. You were free, yet we drew you back." It was the voice that had interrogated me in my underground cell.

I said, "If you have walked far in The Way, you know you have less authority over me than the ignorant may believe." (It is not difficult to ape the way such people talk, for it is itself an aping of the speech of ascetics, and such priestesses as the

Pelerines.) "You stole my son, who is also son to The Beast Who Speaks, as you must know by this time if you have much questioned him. To gain his return, I surrendered my sword to your slaves, and for a time submitted myself to you. I will take it up again now."

There is a place in the shoulder that, when pressed firmly with the thumb, paralyzes the entire arm. I laid my hand on the shoulder of the robed man who held *Terminus Est,* and he dropped it at my feet. With more presence of mind than I would have credited in a child, the boy Severian picked it up and handed it to me. The midmost robed man lifted his staff and shouted, "Arms!" and his followers rose as one man. Many had the talons I have described, and many of the others drew knives.

I fastened *Terminus Est* over my shoulder in her accustomed place and said, "You surely do not suppose that I require this ancient sword as a weapon? She has higher properties, as you of all people should know."

The robed man who had produced little Severian said hurriedly, "So Abundantius has just told us." The other man was still rubbing his arm.

I looked at the midmost robed man, who was clearly the one referred to. His eyes were clever, and as hard as stones. "Abundantius is wise," I said. I was trying to think of some way in which I could kill him without drawing the others down on us. "He knows too, I think, of the curse that afflicts those who harm the person of a magus."

"You are a magus then," Abundantius said.

"I, who took the archon's prey from out of his hands and passed invisible through the midst of his army? Yes, I have been called so."

"Prove then that you are a magus and we will hail you as a brother. But if you fail the test or refuse it—we are many, and you have but one sword."

"I will fail no fair assay," I said. "Though neither you nor your followers have authority to make one."

He was too clever to be drawn into such a debate. "The test is known to all here except yourself, and known, too, to be just. Everyone you see about you has succeeded in it, or hopes to."

They took me to a hall I had not seen before, a place substantially built of logs, and hidden among the trees. It had no windows, and only a single entrance. When torches were carried inside, I saw that its one chamber was unfurnished but for a carpet of woven grass, and so long in proportion to its width that it seemed almost a corridor.

Abundantius said, "Here you will have your combat with Decuman." He indicated the man whose arm I had numbed, who was, perhaps, a trifle surprised at being thus singled out. "You bested him by the fire. Now he must best you, if he can. You may sit here, nearest the door, so that you may be assured we cannot enter to give him aid. He will sit at the farther end. You shall not approach one another, or touch one another as you touched him by the fire. You must weave your spells, and in the morning we shall come to see who has mastered."

Taking little Severian by the hand, I led him to the blind end of that dark place. "I'll sit here," I said. "I have every confidence that you will not come to Decuman's aid, but you have no way of knowing whether I have confederates in the jungle outside. You have offered to trust me, and so I shall trust you."

"It would be better," Abundantius said, "if you were to leave the child in our keeping."

I shook my head. "I must have him with me. He is mine, and when you robbed me of him on the path, you robbed me too of half my power. I will not be separated from him again."

After a moment, Abundantius nodded. "As you wish. We but desired that he might come to no harm."

"No harm will come to him," I said.

There were iron brackets on the walls, and four of the naked men thrust their torches into them before they left. Decuman seated himself cross-legged near the door, his staff upon his lap. I sat too, and drew the boy to me. "I'm scared," he said; he buried his little face in my cloak.

"You have every right to be. The past three days have been bad ones for you."

Decuman had begun a slow, rhythmic chant.

"Little Severian, I want you to tell me what happened to you on the path. I looked around and you were gone."

It took some comforting and coaxing, but at last his sobs ceased. "They came out—the three-colored men with claws, and I was afraid and ran away."

"Is that all?"

"And then more three-colored men came out and caught me, and they made me go into a hole in the ground, where it was dark. And then they woke me and lifted me up, and I was inside a man's coat, and then you came and got me."

"Didn't anyone ask you questions?"

"A man in the dark."

"I see. Little Severian, you mustn't ever run away again, the way you did on the path—do you understand? Only run if I run too. If you hadn't run away when we met the three-colored men, we wouldn't be here."

The boy nodded.

"Decuman," I called. "Decuman, can we talk?"

He ignored me, save perhaps that his murmured chant grew a trifle louder. His face was lifted so that he appeared to be staring at the roof poles, but his eyes were closed.

"What is he doing?" the boy asked.

"He is weaving an enchantment."

"Will it hurt us?"

"No," I said. "Such magic is mostly fakery—like lifting you up through a hole so it would look as if the other one had made you appear under his robe."

Yet even as I spoke, I was conscious there was something more. Decuman was concentrating his mind on me as few minds can be concentrated, and I felt I was naked in some brightly lit place where a thousand eyes watched. One of the torches flickered, guttered, and went out. As the light in the hall dimmed, the light I could not see seemed to grow brighter.

I rose. There are ways of killing that leave no mark, and I reviewed them mentally as I stepped forward.

At once, pikes sprang from the walls, an ell on either side. They were not such spears as soldiers have, energy weapons whose heads strike bolts of fire, but simple poles of wood tipped with iron, like the pilets the villagers of Saltus had used. Nevertheless, they could kill at close range, and I sat down again. The boy said, "I think they're outside watching us through the cracks between the logs."

"Yes, I know that now too."

"What can we do?" he asked. And then when I did not reply, "Who are these people, Father?"

It was the first time he had called me that. I drew him closer, and it seemed to weaken the net Decuman was knotting about my mind. I said, "I'm only guessing, but I would say this is an academy of magicians—of those cultists who practice what they believe are secret arts. They are supposed to have followers everywhere—though I choose to doubt that— and they are very cruel. Have you heard of the New Sun, little Severian? He is the man who prophets say will come and drive back the ice and set the world right."

"He will kill Abaia," the boy answered, surprising me.

"Yes, he is supposed to do that as well, and many other things. He is said to have come once before, long ago. Did you know that?"

He shook his head.

"Then his task was to forge a peace between humanity and the Increate, and he was called the Conciliator. He left behind a famous relic, a gem called the Claw." My hand went to it as I spoke, and though I did not loosen the drawstrings of the little sack of human skin that held it, I could feel it through the soft leather. As soon as I touched it, the invisible glare Decuman had created in my mind fell almost to nothing. I cannot say now just why I had presumed for so long that it was necessary for the Claw to be taken from its place of concealment for it to be effective. I learned that night that it was not so, and I laughed.

For a moment Decuman halted his chant, and his eyes opened. Little Severian clutched me more tightly. "Aren't you afraid anymore?"

"No," I said. "Could you see that I was frightened?"

He nodded solemnly.

"What I was going to tell you was that the existence of that relic seems to have given some people the idea that the Conciliator used claws as weapons. I have sometimes doubted that he existed; but if such a person ever lived, I'm sure that he used his weapons largely against himself. Do you understand what I am saying?"

I doubt that he did, but he nodded.

"When we were on the path, we found a charm against the coming of the New Sun. The three-colored men, who I think are the ones who have passed this test, use claws of steel. I think they must want to hold back the coming of the New Sun so they can take his place and perhaps usurp his powers. If—"

Outside, someone screamed.

XXII

The Skirts of the Mountain

MY LAUGH HAD broken Decuman's concentration, if only for a moment. The scream from outside did not. His net, so much of which had fallen in ruins when I gripped the Claw, was being knotted again, more slowly but more tightly.

It is always a temptation to say that such feelings are indescribable, though they seldom are. I felt that I hung naked between two sentient suns, and I was somehow aware that these suns were the hemispheres of Decuman's brain. I was bathed in light, but it was the glare of furnaces, consuming and somehow immobilizing. In that light, nothing seemed worthwhile; and I myself infinitely small and contemptible.

Thus my concentration too, in a sense, remained unbroken. Yet I was aware, however dimly, that the scream might signal an opportunity for me. Much later than I should have, after perhaps a dozen breaths had passed my nostrils, I stumbled to my feet.

Something was coming through the doorway. My first thought, absurd as it may sound, was that it was mud—that a convulsion had rocked Urth, and the hall was about to be inundated in what had been the bottom of some fetid marsh. It flowed around the doorposts blindly and softly, and as it did, another torch went out. Soon it was about to touch Decuman, and I shouted to warn him.

I am not sure whether it was the touch of the creature or my voice, but he recoiled. I was conscious again of the breaking of the spell, the ruin of the snare that had held me between the twin suns. They flew apart and dimmed as they vanished, and I seemed to expand, and to turn in a direction neither up nor down, left nor right, until I stood wholly in the hall of testing, with little Severian clinging to my cloak.

Decuman's hand flashed with talons then. I had not even realized he had them. Whatever that black and nearly shapeless creature was, its side cut as fat does under the lash. Its blood was black too, or perhaps darkly green. Decuman's was red; when the creature flowed over him, it seemed to melt his skin like wax.

I lifted the boy and made him cling to my neck and clasp my waist with his legs, then jumped with all my strength. But though my fingertips touched a roof pole, I could not grasp it. The creature was turning, blindly but purposefully. Perhaps it hunted by scent, yet I have always felt it was by thought— that would explain why it was so slow to find me in the antechamber, where I had dreamed myself to Thecla, and so swift in the hall of testing, when Decuman's mind was focused on mine.

I jumped again, but this time I missed the pole by a span at least. To get one of the two remaining torches, I had to run toward the creature. I did and seized the torch, but it went out as I took it from its bracket.

Holding the bracket with one hand, I jumped a third time, assisting my legs with the strength of my arm; and now I caught a smooth, narrow pole with my left hand. The pole bent beneath my weight, but I was able to draw myself up, with the boy on my shoulders, until I could get one foot on the bracket.

Below me, the dark, shapeless creature reared, fell, and lifted itself again. Still holding the pole, I drew *Terminus Est*. A slash bit deep into the oozing flesh, but the blade was no sooner clear than the wound seemed to close and knit. I turned my sword on the roof thatch then, an expedient I confess to stealing from Agia. It was thick, of jungle leaves bound with tough fibers; my first frantic strokes seemed to make little impression on it, but at the third a great swath fell. Part of it struck the remaining torch, smothering it, then sending up a gout of flame. I vaulted through the gap and into the night.

Leaping blindly as I did with that sharp blade drawn, it is a wonder that I did not kill both the boy and myself. I dropped it and him when I struck the ground, and fell to my knees. The red blaze of the thatch grew brighter with the passing of every moment. I heard the boy whimper and called to him not to run, then pulled him to his feet with one hand and snatched up *Terminus Est* with the other and ran myself.

All the rest of that night we fled blindly through the jungle. In so far as I could, I tried to direct our steps uphill—not only because our way north would mean climbing, but because I knew we were less likely to tumble over some drop. When morning came, we were in the jungle still, with no more idea than we had before of where we were. I carried the boy then, and he fell asleep in my arms.

In another watch there could be no doubt the ground was rising steeply before us, and at last we came to a curtain of vines such as I had cut through the day before. Just as I was ready to try to put down the boy without waking him, so that I could draw my sword, I saw bright daylight streaming through a rent to my left. I went to it, walking as quickly as I could, almost running; then through it, and out onto a rocky upland of coarse grass and shrubs. A few more steps brought me to a clear stream that sang over rocks—unquestionably the stream beside which the boy and I had slept two nights before. Not knowing or caring whether the shapeless creature was on our track still, I lay down beside it and slept again.

I was in a maze, like and yet unlike the dark underground maze of the magicians. The corridors were wider here, and sometimes seemed galleries as mighty as those of the House Absolute. Some, indeed, were lined with pier glasses, in which I saw myself with ragged cloak and haggard face, and Thecla, half-transparent in a lovely, trailing gown, close beside me. Planets whistled down long, oblique, curving tracks that only they could see. Blue Urth carried the green moon like an infant, but did not touch her. Red Verthandi became Decuman, his skin eaten away, turning in his own blood.

I fled and fell, jerking all my limbs. I saw true stars in the sun-drenched sky for a moment, but sleep drew me as irresistibly as gravity. Beside a wall of glass, I walked; and through it I saw the boy, running and frightened, in the old, patched, gray shirt I had worn as an apprentice, running from the fourth level, I thought, to the Atrium of Time. Dorcas and Jolenta came hand in hand, smiling at each other, and did not see me. Then autochthons, copper-skinned and bowlegged, feathered and jeweled, were dancing behind their shaman, dancing in the rain. The undine swam in air, vast as a cloud, blotting out the sun.

I woke. Soft rain pattered on my face. Beside me, little Severian slept still. I wrapped him as well as I could in my cloak and carried him again to the rent in the curtain of vines. Beyond that curtain under the wide-boughed trees, the rain hardly penetrated; and there we lay and slept once more. This time there were no dreams, and when I woke we had slept a day and a night, and the pale light of dawn lay everywhere.

The boy was already up, wandering among the boles of the trees. He showed me where the brook was in this place, and I washed, and shaved as well as I could without hot water, which I had not done since the first afternoon in the house beneath the cliff. Then we found the familiar path and made our way north again.

"Won't we meet the three-colored men?" he asked, and I told him not to worry and not to run—that I would handle the three-colored men. The truth was that I was far more concerned about Hethor and the creature he had set upon my track. If it had not perished in the fire, it might be moving toward us now; for though it had seemed an animal that would fear the sun, the dimness of the jungle was the very stuff of twilight.

Only one painted man stepped into the path, and he did so not to bar the way but to prostrate himself. I was tempted to kill him and be done with it; we are taught strictly to kill and maim only at the order of a judge, but that training had been weakening in me as I moved farther and farther from Nessus and toward the war and the wild mountains. Some mystics hold that the vapors arising from battles affect the brain, even a long way downwind; and it may be so. Nevertheless, I lifted him up, and merely told him to stand aside.

"Great Magus," he said, "what have you done with the creeping dark?"

"I have sent it back to the pit, from which I drew it," I told him, for since we had not encountered the creature, I was fairly certain Hethor had recalled it, if it was not dead.

"Five of us transmigrated," the painted man said.

"Your powers, then, are greater than I would have credited. It has killed hundreds in a night."

I was far from sure he would not attack us when our backs were to him, but he did not. The path down which I had walked as a prisoner the day before seemed deserted now. No more guards appeared to challenge us; some of the strips of red cloth had been torn down and trampled under foot, though I could not imagine why. I saw many footprints on the path, which had been smooth (perhaps raked smooth) before.

"What are you looking for?" the boy asked.

I kept my voice low, still not sure there were no listeners behind the trees. "The slime of the animal we ran away from last night."

"Do you see it?"

I shook my head.

For a time, the boy was silent. Then he said, "Big Severian, where did it come from?"

"Do you remember the story? From one of the mountaintops beyond the shores of Urth."

"Where Spring Wind lived?"

"I don't think it was the same one."

"How did he get here?"

"A bad man brought him," I said. "Now be quiet for a while, little Severian."

If I was short with the boy, it was because I had been troubled by the same thought. Hethor must have smuggled his pets aboard the ship on which he served, that seemed clear enough; and when he had followed me out of Nessus, he might easily have carried the notules in some small, sealed container on his person—terrible though they were, they were no thicker than tissue, as Jonas had known.

But what of the creature we had seen in the hall of testing? It had appeared in the antechamber of the House Absolute too, after Hethor had come, but how? And had it followed Hethor and Agia like a dog as they journeyed north to Thrax? I summoned the memory of it, as I had seen it when it killed Decuman, and tried to estimate its weight: it must have been as heavy as several men, and perhaps as heavy as a destrier. A large cart, surely, would have been required to transport and conceal it. Had Hethor driven such a cart through these mountains? I could not believe it. Had the viscid horror we had seen shared such a cart with the salamander I had seen destroyed in Thrax? I could not believe that either.

The village seemed deserted when we reached it. Some parts of the hall of testing still stood and smoldered. I looked in vain for the remains of Decuman's body there, though I found his half-burned staff. It had been hollow, and from the smoothness of its interior, I suspected that with the head removed it had formed a sabarcane for shooting poisoned darts. No doubt it would have been used if I had proved overly resistant to the spell he wove.

The boy must have been following my thoughts from my expression and the direction of my glance. He said, "That man really was magic, wasn't he? He almost magicked you."

I nodded.

"You said it wasn't real."

"In some ways, little Severian, I am not much wiser than you. I didn't think it was. I had seen so much fakery—the secret door into the underground room where they kept me, and the way they made you appear under the other man's robe. Still, there are dark things everywhere, and I suppose that those who look hard enough for them cannot help but find some. Then they become, as you said, real magicians."

"They could tell everybody what to do, if they know real magic."

I only shook my head to that, but I have thought much about it since. It seems to me there are two objections to the boy's idea, though expressed in a more mature form it must appear more convincing.

The first is that so little knowledge is passed from one generation to the next by the magicians. My own training was in what may be called the most fundamental of the applied sciences; and I know from it that the progress of science depends much less upon either theoretical considerations or systematic investigation than is commonly believed, but rather on the transmittal of reliable information, gained by chance or insight, from one set of men to their successors. The nature of those who hunt after dark knowledge is to hoard it even in death, or to transmit it so wrapped in disguise and beclouded with self-serving lies that it is of little value. At times, one hears of those who teach their lovers well, or their children; but it is the nature of such people seldom to have either, and it may be that their art is weakened when they do.

The second is that the very existence of such powers argues a counterforce. We call powers of the first kind dark, though they may use a species of deadly light as Decuman did; and we call those of the second kind bright, though I think that they may at times employ darkness, as a good man nevertheless draws the curtains of his bed to sleep. Yet there is truth to the talk of darkness and light, because it shows plainly that one implies the other. The tale I read to little Severian said that the universe was but a long word of the Increate's. We, then, are the syllables of that word. But the speaking of any word is futile unless there are other words, words that are not spoken. If a beast has but one cry, the cry tells nothing; and even the wind has a multitude of voices, so that those who sit indoors may hear it and know if the weather is tumultuous or mild. The powers we call dark seem to me to be the words the Increate did *not* speak, if the Increate exists at all; and these words must be maintained in a quasi-existence, if the other word, the word spoken, is to be distinguished. What is not said can be important—but what is said is more important. Thus my very knowledge of the existence of the Claw was almost sufficient to counter Decuman's spell.

And if the seekers after dark things find them, may not the seekers after bright find them as well? And are they not more apt to hand their wisdom on? So the Pelerines had guarded the Claw, from generation unto generation; and thinking of this, I became more determined than ever to find them and restore it to them; for if I had not known it before, the night with the alzabo had brought home to me that I was only flesh, and would die in time certainly, and perhaps would die soon.

Because the mountain we approached stood to the north and thus cast its shadow toward the saddle of jungle, no curtain of vines grew on that side. The pale green of the leaves only faded to one more pale still, and the number of dead trees increased, though all the trees were smaller. The canopy of leaves beneath which we had walked all day broke, and in another hundred strides broke again, and at last vanished altogether.

Then the mountain rose before us, too near for us to see it as the image of a man. Great folded slopes rolled down out of a bank of cloud; they were, I knew, but the sculptured drapery of his robes. How often he must have risen from sleep and put them on, perhaps without reflecting that they would be preserved here for the ages, so huge as almost to escape the sight of humankind.

XXIII

The Cursed Town

AT ABOUT NOON of the next day we found water again, the only water the two of us were to taste upon that mountain. Only a few strips of the dried meat Casdoe had left for me remained. I shared them out, and we drank from the stream, which was no more than a trickle the size of a man's thumb. That seemed strange, because I had seen so much snow on the head and shoulders of the mountain; I was to discover later that the slopes below the snow, where snow might have melted with the coming of summer, were blown clear by the wind. Higher, the white drifts might accumulate for centuries.

Our blankets were damp with dew, and we spread them there on stones to dry. Even without the sun, the dry gusts of mountain air dried them in a watch or so. I knew that we would be spending the coming night high up the slopes, much as I had spent the first night after leaving Thrax. Somehow, the knowledge was powerless to depress my spirits. It was not so much that we were leaving the dangers we had found in the saddle of jungle, as that we were leaving behind a certain sordidness there. I felt that I had been befouled, and that the cold atmosphere of the mountain would cleanse me. For a time that feeling remained with me almost unexamined; then, as we began to climb in earnest, I realized that what disturbed me was the memory of the lies I had told the magicians, pretending, as they did, to command great powers and be privy to vast secrets. Those lies had been wholly justifiable—they had helped to save my life and little Severian's. Nevertheless, I felt myself somewhat less of a man because I had resorted to them. Master Gurloes, whom I had come to hate before I left the guild, had lied frequently; and now I was not sure whether I had hated him because he lied, or hated lying because he did it.

And yet Master Gurloes had possessed as good an excuse as I did, and perhaps a better one. He had lied to preserve the guild and advance its fortunes, giving various officials and officers exaggerated accounts of our work, and when necessary concealing our mistakes. In doing that, he, the de facto head of the guild, had been advancing his own position, to be sure; yet he had also been advancing mine, and that of Drotte, Roche, Eata, and all the other apprentices and journeymen who would eventually inherit it. If he had been the simple, brutal man he wished everyone to believe he was, I could have been certain now that his dishonesty had been for his benefit alone. I knew that he was not; perhaps for years he had seen himself as I now saw myself.

And yet I could not be certain I had acted to save little Severian. When he had run and I had surrendered my sword, it might have been more to his advantage if I had fought—I myself was the one whose immediate advantage had been served by my docile capitulation, since if I had fought I might have been killed. Later, when I had escaped, I had surely returned as much for *Terminus Est* as for the boy; I had returned for her in the mine of the man-apes, when he had not been with me; and without her, I would have become a mere vagabond.

A watch after I entertained these thoughts, I was scaling a rock face with both the sword and the boy on my back, and with no more certainty concerning how much I cared for either than I had before. Fortunately I was fairly fresh, it was not a difficult climb as such things go, and at the top we struck an ancient highway.

Although I have walked in many strange places, I have walked in none that gave me so great a sensation of anomaly. To our left, no more than twenty paces off, I could see the termination of this broad road, where some rockslide had carried its lower end away. Before us it stretched as perfect as on the day it was completed, a ribbon of seamless black stone winding up toward that immense figure whose face was lost above the clouds.

The boy gripped my hand when I put him down. "My mother said we couldn't use the roads, because of the soldiers."

"Your mother was right," I told him. "But she was going to go down, where the soldiers are. No doubt there were soldiers on this road once, but they died a long time before the biggest tree in the jungle down there was a seed." He was cold, and I gave him one of the blankets and showed him how to wrap it about him and hold it closed to make a cloak. If anyone had seen us then, we would have appeared a small, gray figure followed by a disproportionate shadow.

We entered a mist, and I thought it strange to find one that high up. It was only after we had climbed above it and could look down upon its sunlit top that I realized it had been one of the clouds that had seemed so remote when I had looked up at them from the saddle.

And yet that saddle of jungle, so far below us now, was itself no doubt thousands of cubits above Nessus and the lower reaches of Gyoll. I thought then how far I must have come, that jungles could exist at such altitudes—nearly to the waist of the world, where it was always summer, and only height produced any difference in the climate. If I were to journey to the west, out of these mountains, then from what I had learned from Master Palaemon, I would find myself in a jungle so pestilential as to make the one we had left seem a paradise, a coastal jungle of steaming heat and swarming insects; and yet there too I would see the evidences of death, for though that jungle received as much of the sun's strength as any spot on Urth, still it was less than it had received in times past, and just as the ice crept forward in the south and the vegetation of the temperate zone fled from it, so the trees and other plants of the tropics died to give the newcomers space.

While I looked down at the cloud, the boy had been walking ahead. Now he looked back at me with shining eyes and called, "Who made this road?"

"No doubt the workers who carved the mountain. They must have had great energies at their command and machines more powerful than any we know about. Still, they would have had to carry the rubble away in some fashion. A thousand carts and wains must have rolled here once." And yet I wondered, because the iron wheels of such vehicles score even the hard cobbles of Thrax and Nessus, and this road was as smooth as a processional way. Surely, I thought, only the sun and wind have passed here.

"Big Severian, look! Do you see the hand?"

The boy was pointing toward a spur of the mountain high above us. I craned my neck, but for a moment I saw nothing but what I had seen before: a long promontory of inhospitable gray rock. Then the sunlight flashed on something near the end. It seemed, unmistakably, the gleam of gold; when I had seen that, I saw also that the gold was a ring, and under it I saw the thumb lying frozen in stone along the rock, a thumb perhaps a hundred paces long, with the fingers above it hills.

We had no money, and I knew how valuable money might be when we were forced, as eventually we must be, to reenter the inhabited lands. If I was still searched for, gold might persuade the searchers to look elsewhere. Gold might also buy little Severian an apprenticeship in some worthy guild, for it was clear he could not continue to travel with me. It seemed most probable that the great ring was only gold leaf over stone; even so, so vast a quantity of gold leaf, if it could be peeled away and rolled up, must amount to a considerable total. And though I made an effort not to, I found myself wondering if mere gold leaf could have endured so many centuries. Would it not have loosened and fallen away long ago? If the ring were of solid gold, it would be worth a fortune; but all the fortunes of Urth could not have bought this mighty image, and he who had ordered its construction must have possessed wealth incalculable. Even if the ring were not solid through to the finger beneath, there might be some substantial thickness of metal.

As I considered all this, I toiled upward, my long legs soon outstripping the boy's short ones. At times the road climbed so steeply I could hardly believe vehicles burdened with stone had ever traversed it. Twice we crossed fissures, one so wide that I was forced to throw the boy across it before leaping over it myself. I was hoping to find water before we halted; I found none, and when night fell we had no better shelter than a crevice of stone where we wrapped ourselves in the blankets and my cape and slept as well as we could.

* * *

In the morning we were both thirsty. Although the rainy season would not come until autumn, I told the boy I thought it might rain today, and we started forward again in good spirits. Then too, he showed me how carrying a small stone in the mouth helps to quench thirst. It is a mountain trick, one I had not known. The wind was colder now than it had been before, and I began to feel the thinness of the air. Occasionally the road twisted to some point where we received a few moments of sunshine.

In doing so, it wound farther and farther from the ring, until at last we found ourselves in full shadow, out of sight of the ring altogether and somewhere near the knees of the seated figure. There was a last steep climb, so abrupt that I would have been grateful for steps. And then, ahead of us where they seemed to float in the clear air, a cluster of slender spires. The boy called out "Thrax!" so happily that I knew his mother must have told him tales of it, and told him too, when she and the old man took him from the house where he had been born, that she would bring him there.

"No," I said. "It is not Thrax. This looks more like my own Citadel—our Matachin Tower, and the witches' tower, and the Bear Tower and the Bell Tower."

He looked at me, wide-eyed.

"No, it isn't that either, of course. Only I have been to Thrax, and Thrax is a city of stone. Those towers are of metal, as ours were."

"They have eyes," little Severian said.

So they did. At first I thought my imagination was deceiving me, particularly since not all the towers possessed them. At last I came to realize that some faced away from us, and that the towers had not only eyes but shoulders and arms as well; that they were, in fact, the metallic figures of cataphracts, warriors armored from head to toe. "It isn't a real city," I told the boy. "What we have found are the guardsmen of the Autarch, waiting in his lap to destroy those who would harm him."

"Will they hurt us?"

"It's a frightening thought, isn't it? They could crush you and me beneath their feet like mice. I'm sure they won't, however. They're only statues, spiritual guards left here as memorials to his powers."

"There are big houses too," the boy said.

He was right. The buildings were no more than waist-high to the towering metal figures, so that we had overlooked them at first. That again reminded me of the Citadel, where structures never meant to brave the stars are mingled with the towers. Perhaps it was merely the thin air, but I had a sudden vision of these metal men rising slowly, then ever more swiftly, lifting hands toward the sky as they dove into it as we used to dive down to the dark waters of the cistern by torchlight.

Although my boots must have grated on the wind-swept rock, I find I have no memory of such a sound. Perhaps it was lost in the immensity of the mountaintop, so that we approached the standing figures as silently as if we walked over moss. Our shadows, which had spread behind us and to our left when they had first appeared, were contracted into pools about our feet; and I noticed that I could see the eyes of every figure. I told myself that I had overlooked some at first, yet they glittered in the sun.

At last we threaded a path among them, and among the buildings that surrounded them. I had expected these buildings to be ruinous, like those in the forgotten city of Apu-Punchau. They were closed, secretive, and silent; but they might have been constructed only a few years before. No roofs had fallen in; no vines had dislodged the square gray stones of their walls. They were windowless, and their architecture did not suggest temples, fortresses, tombs, or any other type of structure with which I was familiar. They were utterly without ornament and without grace; yet their workmanship was excellent, and their differing forms seemed to indicate differences in function. The shining figures stood among them as if they had been halted in their places by some sudden, freezing wind, not as monuments stand.

I selected a building and told the boy we would break into it, and that if we were fortunate we might find water there, and perhaps even preserved food. It proved a foolish boast. The doors were as solid as the walls, the roof as strong as the foundation. Even if I had possessed an ax, I do not think I could have smashed my way in, and I dared not hew with *Terminus Est.* Poking and prying for some weakness, we wasted several watches. The second and third buildings we attempted proved no easier than the first.

"There's a round house over there," the boy said at last. "I'll go and look at it for you."

Because I felt sure there was nothing in this deserted place that could harm him, I told him to go ahead.

Soon he was back. "The door's open!"

XXIV

The Corpse

I HAD NEVER discovered what uses the other buildings had
served. No more did I understand this one, which was circular
and covered by a dome. Its walls were metal—not the darkly
lustrous metal of our Citadel towers, but some bright alloy
like polished silver.

This gleaming building stood atop a stepped pedestal, and I
wondered to see it there when the great images of the cataphracts in their antique armor stood plainly in the streets.
There were five doorways about its circumference (for we
walked around it before venturing inside), and all of them
stood open. By examining them and the floor before them, I
tried to judge whether they had stood so for so many years;
there was little dust at this elevation, and in the end I could
not be certain. When we had completed our inspection, I told
the boy to let me go first, and stepped inside.

Nothing happened. Even when the boy followed me, the
doors did not close, no enemy rushed at us, no energy colored
the air, and the floor remained firm beneath our feet. Nevertheless, I had the feeling that we had somehow entered a trap:
that outside on the mountain we had been free, however hungry and thirsty we were, and that here we were free no longer.
I think I would have turned and run if he had not been with
me. As it was, I did not want to appear superstitious or afraid,
and I felt an obligation to try to find food and water.

There were many devices in that building to which I can give no name. They were not furniture, nor boxes, nor machines as I understand the term. Most were oddly angled; I saw some that appeared to have niches in which to sit, though the sitter would have been cramped, and would have faced some part of the device instead of his companions. Others contained alcoves where someone might once, perhaps, have rested.

These devices stood beside aisles, wide aisles that ran toward the center of the structure as straight as the spokes of a wheel. Looking down the one we had entered, I could see, dimly, some red object, and upon it, much smaller, something brown. At first, I did not pay great attention to either, but when I had satisfied myself that the devices I have described were of no value and no danger to us, I led the boy toward them.

The red object was a sort of couch, a very elaborate one, with straps so that a prisoner might be confined upon it. Around it were mechanisms that seemed intended to provide for nourishment and elimination. It stood upon a small dais, and on it lay what had once been the body of a man with two heads. The thin, dry air of the mountain had desiccated the body long ago—like the mysterious buildings, it might have been a year old or a thousand. He had been a man taller than I, perhaps even an exultant, and powerfully muscled. Now I might, I thought, tear one of his arms from its socket with a gesture. He wore no loincloth, or any other garment, and though we are accustomed to sudden changes in the size of the organs of procreation, it was strange to see them so shriveled here. Some hair remained upon the heads, and it appeared to me that the hair of the right had been black; that of the head on the left was yellowish. The eyes of both were closed, and the mouths open, showing a few teeth. I noticed that the straps that might have bound this creature to the couch were not buckled.

At the time, however, I was far more concerned with the mechanism that had once fed him. I told myself that ancient machines were often astoundingly durable, and though it had long been abandoned, it had enjoyed the most favorable conditions for its preservation; and I twisted every dial I could find, and shifted each lever, in an attempt to make it produce some nutriment. The boy watched me, and when I had been moving things here and there for some time asked if we were going to starve.

"No," I told him. "We can go a great deal longer without food than you would think. Getting something to drink is a great deal more urgent, but if we can't find anything here, there is sure to be snow further up the mountain.".

"How did he die?" For some reason I had never brought myself to touch the corpse; now the boy ran his plump fingers along one withered arm.

"Men die. The wonder is that such a monster lived. Such things usually perish at birth."

"Do you think the others left him here when they went away?" He asked.

"Left him here alive, you mean? I suppose they could have. There would have been no place for him, perhaps, in the lands below. Or perhaps he did not want to go. Maybe they confined him here on this couch when he misbehaved. Possibly he was subject to madness, or fits of violent rage. If any of those things are true, he must have spent his last days wandering over the mountain, returning here to eat and drink, and dying when the food and water he depended on were exhausted."

"Then there isn't any water in there," the boy said practically.

"That's true. Still, we don't know it happened like that. He may have died for some other reason before his supplies ran out. Then too, the kind of thing we've been saying would seem to assume that he was a sort of pet or mascot for the people who carved the mountain. This is a very elaborate place in which to keep a pet. Just the same, I don't think I'm ever going to be able to reactivate this machine."

"I think we ought to go down," the boy announced as we were leaving the circular building.

I turned to look behind us, thinking how foolish all my fears had been. Its doors remained open; nothing had moved, nothing had changed. If it had ever been a trap, it seemed certain it was a trap that had rusted open centuries before.

"So do I," I said. "But the day is nearly over—see how long our shadows are now. I don't want to be overtaken by the night when we're climbing down the other side, so I'm going to find out whether I can reach the ring we saw this morning. Perhaps we'll find water as well as gold. Tonight we'll sleep in that round building out of the wind, and tomorrow we'll start down the north side by the first light."

He nodded to show that he understood, and accompanied me willingly enough as I set off to look for a path to the ring. It had been on the southern arm, so that we were in some sense returning to the side we had first climbed, though we had approached the cluster of sculptured cataphracts and buildings from the southeast. I had feared that the ascent to the arm would be a difficult climb; instead, just where the vast height of the chest and upper arm rose before us, I found what I had been wishing for much earlier: a narrow stair. There were many hundreds of steps, so it was a weary climb still, and I carried the boy up much of it.

The arm itself was smooth stone, yet so wide there seemed to be little danger that the boy would fall off as long as we kept to the center. I made him hold my hand and strode along quite eagerly, my cloak snapping in the wind.

To our left lay the ascent we had begun the day before; beyond it was the saddle between the mountains, green under its blanket of jungle. Beyond even that, hazy now with distance, rose the mountain where Becan and Casdoe had built their home. As I walked, I tried to distinguish their cabin, or at least the area in which it stood, and at last I found what seemed to me the cliff face I had descended to reach it, a tiny fleck of color on the side of that less lofty mountain, with the glint of the falling water in its center like an iridescent mote.

When I had seen it, I halted and turned to look up at the peak on whose slope we walked. I could see the face now and its mitre of ice, and below it the left shoulder, where a thousand cavalrymen might have been exercised by their chiliarch.

Ahead of me, the boy was pointing and shouting something I could not understand, pointing down toward the buildings and the standing figures of the metal guardsmen. It was a moment before I realized what he meant—their faces were turned three-quarters toward us, as they had been turned three-quarters toward us that morning. Their heads had moved. For the first time, I followed the direction of their eyes—and found that they were looking at the sun.

I nodded to the boy and called, "I see!"

We were on the wrist, with the little plain of the hand spread before us, broader and safer even than the arm. As I strode over it, the boy ran ahead of me. The ring was on the second finger, a finger larger than a log cut from the greatest tree. Little Severian ran out upon it, balancing himself without difficulty on the crest, and I saw him throw out his hands to touch the ring.

There was a flash of light—bright, yet not blindingly so in the afternoon sunshine; because it was tinted with violet, it seemed almost a darkness.

It left him blackened and consumed. For a moment, I think, he still lived; his head jerked back and his arms were flung wide. There was a puff of smoke, carried away at once by the wind. The body fell, its limbs contracting as the legs of a dead insect do, and rolled until it had tumbled out of sight in the crevice between the second and third fingers.

I, who had seen so many brandings and abacinations, and had even used the iron myself (among the billion things I recall perfectly is the flesh of Morwenna's cheeks blistering), could scarcely force myself to go and look at him.

There were bones there, in that narrow place between the fingers, but they were old bones that broke beneath my feet when I leaped down like the bones strewn upon the paths in our necropolis, and I did not trouble to examine them. I took out the Claw. When I had cursed myself for not using it when Thecla's body was brought forth at Vodalus's banquet, Jonas had told me not to be a fool, that whatever powers the Claw might possess could not possibly have restored life to that roasted flesh.

And I could not help but think that if it acted now and restored little Severian to me, for all my joy I would take him to some safe place and slash my own throat with *Terminus Est*. Because if the Claw would do that, it would have called Thecla back too, if only it had been used; and Thecla was a part of myself, now forever dead.

For a moment it seemed that there was a glimmering, a bright shadow or aura; then the boy's corpse crumbled to black ash that stirred in the unquiet air.

I stood, and put the Claw away, and began to walk back, vaguely wondering how much trouble I would have in leaving that narrow place and regaining the back of the hand. (In the end, I had to stand *Terminus Est* on the tip of her own blade and put one foot on a quillion to get up, then crawl back, head down, until I could grasp her pommel and pull her up after me.) There was no confusion of memory, but for a time a confusion of mind, in which the boy was merged in that other boy, Jader, who had lived with his dying sister in the jacal upon the cliff in Thrax. The one, who had come to mean so much to me, I could not save; the other, who had meant little, I had cured. In some way, it seemed to me they were the same boy. No doubt that was merely some protective reaction of my mind, a shelter it sought from the storm of madness; but it seemed to me somehow that so long as Jader lived, the boy his mother had named Severian could not truly perish.

I had meant to halt upon the hand and look back; I could not—the truth is that I feared I would go to the edge and throw myself over. I did not actually stop until I had nearly regained the narrow stair that led down so many hundreds of steps to the broad lap of the mountain. Then I seated myself and once more found that fleck of color that was the cliff below which Casdoe's home had stood. I remembered the barking of the brown dog as I had come through the forest toward it. He had been a coward, that dog, when the alzabo came, but he had died with his teeth in the defiled flesh of a zoanthrop, while I, a coward too, had hung back. I remembered Casdoe's tired, lovely face, the boy peeping from behind her skirt, the way the old man had sat cross-legged with his back to the fire, talking of Fechin. They were all dead now, Severa and Becan, whom I had never seen; the old man, the dog, Casdoe, now little Severian, even Fechin, all dead, all lost in the mists that obscure our days. Time itself is a thing, so it seems to me, that stands solidly like a fence of iron palings with its endless row of years; and we flow past like Gyoll, on our way to a sea from which we shall return only as rain.

I knew then, on the arm of that giant figure, the ambition to conquer time, an ambition beside which the desire of the distant suns is only the lust of some petty, feathered chieftain to subjugate some other tribe.

There I sat until the sun was nearly hidden by the rising of the mountains in the west. It should have been easier to descend the stair than it had been to climb it, but I was very thirsty now, and the jolt of each step hurt my knees. The light was nearly gone, and the wind like ice. One blanket had been burned with the boy; I unfolded the other and wrapped my chest and shoulders in it under my cloak.

When I was perhaps halfway down, I paused to rest. Only a thin crescent of reddish brown remained of the day. That narrowed, then vanished; and as it did, each of the great metal cataphracts below me raised a hand in salute. So quiet they were, and so steady, that I could almost have believed them sculptured with lifted arms, as I saw them.

For a time the wonder of it washed all my sorrow from me, and I could only marvel. I remained where I was, staring at them, not daring to move. Night rushed across the mountains; in the last, dim twilight I watched the mighty arms come down.

Still dazed, I reentered the silent cluster of buildings that stood in the figure's lap. If I had seen one miracle fail, I had witnessed another; and even a seemingly purposeless miracle is an inexhaustible source of hope, because it proves to us that since we do not understand everything, our defeats—so much more numerous than our few and empty victories—may be equally specious.

By some idiotic error, I contrived to lose my way when I tried to return to the circular building where I had told the boy we would spend the night, and I was too fatigued to search for it. Instead I found a sheltered spot well away from the nearest metal guardsman, where I rubbed my aching legs and wrapped myself against the cold as well as I could. Although I must have fallen asleep almost at once, I was soon awakened by the sound of soft footsteps.

XXV

Typhon and Piaton

WHEN I HEARD the footsteps, I had risen and drawn my sword, and I waited in a shadow for what seemed a watch at least, though it was no doubt much less. Twice more I heard them, quick and soft, yet somehow suggestive of a large man—a powerful man hurrying, almost running, light-footed and athletic.

Here the stars were in all their glory; as bright as they must be seen by the sailors whose ports they are, when they go aloft to spread the golden gauze that would wrap a continent. I could see the motionless guardsmen almost as if by day, and the buildings around me, bathed in the many-colored lights of ten thousand suns. We think with horror of the frozen plains of Dis, the outermost companion of our sun—but of how many suns are we the outermost companion? To the people of Dis (if such exist) it is all one long, starry night.

Several times, standing there under the stars, I nearly slept; and at the borders of sleep I worried about the boy, thinking that I had probably awakened him when I rose and wondering where I should find food for him when the sun could be seen again. After such thoughts, the memory of his death would come to my mind as night had come to the mountain, a wave of blackness and despair. I knew then how Dorcas had felt when Jolenta died. There had been no sexual play between the boy and me, as I believe there had at some time been between Dorcas and Jolenta; but then it had never been their fleshly love that had aroused my jealousy. The depth of my feeling for the boy had been as great as Dorcas's for Jolenta, surely (and surely greater far than Jolenta's for Dorcas). If Dorcas had known of it, she would have been as jealous as I had sometimes been, I thought, if only she had loved me as I had loved her.

At last, when I heard the footsteps no longer, I concealed myself as well as I could and lay down and slept. I half expected I would not wake from that sleep, or that I would wake with a knife at my throat, but no such thing happened. Dreaming of water, I slept well past the dawn and woke alone, cold and stiff in every limb.

I cared nothing then for the secret of the footsteps, or the guardsmen, or the ring, or for anything else in that accursed place. My only wish was to leave it, and as quickly as possible; and I was delighted—though I could not have explained why—when I found that I would not have to repass the circular building on my way to the northwestern side of the mountain.

There have been many times when I have felt I have gone mad, for I have had many great adventures, and the greatest adventures are those that act most strongly upon our minds. So it was then. A man, larger than I and far broader of shoulder, stepped from between the feet of a cataphract, and it was as though one of the monstrous constellations of the night sky had fallen to Urth and clothed itself in the flesh of humankind. For the man had two heads, like an ogre in some forgotten tale in *The Wonders of Urth and Sky*.

Instinctively, I put my hand on the sword hilt at my shoulder. One of the heads laughed; I think it was the only laughter I was ever to hear at the baring of that great blade.

"Why are you alarmed?" he called. "I see you are as well equipped as I am. What is your friend's name?"

Even in my surprise, I admired his boldness. "She is *Terminus Est,*" I said, and I turned the sword so he could see the writing on the steel.

" 'This is the place of parting.' Very good. Very good indeed, and particularly good that it should be read here and now, because this time will truly be a line between old and new such as the world has not seen. My own friend's name is Piaton, which I fear means nothing much. He is an inferior servant to that you have, though perhaps a better steed."

Hearing its name, the other head opened wide its eyes, which had been half closed, and rolled them. Its mouth moved as though to speak, but no sound emerged. I thought it a species of idiot.

"But now you may put up your weapon. As you see, I am unarmed, though already be-headed, and in any case, I mean you no hurt."

He raised his hands as he spoke, and turned to one side and then the other, so that I might see that he was entirely naked, something that was already clear enough.

I asked, "Are you perhaps the son of the dead man I saw in the round building back there?"

I had sheathed *Terminus Est* as I spoke, and he took a step nearer, saying, "Not at all. I am the man himself."

Dorcas rose in my thoughts as if through the brown waters of the Lake of Birds, and I felt again her dead hand clutch mine. Before I knew that I was speaking, I blurted, "I restored you to life?"

"Say rather that your coming awakened me. You thought me dead when I was only dry. I drank, and as you see, I live again. To drink is to live, to be bathed in water is to have a new birth."

"If what you tell me is true, it is wonderful. But I am too much in need of water myself to think much about it now. You say that you have drunk, and the way you say it implies at least that you're friendly toward me. Prove it, please. I haven't eaten or drunk for a long time."

The head that spoke smiled. "You have the most marvelous way of falling in with whatever I plan—there is an appropriateness about you, even to your clothing, that I find delightful. I was just about to suggest that we go where there is food and drink in plenty. Follow me."

At that time, I think I would have followed anyone who promised me water anywhere. Since then I have tried to convince myself that I went out of curiosity, or because I hoped to learn the secret of the great cataphracts; but when I recall those moments and search my mind as it was then, I find nothing other than despair and thirst. The waterfall above Casdoe's house wove its silver columns before my eyes, and I remembered the Vatic Fountain of the House Absolute, and the rush of water from the cliff top in Thrax when I opened the sluice gate to flood the Vincula.

The two-headed man walked before me as if he were confident I would follow him, and equally confident that I would not attack him. When we rounded a corner, I realized for the first time that I had not been, as I had thought, on one of the radiating streets that led to the circular building. It stood before us now. A door—though it was not the one through which little Severian and I had passed—was open as before, and we entered.

"Here," the head that spoke said. "Get in."

The thing toward which he gestured was like a boat, and padded everywhere within as the nenuphar boat in the Autarch's garden had been; yet it floated not on water but in air. When I touched the gunwale, the boat rocked and bobbed beneath my hand, though the motion was almost too small to be seen. I said, "This must be a flyer. I've never seen one so close before."

"If a flyer were a swallow, this would be—I don't know—a sparrow, perhaps. Or a mole, or the toy bird that children strike with paddles to make it fly back and forth between them. Courtesy, I fear, demands that you enter first. I assure you there is no danger."

Still, I hung back. There seemed something so mysterious about that vessel that for the moment I could not bring myself to set foot in it. I said, "I come from Nessus and from the eastern bank of Gyoll, and we were taught there that the place of honor in any craft is to be the last to enter and the first to leave."

"Precisely," the head that spoke replied, and before I realized what was happening, the two-headed man seized me about the waist and tossed me into the boat as I might have tossed the boy. It dipped and rolled under the impact of my body, and a moment later yawed violently as the two-headed man sprang in beside me. "You didn't think, I hope, that you were to take precedence over me?"

He whispered something and the vessel began to move. It glided forward slowly at first, but it was picking up speed.

"True courtesy," he continued, "earns the name. It is courtesy that is truthful. When the plebeian kneels to the monarch, he is offering his neck. He offers it because he knows his ruler can take it if he wishes. Common people like that say—or rather, they used to say, in older and better times—that I have no love of truth. But the truth is that it is precisely truth that I love, an open acknowledgment of fact."

All this time we were lying at full length, with hardly the width of a hand between us. The idiotic head the other had called Piaton goggled at me and moved its lips as he spoke, making a confused mumbling.

I tried to sit up. The two-headed man caught me with an arm of iron and pulled me down again, saying, "It's dangerous. These things were built to lie in. You wouldn't want to lose your head, would you? It's nearly as bad, believe me, as getting an extra one."

The boat nosed down and plunged into the dark. For a moment I thought we were going to die, but the sensation became one of exhilarating speed, the kind of feeling I had known as a boy when we used to slide on evergreen boughs among the mausoleums in winter. When I had become somewhat accustomed to it, I asked, "Were you born as you are? Or was Piaton actually thrust upon you in some way?" Already, I think, I had begun to realize that my life would depend on finding out as much as I could about this strange being.

The head that spoke laughed. "My name is Typhon. You might as well call me by it. Have you heard of me? Once I ruled this planet, and many more."

I was certain he lied, so I said, "Rumors of your might echo still . . . Typhon."

He laughed again. "You were on the point of calling me Imperator or something of the sort, weren't you? You shall yet. No, I was not born as I am, or born at all, as you meant it. Nor was Piaton grafted to me. I was grafted to him. What do you think of that?"

The boat moved so rapidly now that the air was whistling above our heads, but the descent seemed less steep than it had been. As I spoke, it became nearly level. "Did you wish it?"

"I commanded it."

"Then I think it very strange. Why should you desire to have such a thing done?"

"That I might have life, of course." It was too dark now for me to see either face, though Typhon's was less than a cubit from my own. "All life acts to preserve its life—that is what we call the Law of Existence. Our bodies, you see, die long before we do. In fact, it would be fair to say that we only die because they do. My physicians, of whom I naturally had the best of many worlds, told me it might be possible for me to take a new body, their first thought being to enclose my brain in the skull previously occupied by another. You see the flaw in that?"

Wondering if he were serious, I said, "No, I'm afraid I do not."

"The face—the face! The face would be lost, and it is the face that men are accustomed to obey!" His hand gripped my arm in the dark. "I told them it wouldn't do. Then one came who suggested that the entire head might be substituted. It would even be easier, he said, because the complex neural connections controlling speech and vision would be left intact. I promised him a palatinate if he should succeed."

"It would appear to me—" I began.

Typhon laughed once more. "That it would be better if the original head were removed first. Yes, I always thought so myself. But the technique of making the neural connections was difficult, and he found that the best way—all this was with experimental subjects I provided for him—was to transfer only the voluntary functions by surgery. When that was done, the involuntary ones transferred themselves, eventually. Then the original head could be removed. It would leave a scar, of course, but a shirt would cover it."

"But something went wrong?" I had already moved as far from him as I could in the narrow boat.

"Mostly it was a matter of time." The terrible vigor of his voice, which had been unrelenting, now seemed to wane. "Piaton was one of my slaves—not the largest, but the strongest of all. We tested them. It never occurred to me that someone with his strength might be strong, too, in holding to the action of the heart . . ."

"I see," I said, though in truth I saw nothing.

"It was a period of great confusion as well. My astronomers had told me that this sun's activity would decay slowly. Far too slowly, in fact, for the change to be noticeable in a human lifetime. They were wrong. The heat of the world declined by nearly two parts in a thousand over a few years, then stabilized. Crops failed, and there were famines and riots. I should have left then."

"Why didn't you?" I asked.

"I felt a firm hand was needed. There can only be one firm hand, whether it is the ruler's or someone else's . . .

"Then too, a wonder-worker had arisen, as such people do. He wasn't really a troublemaker, though some of my ministers said he was. I had withdrawn here until my treatment should be complete, and since diseases and deformities seemed to flee from him, I ordered him brought to me."

"The Conciliator," I said, and a moment later could have opened my own wrist for it.

"Yes, that was one of his names. Do you know where he is now?"

"He has been dead for many chiliads."

"And yet he remains, I think?"

That remark startled me so that I looked down at the sack suspended from my neck to see if azure light were not escaping from it.

At that moment, the vessel in which we rode lifted its prow and began to ascend. The moaning of the air about us became the roaring of a whirlwind.

XXVI

The Eyes of the World

PERHAPS THE BOAT was controlled by light—when light flashed about us, it stopped at once. In the lap of the mountain I had suffered from the cold, but that was nothing to what I felt now. No wind blew, but it was colder than the bitterest winter I could recall, and I grew dizzy with the effort of sitting up.

Typhon sprang out. "It's been a long time since I was here last. Well, it's good to be home again."

We were in an empty chamber hewn from solid rock, a place as big as a ballroom. Two circular windows at the far end admitted the light; Typhon hastened toward them. They were perhaps a hundred paces apart, and each was some ten cubits wide. I followed him until I noticed that his bare feet left distinct, dark prints. Snow had drifted through the windows and spilled upon the stone floor. I fell to my knees, scooped it up, and stuffed my mouth with it.

I have never tasted anything so delicious. The heat of my tongue seemed to melt it to nectar at once; I truly felt that I could remain where I was all my life, on my knees devouring the snow. Typhon turned back, and seeing me, laughed. "I had forgotten how thirsty you were. Go ahead. We have plenty of time. What I wanted to show you can wait."

Piaton's mouth moved too as it had before, and I thought I caught an expression of sympathy on the idiot face. That brought me to myself again, possibly only because I had already gulped several mouthfuls of the melting snow. When I had swallowed again, I remained where I was, scraping a new heap together, but I said, "You told me about Piaton. Why can't he speak?"

"He can't get his breath, poor fellow," Typhon said. Now I saw that he had an erection, which he nursed with one hand. "As I told you, I control all the voluntary functions—I will control the involuntary ones too, soon. So although poor Piaton can still move his tongue and shape his lips, he is like a musician who fingers the keys of a horn he cannot blow. When you've had enough of that snow, tell me, and I'll show you where you can get something to eat."

I filled my mouth again and swallowed. "This is enough. Yes, I am very hungry."

"Good," he said, and turning away from the windows went to the wall at one side of the chamber. When I neared it, I saw that it, at least, was not (as I had thought) plain stone. Instead, it seemed a kind of crystal, or thick, smoky glass; through it I could see loaves and many strange dishes, as still and perfect as food in a painting.

"You have a talisman of power," Typhon told me. "Now you must give it to me, so that we can open this cupboard."

"I'm afraid I don't understand what you mean. Do you want my sword?"

"I want the thing you wear at your neck," he said, and stretched out a hand for it.

I stepped back. "There is no power in it."

"Then you lose nothing. Give it to me." As Typhon spoke, Piaton's head moved almost imperceptibly from side to side.

"It is only a curio," I said. "Once I thought it had great power, but when I tried to revive a beautiful woman who was dying, it had no effect, and yesterday it could not restore the boy who traveled with me. How did you know of it?"

"I was watching you, of course. I climbed high enough to see you well. When my ring killed the child and you went to him, I saw the sacred fire. You don't have to actually put it in my hand if you don't want to—just do what I tell you."

"You could have warned us, then," I said.

"Why should I? At that time you were nothing to me. Do you want to eat or not?"

I took out the gem. After all, Dorcas and Jonas had seen it, and I had heard the Pelerines had displayed it in a monstrance on great occasions. It lay on my palm like a bit of blue glass, all fire gone.

Typhon leaned over it curiously. "Hardly impressive. Now kneel."

I knelt.

"Repeat after me: I swear by all this talisman represents that for the food I shall receive, I shall be the creature of him I know as Typhon, evermore—"

A snare was closing beside which Decuman's net was a primitive first attempt. This one was so subtle I scarcely knew it was there, and yet I sensed that every strand was of hard-drawn steel.

"—rendering to him all I have and all I shall be, what I own now and what I shall own in days to come, living or dying at his pleasure."

"I have broken oaths before," I said. "If I took it, I should break that one."

"Then take it," he said. "It is no more than a form we must follow. Take it, and I can release you as soon as you have finished eating."

I stood instead. "You said you loved truth. Now I see why—it is truth that binds men." I put the Claw away.

If I had not done so, it would have been lost forever a moment later. Typhon seized me, pinning my arms to my sides so I could not draw *Terminus Est*, and ran with me to one of the windows. I struggled, but it was as a puppy struggles in the hands of a strong man.

As we approached it, the great size of the window made it seem not a window at all; it was as though a part of the outer world had intruded itself into the chamber, and it was a part consisting not of the fields and trees at the mountain's base, which was what I had expected, but of mere extension, a fragment of the sky. The chamber's rock wall, less than a cubit thick, floated backward at the corner of my vision like the muddled line we see, swimming with open eyes, that is the demarcation between the water and the air.

Then I was outside. Typhon's hold had shifted to my ankles, but whether because of the thickness of my boots or merely because of my panic, for a moment I felt I was not held at all. My back was to the mass of the mountain. The Claw, in its soft bag, dangled below my head, held by my chin. I remember feeling a sudden, absurd fear that *Terminus Est* would slip from her sheath.

I pulled myself up with my belly muscles, as a gymnast does when he hangs from the bar by his feet. Typhon released one of my ankles to strike my mouth with his fist, so that I fell back again. I cried out, and tried to wipe my eyes clear of the blood trickling into them from my lips.

The temptation to draw my sword, raise myself again, and strike with it was almost too great to resist. Yet I knew that I could not do so without giving Typhon ample time to see what I intended and let me fall. Even if I succeeded, I would die.

"I urge you now . . ." Typhon's voice came above me, seeming distant in that golden immensity. ". . . to require of your talisman such help as it can provide you."

He paused, and every moment seemed Eternity itself.

"Can it aid you?"

I managed to call, "No."

"Do you understand where you are?"

"I saw. On the face. The mountain autarch."

"It is my face—did you see that? I was the autarch. It is I who come again. You are at my eyes, and it is the iris of my right eye that is to your back. Do you comprehend? You are a tear, a single black tear I weep. In an instant, I may let you fall away to stain my garment. Who can save you, Talisman-bearer?"

"You. Typhon."

"Only I?"

"Only Typhon."

He pulled me back up, and I clung to him as the boy had once clung to me, until we were well inside the great chamber that was the cranial cavity of the mountain.

"Now," he said, "we will make one more attempt. You must come with me to the eye again, and this time you must go willingly. Perhaps it will be easier for you if we go to the left eye instead of the right."

He took my arm. I suppose I could be said to have gone by my own will, since I walked; but I think I have never in my life walked with less heart. It was only the memory of my recent humiliation that kept me from refusing. We did not halt until we stood upon the very rim of the eye; then with a gesture, Typhon forced me to look out. Below us lay an ocean of undulating cloud, blue with shadow where it was not rose with sunlight.

"Autarch," I said, "how are we here, when the vessel in which we rode plunged down so long a tunnel?"

He shrugged my question aside. "Why should gravity serve Urth, when it can serve Typhon? Yet Urth is fair. Look! You see the robe of the world. Is it not beautiful?"

"Very beautiful," I agreed.

"It can be your robe. I have told you that I was autarch on many worlds. I shall be autarch again, and this time on many more. This world, the most ancient of all, I made my capital. That was an error, because I lingered too long when disaster came. By the time I would have escaped, escape was no longer open to me—those to whom I had given control of such ships as could reach the stars had fled in them, and I was besieged on this mountain. I shall not make that mistake again. My capital will be elsewhere, and I will give this world to you, to rule as my steward."

I said, "I have done nothing to deserve so exalted a position."

"Talisman-bearer, no one, not even you, can require me to justify my acts. Instead, view your empire."

Far below us, a wind was born as he spoke. The clouds seethed under its lash and gathered themselves like soldiers into serried ranks moving eastward. Beneath them I saw mountains, and the coastal plains, and beyond the plains the faint, blue line of the sea.

"Look!" Typhon pointed, and as he did so, a pinprick of light appeared in the mountains to the northeast. "Some great energy weapon has been used there," he said. "Perhaps by the ruler of this age, perhaps by his foes. Whichever it may be, its location is revealed now, and it will be destroyed. The armies of this age are weak. They will fly before our flails as chaff at the harvest."

"How can you know all this?" I asked. "You were as dead, until my son and I came upon you."

"Yes. But I have lived almost a day and have sent my thought into far places. There are powers in the seas now who would rule. They will become our slaves, and the hordes of the north are theirs."

"What of the people of Nessus?" I was chilled to the bone; my legs trembled under me.

"Nessus shall be your capital, if you wish it. From your throne in Nessus you will send me tribute of fair women and boys, of the ancient devices and books, and all the good things this world of Urth produces."

He pointed again. I saw the gardens of the House Absolute like a shawl of green and gold cast upon a lawn, and beyond it the Wall of Nessus, and the mighty city itself, the City Imperishable, spreading for so many hundreds of leagues that even the towers of the Citadel were lost in that endless expanse of roofs and winding streets.

"No mountain is so high," I said. "If this one were the greatest in all the world, and if it stood upon the crown of the second greatest, a man could never see as far as I do now."

Typhon took me by the shoulder. "This mountain is as lofty as I wish it to be. Have you forgotten whose face it bears?"

I could only stare at him.

"Fool," he said. "You see through my eyes. Now get out your talisman. I will have your oath upon it."

I drew forth the Claw—for the last time, as I thought—from the leathern bag Dorcas had sewn for it. As I did, there was some slight stirring far below me. The sight of the world from out of the window of the chamber was still grand beyond imagining, but it was only what a man might discern from a mighty peak: the blue dish of Urth. Through the clouds below I could glimpse the lap of the mountain, with many rectangular buildings, the circular building in the center, and the cataphracts. Slowly they were turning their faces away from the sun, upward, to look at us.

"They honor me," Typhon said. Piaton's mouth moved too, but not with his. This time I heeded it.

"You were at the other eye, previously," I told Typhon, "and they did not honor you then. They salute the Claw. Autarch, what of the New Sun, if at last he comes? Will you be his enemy too, as you were the enemy of the Conciliator?"

"Swear to me, and believe me, when he comes I shall be his master, and he my most abject slave."

I struck then.

There is a way of smashing the nose with the heel of one's hand so that the splintered bone is driven into the brain. One must be very quick, however, because without the need for thought a man will lift his hands to protect his face when he sees the blow. I was not so swift as Typhon, but it was his own face his hands were thrown up to guard. I struck at Piaton, and felt the small and terrible cracking that is the sigil of death. The heart that had not served him for so many chiliads ceased to beat.

After a moment, I pushed Typhon's body over the drop with my foot.

XXVII

On High Paths

THE FLOATING BOAT would not obey me, for I had not the word for it. (I have often thought that its word may have been among the things Piaton had tried to tell me, as he had told me to take his life; and I wish I had come to heed him sooner.) In the end, I was forced to climb from the right eye—the worst climb of my life. In this overlong account of my adventures, I have said often that I forget nothing; but I have forgotten much of that, because I was so exhausted that I moved as though in sleep. When I staggered at last into the silent, sealed town that stood among the feet of the cataracts, it must have been nearly night, and I lay down beside a wall that gave me shelter from the wind.

There is a terrible beauty in the mountains, even when they bring one near to death; indeed, I think it is most evident then, and that the hunters who enter the mountains well clothed and well fed and leave them well fed and well clothed seldom see them. There all the world can seem a natural basin of clear water, still and icy cold.

I descended far that day, and found high plains that stretched for leagues, plains filled with sweet grass and such flowers as are never seen at lower altitudes, flowers small and quick to bloom, perfect and pure as roses can never be.

These plains were bordered as often as not by cliffs. More

than once I thought I could not go north anymore and would have to retrace my steps; but I always found a way in the end, up or down, and so pressed on. I saw no soldiers riding or marching below me, and though that was in some sense a relief—for I had been afraid the archon's patrol might still be tracking me—it was also unsettling, because it showed I was no longer near the routes by which the army was supplied.

The memory of the alzabo returned to haunt me; I knew that there must be many more of its kind in the mountains. Then too, I could not feel certain it was truly dead. Who could say what recuperative powers such a creature might possess? Though I could forget it by daylight, forcing it, so to speak, away from my consciousness with worries about the presence or absence of soldiers, and the thousand lovely images of peak and cataract and swooping valley that assailed my eyes on every side, it returned by night, when, huddled in my blanket and cloak and burning with fever, I believed I heard the soft padding of its feet, the scraping of its claws.

If as is often said, the world is ordered to some plan (whether one formed prior to its creation or one derived during the billion aeons of its existence by the inexorable logic of order and growth makes no difference) then in all things there must be both the miniature representation of higher glories and the enhanced depiction of smaller matters. To hold my circling attention from the recollection of its horror, I tried sometimes to fix it on that facet of the nature of the alzabo that permits it to incorporate the memories and wills of human beings into its own. The parallel to smaller matters gave me little difficulty. The alzabo might be likened to certain insects, that cover their bodies with twigs and bits of grass, so that they will not be discovered by their enemies. Seen in one way, there is no deception—the twigs, the fragments of leaves are there and are real. Yet the insect is within. So with the alzabo. When Becan, speaking through the creature's mouth, told me he wished his wife and the boy with him, he believed himself to be describing his own desires, and so he was; yet those desires would serve to feed the alzabo, who was within, whose needs and consciousness hid behind Becan's voice.

Not surprisingly, the problem of correlating the alzabo with some higher truth was more difficult; but at last I decided that it might be likened to the absorption by the material world of the thoughts and acts of human beings who, though no longer living, have so imprinted it with activities that in the wider sense we may call works of art, whether buildings, songs, battles, or explorations, that for some time after their demise it may be said to carry forward their lives. In just this fashion the child Severa suggested to the alzabo that it might shift the table in Casdoe's house to reach the loft, though the child Severa was no more.

I had Thecla, then, to advise me, and though I had little hope when I called on her, and she little advice to give, yet she had been warned often against the dangers of the mountains, and she urged me up and onward, and down, always down to lower lands and warmth, at the first light.

I hungered no longer, for hunger is a thing that passes if one does not eat. Weakness came instead, bringing with it a pristine clarity of mind. Then, in the evening of the second day after I had climbed from the pupil of the right eye, I came upon a shepherd's bothy, a sort of beehive of stone, and found in it a cooking pot and a quantity of ground corn.

A mountain spring was only a dozen steps away, but there was no fuel. I spent the evening collecting the abandoned nests of birds from a rock face a half league distant, and that night I struck fire from the tang of *Terminus Est* and boiled the coarse meal (which took a long time to cook, because of the altitude) and ate it. It was, I think, as good a dinner as I have ever tasted, and it had an elusive yet unmistakable flavor of honey, as if the nectar of the plant had been retained in the dry grains as the salt of seas that only Urth herself recalls is held within the cores of certain stones.

I was determined to pay for what I had eaten, and went through my sabretache looking for something of at least equal value that I might leave for the shepherd. Thecla's brown book I would not give up; I soothed my conscience by reminding myself that it was unlikely the shepherd could read in any case. Nor would I surrender my broken whetstone—both because it recalled the green man, and because it would be only a tawdry gift here, where stones nearly as good lay among the young grass on every side. I had no money, having left every coin I had possessed with Dorcas. At last I settled on the scarlet cape she and I had found in the mud of the stone town, long before we reached Thrax. It was stained and too thin to provide much warmth, but I hoped that the tassels and bright color would please him who had fed me.

I have never fully understood how it came to be where we found it, or even whether the strange individual who had called us to him so that he might have that brief period of renewed life had left it behind intentionally or accidentally when the rain dissolved him again to that dust he had been for so long. The ancient sisterhood of priestesses beyond question possesses powers it seldom or never uses, and it is not absurd to suppose that such raising of the dead is among them. If that is so, he may have called them to him as he called us, and the cape may have been left behind by accident.

Yet even if that is so, some higher authority may have been served. It is in such fashion most sages explain the apparent paradox that though we freely choose to do this or the other, commit some crime or by altruism steal the sacred distinction of the Empyrian, still the Increate commands the entirety and is served equally (that is, totally) by those who would obey and those who would rebel.

Not only this. Some, whose arguments I have read in the brown book and several times discussed with Thecla, have pointed out that fluttering in the Presence there abide a multitude of beings that though appearing minute—indeed, infinitely small—by comparison are correspondingly vast in the eyes of men, to whom their master is so gigantic as to be invisible. (By this unlimited size he is rendered minute, so that we are in relation to him like those who walk upon a continent but see only forests, bogs, hills of sand, and so on, and though feeling, perhaps, some tiny stones in their shoes, never reflect that the land they have overlooked all their lives is there, walking with them.)

There are other sages too, who doubting the existence of that power these beings, who may be called the amschaspands, are said to serve, nonetheless assert the fact of their existence. Their assertions are based not on human testimony—of which there is much and to which I add my own, for I saw such a being in the mirror-paged book in the chambers of Father Inire—but rather on irrefutable theory, for they say that if the universe was not created (which they, for reasons not wholly philosophical, find it convenient to disbelieve), then it must have existed forever to this day. And if it has so existed, time itself extends behind the present day without end, and in such a limitless ocean of time, all things conceivable must of necessity have come to pass. Such beings as the amschaspands are conceivable, for they, and many others, have conceived of them. But if creatures so mighty once entered existence, how should they be destroyed? Therefore they are still extant.

Thus by the paradoxical nature of knowledge, it is seen that though the existence of the Ylem, the primordial source of all things, may be doubted, yet the existence of his servants may not be doubted.

And as such beings certainly exist, may it not be that they interfere (if it can be called interference) in our affairs by such accidents as that of the scarlet cape I left in the bothy? It does not require illimitable might to interfere with the internal economy of a nest of ants—a child can stir it with a stick. I know of no thought more terrible than this. (That of my own death, which is popularly supposed to be so awful as to be inconceivable, does not much trouble me; it is of my life that I find, perhaps because of the perfection of my memory, that I cannot think.)

Yet there is another explanation: It may be that all those who seek to serve the Theophany, and perhaps even all those who allege to serve him, though they appear to us to differ so widely and indeed to wage a species of war upon one another, are yet linked, like the marionettes of the boy and the man of wood that I once saw in a dream, and who, although they appeared to combat each other, were nevertheless under the control of an unseen individual who operated the strings of both. If this is the case, then the shaman we saw may have been the friend and ally of those priestesses who range so widely in their civilization across the same land where he, in primitive savagery, once sacrificed with liturgical rigidity of drum and crotal in the small temple of the stone town.

In the last light of the day after I slept in the shepherd's bothy, I came to the lake called Diuturna. It was that, I think, and not the sea, that I had seen on the horizon before my mind was enchained by Typhon's—if indeed my encounter with Typhon and Piaton was not a vision or a dream, from which I awoke of necessity at the spot where I began it. Yet Lake Diuturna is nearly a sea itself, for it is sufficiently vast to be incomprehensible to the mind; and it is the mind, after all, that creates the resonances summoned by that word—without the mind there is only a fraction of Urth covered with brackish water. Though this lake lies at an altitude substantially higher than that of the true sea, I spent the greater part of the afternoon descending to its shore.

The walk was a remarkable experience, and one I treasure even now, perhaps the most beautiful I can recall, though I now hold in my mind the experiences of so many men and women, for as I descended I strode through the year. When I left the bothy, I had above me, behind me, and to my right great fields of snow and ice, through which showed dark crags colder even than they, crags too wind-swept to retain the snow, which sifted down to melt on the tender meadow grass I trod, the grass of earliest spring. As I walked, the grass grew coarser, and of a more virile green. The sounds of insects, of which I am seldom conscious unless I have not heard them in some time, resumed, with a noise that reminded me of the tuning of the strings in the Blue Hall before the first cantilena began, a noise I sometimes used to listen to when I lay on my pallet near the open port of the apprentices' dormitory.

Bushes, which for all their appearance of wiry strength had not been able to endure the heights where the tender grasses lived, appeared now; but when I examined them with care, I found that they were not bushes at all, but plants I had known as towering trees, stunted here by the shortness of the summer and the savagery of the winter, and often split by that ill use into severe straggling trunks. In one of these dwarfed trees, I found a thrush upon a nest, the first bird I had seen in some time except for the soaring raptors of the peaks. A league farther on, and I heard the whistling of cavies, who had their holes among the rocky outcrops, and who thrust up brindled heads with sharp black eyes to warn their relatives of my coming.

A league farther on, and a rabbit went skipping ahead of me in dread of the whirling astara I did not possess. I was descending rapidly at this point, and I became aware of how much strength I had lost, not only to hunger and illness, but to the thinness of the air. It was as though I had been afflicted with a second sickness, of which I had been unaware until the return of trees and real shrubs brought its cure.

At this point, the lake was no longer a line of misted blue; I could see it as a great and almost featureless expanse of steely water, dotted by a few boats I was later to learn were built for the most part of reeds, with a perfect little village at the end of a bay only slightly to the right of my present line of travel.

Just as I had not known my weakness, until I saw the boats and the rounded curves of the thatched roofs of the village I had not known how solitary I had been since the boy died. It was more than mere loneliness, I think. I have never had much need for companionship, unless it was the companionship of someone I could call a friend. Certainly I have seldom wished the conversation of strangers or the sight of strange faces. I believe rather that when I was alone I felt I had in some fashion lost my individuality; to the thrush and the rabbit I had been not Severian, but Man. The many people who like to be utterly alone, and particularly to be utterly alone in a wilderness, do so, I believe, because they enjoy playing that part. But I wanted to be a particular person again, and so I sought the mirror of other persons, which would show me that I was not as they were.

XXVIII

The Hetman's Dinner

IT WAS NEARLY evening before I reached the first houses. The sun spread a path of red gold across the lake, a path that appeared to extend the village street to the margin of the world, so that a man might have walked down it and out into the larger universe. But the village itself, small and poor though I saw it to be when I reached it, was good enough for me, who had been walking so long in high and remote places.

There was no inn, and since none of the people who peered at me over the sills of their windows seemed at all eager to admit me, I asked for the hetman's house, pushed aside the fat woman who answered the door, and made myself comfortable. By the time the hetman arrived to see who had appointed himself his guest, I had my broken stone and my oil out and was leaning over the blade of *Terminus Est* as I warmed myself before his fire. He began by bowing, but he was so curious about me that he could not resist looking up as he bowed; so that I had difficulty in refraining from laughing at him, which would have been fatal to my plans.

"The optimate is welcome," the hetman said, blowing out his wrinkled cheeks. "Most welcome. My poor house—all our poor little settlement—is at his disposal."

"I am not an optimate," I told him. "I am the Grand Master Severian, of the Order of the Seekers for Truth and Penitence, commonly called the guild of torturers. You, Hetman, will address me as *Master.* I have had a difficult journey, and if you will provide me with a good dinner and a tolerable bed, it is not likely I will have to trouble you or your people for much else before morning."

"You will have my own bed," he said quickly. "And such food as we can provide."

"You must have fresh fish here, and waterfowl. I'll have both. Wild rice, too." I remembered that once, when Master Gurloes was discussing our guild's relations with the others in the Citadel, he had told me that one of the easiest ways to dominate a man is to demand something he cannot supply. "Honey, new bread, and butter should do it, except for the vegetable and the salad, and since I'm not particular about those, I will let you surprise me. Something good, and something I haven't had before, so that I'll have a tale to carry back to the House Absolute."

The hetman's eyes had been growing rounder and rounder as I spoke, and at the mention of the House Absolute, which was doubtless no more than the most distant of rumors in his village, they seemed about to pop out of his skull. He tried to murmur something about cattle (presumably that they could not live to supply butter at these altitudes) but I waved him out, then caught him by the scruff of the neck for not closing the door behind him.

When he was gone, I risked taking off my boots. It never pays to appear relaxed around prisoners (and he and his village were mine now, I thought, though they were not confined), but I felt sure no one would dare enter the room until some sort of meal was ready. I finished cleaning and oiling *Terminus Est,* and gave her enough strokes with the whetstone to restore her edges.

That done, I withdrew my other treasure (though it was not in fact mine) from its bag and examined it in the light of the hetman's pungent fire. Since I had left Thrax it no longer pressed against my chest like a finger of iron—indeed, while I tramped in the mountains I had sometimes forgotten for half a day that I wore it, and once or twice I had clasped it in panic, thinking, when I recalled it at last, that I had lost it. In this low-ceilinged, square room of the hetman's, where the rounded stones in the walls seemed to warm their bellies like burgesses, it did not flash as it had in the one-eyed boy's jacal;

but neither was it so lifeless as it had been when I showed it to Typhon. Now, rather, it seemed to glow, and I could almost have imagined that its energies played upon my face. The crescent-shaped mark in its heart had never appeared more distinct, and though it was dark, a star-point of light emanated from it.

I put away the gem at last, a little ashamed of having toyed with so entheal a thing as if it were a bauble. I took out the brown book and would have read from it if I could; but though my fever seemed to have left me, I was still very fatigued, and the flickering firelight made the cramped, old-fashioned letters dance on the page and soon defeated my eyes, so that the story I was reading appeared at some times to be no more than nonsense, and at others to deal with my own concerns—endless journeyings, the cruelty of crowds, streams running with blood. Once I thought I saw Agia's name, but when I looked a second time it had become the word *again:* "Agia she leaped, and twisting round the columns of the carapace . . ."

The page seemed luminous yet indecipherable, like the reflection of a looking glass seen in a quiet pool. I closed the book and put it back in my sabretache, not certain I had in fact seen any of the words I had thought an instant ago I had read. Agia must indeed have leaped from the thatched roof of Casdoe's house. Certainly she twisted, for she had twisted the execution of Agilus into murder. The great tortoise that in myth is said to support the world and is thus an embodiment of the galaxy, without whose swirling order we would be a lonely wanderer in space, is supposed to have revealed in ancient times the Universal Rule, since lost, by which one might always be sure of acting rightly. Its carapace represented the bowl of heaven, its plastron the plains of all the worlds. The columns of the carapace would then be the armies of the Theologoumenon, terrible and gleaming . . .

Yet I was not sure I had read any of this, and when I took out the book again and tried to find the page, I could not. Though I knew my confusion was only the result of fatigue, hunger, and the light, I felt the fear that has always come upon me on the many occasions of my life when some small incident has made me aware of an incipient insanity. As I stared into the fire, it seemed more possible than I would have liked to believe that someday, perhaps after a blow on the head, perhaps for no discernible cause, my imagination and my reason might reverse their places—just as two friends who come every day to the same seats in some public garden might at last decide for novelty's sake to exchange them. Then I would see as if in actuality all the phantoms of my mind, and only perceive in that tenuous way in which we behold our fears and ambitions the people and things of the real world. These thoughts, occurring at this point in my narrative, must seem prescient; I can only excuse them by saying that tormented as I am by my memories, I have meditated in the same way very often.

A faint knock at the door ended my morbid revery. I pulled on my boots and called, "Come in!"

A person who took care to remain out of my sight, though I am fairly sure it was the hetman, pushed back the door; and a young woman entered carrying a brass tray heaped with dishes. It was not until she set it down that I realized she was quite naked except for what I at first took to be rude jewelry, and not until she bowed, lifting her hands to her head in the northern fashion, that I saw that the dully shining bands about her wrists, which I had taken for bracelets, were in fact gyves of watered steel joined by a long chain.

"Your supper, Grand Master," she said, and backed toward the door until I could see the flesh of her rounded hips flattened where they pressed against it. With one hand she attempted to lift the latch; but though I heard its faint rattle, the door did not give. No doubt the person who had admitted her was holding it closed from the outside.

"It smells delicious," I told her. "Did you cook it yourself?"

"A few things. The fish, and the fried cakes."

I stood, and leaning *Terminus Est* against the rough masonry of the wall so as not to frighten her, went over to examine the meal: a young duck, quartered and grilled, the fish she had mentioned, the cakes (which later proved to be of cattail flour mixed with minced clams), potatoes baked in the embers of a fire, and a salad of mushrooms and greens.

"No bread," I said. "No butter and no honey. They will hear of this."

"We hoped, Grand Master, that the cakes would be acceptable."

"I realize it isn't your fault."

It had been a long time since I had lain with Cyriaca, and I had been trying not to look at this slave girl, but I did so now. Her long, black hair hung to her waist and her skin was nearly the color of the tray she held, yet she had a slender waist, a thing seldom found in autochthon women, and her face was piquant and even a trifle sharp. Agia, for all her fair skin and freckles, had broader cheeks by far.

"Thank you, Grand Master. He wants me to stay here to serve you while you eat. If you do not want that, you must tell him to open the door and let me out."

"I will tell him," I said, raising my voice, "to go away from the door and cease eavesdropping on my conversation. You are speaking of your owner, I suppose? Of the hetman of this place?"

"Yes, of Zambdas."

"And what is your own name?"

"Pia, Grand Master."

"And how old are you, Pia?"

She told me, and I smiled to find her precisely the same age as myself.

"Now you must serve me, Pia. I'm going to sit over here at the fire, where I was before you came in, and you can bring me the food. Have you served at table before?"

"Oh, yes, Grand Master. I serve at every meal."

"Then you should know what you're doing. What do you recommend first—the fish?"

She nodded.

"Then bring that over, and the wine, and some of your cakes. Have you eaten?"

She shook her head until the black hair danced. "Oh, no, but it would not be right for me to eat with you."

"Still I notice I can count a good many ribs."

"I would be beaten for it, Grand Master."

"Not while I am here, at least. But I won't force you. Just the same, I would like to assure myself that they haven't put anything in any of this that I wouldn't give my dog, if I still had him. The wine would be the most likely place, I think. It will be rough but sweet, if it's like most country wines." I poured the stone goblet half full and handed it to her. "You drink that, and if you don't fall to the floor in fits, I'll try a drop too."

She had some difficulty in getting it down, but she did so at last and, with watering eyes, handed the goblet back to me. I poured some wine for myself and sipped it, finding it every bit as bad as I expected.

I made her sit beside me then, and fed her one of the fish she herself had fried in oil. When she had finished it, I ate a couple too. They were so much superior to the wine as her own delicate face was to the old hetman's—caught that day, I felt sure, and in water much colder and cleaner than the muddy lower reaches of Gyoll, from which the fish I had been accustomed to in the Citadel had come.

"Do they always chain slaves here?" I asked her as we divided the cakes. "Or have you been particularly unruly, Pia?"

She said, "I am of the lake people," as though that answered my question, as no doubt it would have if I had been familiar with the local situation.

"I would think these are the lake people." I gestured to indicate the hetman's house and the village in general.

"Oh, no. These are the shore people. Our people live in the lake, on the islands. But sometimes the wind blows our islands here, and Zambdas is afraid I will see my home then and swim to it. The chain is heavy—you can see how long it is—and I can't take it off. And so the weight would drown me."

"Unless you found a piece of wood to bear the weight while you paddled with your feet."

She pretended not to have heard me. "Would you like some duck, Grand Master?"

"Yes, but not until you eat some of it first, and before you have any, I want you to tell me more about those islands. Did you say the wind blew them here? I confess I have never heard of islands that were blown by the wind."

Pia was looking longingly toward the duck, which must have been a delicacy in that part of the world. "I have heard that there are islands that do not move. That must be very inconvenient, I suppose, and I have never seen any. Our islands travel from one place to another, and sometimes we put sails in their trees to make them go faster. But they will not sail across the wind very well, because they do not have wise bottoms like the bottoms of boats, but foolish bottoms like the bottoms of tubs, and sometimes they turn over."

"I want to see your islands sometime, Pia," I told her. "I also want to get you back to them, since that seems to be where you want to go. I owe something to a man with a name much like yours, and so I'll try to do that before I leave this place. Meanwhile, you had better build up your strength with some of that duck."

She took a piece, and after she had swallowed a few mouthfuls began to peel off slivers for me that she fed me with her fingers. It was very good, still hot enough to steam and imbued with a delicate flavor suggestive of parsley, which perhaps came from some water plant on which these ducks fed; but it was also rich and somewhat greasy, and when I had eaten the better part of one thigh, I took a few bites of salad to clear my palate.

I think I ate some more of the duck after that, then a movement in the fire caught my eye. A fragment of almost-consumed wood glowing with heat had fallen from one of the logs into the ashes under the grate, but instead of lying there and becoming dim and eventually black, it seemed to straighten up, and in doing so became Roche, Roche with his fiery red hair turned to real flames, Roche holding a torch as he used to when we were boys and went to swim in the cistern beneath the Bell Keep.

It seemed so extraordinary to see him there, reduced to a glowing micromorph, that I turned to Pia to point him out to her. She appeared to have seen nothing; but Drotte, no taller than my thumb, was standing on her shoulder, half concealed in her flowing black hair. When I tried to tell her he was there, I heard myself speaking in a new tongue, hissing, grunting, and clicking. I felt no fear at any of this, only a detached wonder. I could tell that what I was saying was not human speech, and observe the horrified expression on Pia's face as though I were contemplating some ancient painting in old Rudisind's gallery in the Citadel; yet I could not turn my noises into words, or even halt them. Pia screamed.

The door flew open. It had been closed for so long that I had almost forgotten it could not be locked; but it was open now, and two figures stood there. When the door opened they were men, men whose faces had been replaced by smooth pelts of fur like the backs of two otters, but men still. An instant later they had become plants, tall stalks of viridian from which protruded the razor-sharp, oddly angled leaves of the avern. Spiders, black and soft and many-legged, had been hiding there. I tried to rise from my chair, and they leaped at me trailing webs of gossamer that shone in the firelight. I had only time to see and remember Pia's face, with its wide eyes and its delicate mouth frozen in a circle of horror before a peregrine with a beak of steel stooped to tear the Claw from my neck.

XXIX

The Hetman's Boat

AFTER THAT I was locked in the dark for what I later found had been the night and the greater part of the following morning. Yet though it was dark where I lay, it was not at first dark to me, for my hallucinations needed no candle. I can recall them still, as I can recall everything; but I will not bore you, my ultimate reader, with the entire catalog of phantoms, though it would be easy enough for me to describe them here. What is not easy is the task of expressing my feelings concerning them.

It would have been a great relief for me to believe that they were all in some way contained in the drug I had swallowed (which was, as I guessed then and learned later, when I could question those who treated the wounded of the Autarch's army, nothing more than the mushrooms that had been chopped into my salad) just as Thecla's thoughts and Thecla's personality, comforting at times and troubling at others, had been contained in the fragment of her flesh I had eaten at Vodalus's banquet. Yet I knew it could not be so, and that all the things I saw, some amusing, some horrible and terrifying, some merely grotesque, were the product of my own mind. Or of Thecla's, which was now a part of my own.

Or rather, as I first began to realize there in the dark as I watched a parade of women from the court—exultants immensely tall and imbued with the stiff grace of costly porcelains, their complexions powdered with the dust of pearls or diamonds and their eyes made large as Thecla's had been by the application of minute amounts of certain poisons in childhood—products of the mind that now existed in the combination of the minds that had been hers and mine.

Severian, the apprentice I had been, the young man who had swum beneath the Bell Keep, who had once nearly drowned in Gyoll, who had idled alone on summer days in the ruined necropolis, who had handed the Chatelaine Thecla, in the nadir of his despair, the stolen knife, was gone.

Not dead. Why had he thought that every life must end in death, and never in anything else? Not dead, but vanished as a single note vanishes, never to reappear, when it becomes an indistinguishable and inseparable part of some extemporized melody. That young Severian had hated death, and by the mercy of the Increate, whose mercy indeed (as is wisely said in many places) confounds and destroys us, he did not die.

The women turned long necks to look down at me. Their oval faces were perfect, symmetrical, expressionless yet lewd; and I understood quite suddenly that they were not—or at least no longer were—the courtiers of the House Absolute, but had become the courtesans of the House Azure.

For some while, as it seemed to me, the parade of those seductive and inhuman women continued, and at each beat of my heart (of which I was conscious at that time as I have seldom been before or since, so that it seemed as if a drum throbbed in my chest) they reversed their roles without changing the least detail of their appearance. Just as I have sometimes known in dreams that a certain figure was in fact someone whom it did not in the least resemble, so I knew at one instant that these women were the ornaments of the Autarchial presence, and at the next that they were to be sold for the night for a handful of orichalks.

During all this time, and all the much longer periods that preceded and followed it, I was acutely uncomfortable. The spiders' webs, which I came gradually to perceive were common fishing nets, had not been removed; but I had been bound with ropes as well, so that one arm was tightly pinioned by my side and the other bent until the fingers of my hand, which soon grew numb, almost touched my face. At the height of the action of the drug I had become incontinent, and now my trousers were soaked with urine, cold and stinking. As my hallucinations grew less violent and the intervals between them longer, the misery of my circumstances afflicted me more, and I became fearful of what would happen to me when I was eventually taken from the windowless storeroom into which I had been cast. I supposed that the hetman had learned from some estafette that I was not what I had pretended to be, and no doubt also that I was fleeing the archon's justice; for I assumed that he would not otherwise have dared to treat me as he had. Under these circumstances, I could only wonder whether he would dispose of me himself (doubtless by noyade, in such a place), deliver me to some petty ethnarch, or return me to Thrax. I resolved to take my own life should the opportunity be afforded me, but it seemed so improbable that I should be given the chance that I was ready to kill myself in my despair.

At last the door opened. The light, though it was only that of a dim room in that thick-walled house, seemed blinding. Two men dragged me forth as they might have pulled out a sack of meal. They were heavily bearded, and so I suppose it was they who had appeared, when they burst in upon Pia and me, to have the pelts of animals for faces. They set me upon my feet, but my legs would not hold, and they were forced to untie me and to remove the nets that had taken me when the net of Typhon had failed. When I could stand again, they gave me a cup of water and a strip of salt fish.

After a time the hetman came in. Although he stood as importantly as he was no doubt accustomed to stand when he directed the affairs of his village, he could not keep his voice from quavering. Why he should still be frightened of me I could not understand, but plainly he still was. Since I had nothing to lose and everything to gain by the attempt, I ordered him to release me.

"That I cannot do, Grand Master," he said. "I am acting under instructions."

"May I ask who has dared tell you to act in this fashion toward the representative of your Autarch?"

He cleared his throat. "Instructions from the castle. My messenger bird carried your sapphire there last night, and another bird came this morning, with a sign that means we are to bring you."

At first I supposed he meant Acies Castle, where one of the squadrons of dimarchi had its headquarters, but after a moment I realized that here, two score leagues at least from the fortifications of Thrax, it was most unlikely that he would be so specific. I said, "What castle is that? And do your instructions preclude my cleaning myself before I present myself there? And having my clothing washed?"

"I suppose that might be done," he said uncertainly; then to one of his men: "How stands the wind?"

The man addressed gave a half shrug that meant nothing to me, though it seemed to convey information to the hetman.

"All right," he told me. "We can't set you free, but we'll wash your clothes and give you something to eat, if you wish it." As he was leaving, he turned back with an expression that was almost apologetic. "The castle is near, Grand Master, the Autarch far. You understand. We have had great difficulties in the past, but now there is peace."

I would have argued with him, but he gave me no chance. The door shut behind him.

Pia, now dressed in a ragged smock, came in a short time later. I was forced to submit to the indignity of being stripped and washed by her; but I was able to take advantage of the process to whisper to her, and I asked her to see that my sword was sent wherever I was—for I was hoping to escape, if only by confessing to the master of the mysterious castle and offering to join forces with him. Just as she had ignored me when I had suggested that she might float the weight of her chain on a stick of firewood, she gave no indication of having heard me now; but a watch or so later, when, dressed once more, I was being paraded to a boat for the edification of the village, she came running after our little procession with *Terminus Est* cradled in her arms. The hetman had apparently wanted to retain such a fine weapon, and remonstrated with her; but I was able to warn him as I was being dragged on board that when I arrived at the castle I would inform whoever received me there of the existence of my sword, and in the end he surrendered.

The boat was a kind I had never seen before. In form it might have been a xebec, sharp fore and aft, wide amidships, with a long, overhanging stern and an even longer prow. Yet the shallow hull was built of bundles of buoyant reeds tied together in a sort of wickerwork. There could be no step for a conventional mast in such a frail hull, and in its place stood a triangular lash-up of poles. The narrow base of the triangle ran from gunwale to gunwale; its long isosceles sides supported a block used, just as the hetman and I clambered aboard, to hoist a slanting yard that trailed a widely striped linen sail. The hetman now held my sword, but just as the painter was cast off, Pia leaped into the boat with her chain jangling.

The hetman was furious and struck her; but it is not an easy matter to take in the sail of such a craft and turn it about with sweeps, and in the end, though he sent her weeping to the bow, he permitted her to stay. I ventured to ask him why she had wanted to come, though I thought I knew.

"My wife is hard on her when I am not at home," he told me. "Beats her and makes her scrub all day. It's good for the child, naturally, and it makes her happy to see me when I come back. But she would rather go with me, and I don't greatly blame her."

"Nor do I," I said, trying to turn my face away from his sour breath. "Besides, she will get to see the castle, which I suppose she has never seen before."

"She's seen the walls a hundred times. She comes of the landless lake people, and they are blown about by the wind and so see everything."

If they were blown by the wind, so were we. Air as pure as spirit filled the striped sail, made even that broad hull heel over, and sent us scudding across the water until the village vanished below the rim of the horizon—though the white peaks of the mountains were still visible, rising as it seemed from the lake itself.

XXX

Natrium

SO PRIMITIVELY ARMED were these lakeshore fisherfolk—indeed, far more primitively than the actual autochthonous primitives I had seen about Thrax—that it was some time before I understood that they were armed at all. There were more on board than were needed to steer and make sail, but I assumed at first that they had come merely as rowers, or to add to the prestige of their hetman when he brought me to his master at the castle. In their belts they carried knives of the straight, narrow-bladed kind fishermen everywhere use, and there was a sheaf of barb-headed fishing spears stowed forward, but I thought nothing of that. It was not until one of the islands I had been so eager to see came into view and I noticed one of the men fingering a club edged with animal teeth that I realized they had been brought as a guard, and there was in fact something to guard against.

The little island itself appeared unexceptional until one saw that it truly moved. It was low and very green, with a diminutive hut (built like our boat of reeds and thatched with the same material) at its highest point. A few willows grew upon it, and a long narrow boat, again built of reeds, was tied at the water's edge. When we were closer, I saw that the island was of reeds too, but of living ones. Their stems gave it its characteristic verdescence; their interlaced roots must have formed its raftlike base. Upon their massed, living tangle, soil had accumulated or been stored up by the inhabitants. The trees had sprouted there to trail their roots in the waters of the lake. A little patch of vegetables flourished.

Because the hetman and all the others on board except Pia scowled at it, I regarded this tiny land with favor; and seeing it as I saw it then, a spot of green against the cold and seemingly infinite blue of the face of Diuturna and the deeper, warmer, yet truly infinite blue of the sun-crowned, star-sprinkled sky, it was easy to love it. If I had looked upon this scene as I might have upon a picture, it would have seemed more heavily symbolic—the level line of the horizon dividing the canvas into equal halves, the dot of green with its green trees and brown hut—than those pictures critics are accustomed to deride for their symbolism. Yet who could have said what it meant? It is impossible, I think, that all the symbols we see in natural landscapes are there only because we see them. No one hesitates to brand as mad the solipsists who truly believe that the world exists only because they observe it and that buildings, mountains, and even ourselves (to whom they have spoken only a moment before) all vanish when they turn their heads. Is it not equally mad to believe that the meaning of the same objects vanishes in the same way? If Thecla had symbolized love of which I felt myself unworthy, as I know now that she did, then did her symbolic force disappear when I locked the door of her cell behind me? That would be like saying that the writing in this book, over which I have labored for so many watches, will vanish into a blur of vermilion when I close it for the last time and dispatch it to the eternal library maintained by old Ultan.

The great question, then, that I pondered as I watched the floating island with longing eyes and chafed at my bonds and cursed the hetman in my heart, is that of determining what these symbols mean in and of themselves. We are like children who look at print and see a serpent in the last letter but one, and a sword in the last.

What message was intended for me in the little homey hut and its green garden suspended between two infinities I do not know. But the meaning I read into it was that of freedom and home, and I felt then a greater desire for freedom, for the liberty to rove the upper and the lower worlds at will, carrying with me such comforts as would suffice me, than I had ever felt before—even when I was a prisoner in the antechamber of the House Absolute, even when I was client of the torturers in the Old Citadel.

Then, just at the time when I desired most to be free and we were as near the island as our course would take us, two men and a boy of fifteen or so came out of the hut. For a moment they stood before their door, looking at us as though they were taking the measure of boat and crew. There were five villagers on board in addition to the hetman, and it seemed clear the islanders could do nothing against us, but they put out in their slender craft, the men paddling after us while the boy rigged a crude sail of matting.

The hetman, who turned from time to time to look back at them, was seated beside me with *Terminus Est* across his lap. It seemed to me that at every moment he was about to set her aside and go astern to speak to the man at the tiller, or go forward to talk to the other four who lounged in the bow. My hands were tied in front of me, and it would have taken only an instant to draw the blade a thumb's width clear of her sheath and cut the cords, but the opportunity did not come.

A second island hove into view, and we were joined by another boat, this bearing two men. The odds were slightly worse now, and the hetman called one of his villagers to him and went a step or two astern, carrying my sword. They opened a metal canister that had been concealed under the steersman's platform there and took out a weapon of a type I had not seen before, a bow made by binding two slender bows, each of which carried its own string, to spacers that held them half a span apart. The strings were lashed together at their centers as well, so that the lashings made a sling for some missile.

While I was looking at this curious contrivance, Pia edged closer. "They're watching me," she whispered. "I can't untie you now. But perhaps . . ." She looked significantly toward the boats that followed ours.

"Will they attack?"

"Not unless there are more to join them. They have only fish spears and pachos." Seeing my look of incomprehension she added, "Sticks with teeth—one of these men has one too."

The villager the hetman had summoned was taking what appeared to be a wadded rag from the canister. He unwrapped it on the open lid and disclosed several silver-gray, oily-looking slugs of metal.

"Bullets of power," Pia said. She sounded frightened.

"Do you think more of your people will come?"

"If we pass more islands. If one or two follow a landboat, then all do, to share in what there is to be gotten from it. But we will be in sight of the shore again soon—" Under her ragged smock, her breasts heaved as the villager wiped his hand on his coat, picked up one of the silvery slugs, and fitted it into the sling of the double bow.

"It's only like a heavy stone—" I began. He drew the strings to his ear and let fly, sending the slug whizzing through the space between the slender bows. Pia had been so frightened that I half expected it to undergo some transformation as it flew, perhaps becoming one of those spiders I still half believed I had seen when, drugged, I had been caught in these fishermen's nets.

Nothing of the sort occurred. The slug flew—a shining streak—across the water and splashed into the lake a dozen paces or so before the bow of the nearer boat.

For the space of a breath, nothing more happened. Then there was a sharp detonation, a fireball, and a geyser of steam. Something dark, apparently the missile itself, still intact and flung up by the explosion it had caused, was thrown into the air only to fall again, this time between the two pursuing boats. A new explosion followed, only slightly less intense than the first, and one of the boats was nearly swamped. The other veered away. A third explosion came, and a fourth, but the slug, whatever other powers it might possess, seemed incapable of tracking the boats the way Hethor's notules had followed Jonas and me. Each blast carried it farther off, and after the fourth it appeared spent. The two pursuing boats fell back out of range, but I admired their courage in keeping up the chase at all.

"The bullets of power bring fire from water," Pia told me.

I nodded. "So I see." I was getting my legs set under me, finding secure footing among the bundles of reeds.

It is no great trick to swim even when your hands are bound behind you—Drotte, Roche, Eata and I used to practice swimming while gripping our own thumbs at the small of the back, and with my hands tied before me, I knew I could stay afloat for a long time if necessary; but I was worried about Pia, and told her to go as far forward as she could.

"But then I will not be able to untie you."

"You'll never be able to while they're watching us," I whispered. "Go forward. If this boat breaks up, hang onto a bunch of reeds. They'll still float. Don't argue."

The men in the bow did not stop her, and she halted only when she had reached the point at which a cable of woven reeds formed the vessel's stem. I took a deep breath and leaped overboard.

If I had wished to I could have dived with hardly a ripple, but I hugged my knees to my chest instead to make as great a splash as I could, and thanks to the weight of my boots I sank far deeper than I would have if I had been stripped for swimming. It was that point that had worried me; I had seen when the hetman's archer had fired his missile that there was a distinct pause before the explosion. I knew that as well as drenching both men, I must have wet every slug lying on the oiled rag—but I could not be certain they would go off before I came to the surface.

The water was cold and grew colder as I went down. Opening my eyes, I saw a marvelous cobalt color that grew darker as it swirled about me. I felt a panicky urge to kick off my boots; but that would have brought me up quickly, and I filled my mind instead with the wonder of the color and the thought of the indestructible corpses I had seen littering the refuse heaps about the mines of Saltus—corpses sinking forever in the blue gulf of time.

Slowly I revolved without effort until I could make out the brown hull of the hetman's boat suspended overhead. For a while that spot of brown and I seemed frozen in our positions; I lay beneath it as dead men lie below a carrion bird that, filling its wings with the wind, appears to hover only just below the fixed stars.

Then with bursting lungs I began to rise.

As if it had been a signal I heard the first explosion, a dull and distant boom. I swam upward as a frog does, hearing another explosion and another, each sounding sharper than the last.

When my head broke water, I saw that the stern of the hetman's boat had opened, the reed bundles spreading like broomstraws. A secondary explosion to my left deafened me for a moment and dashed my face with spray that stung like hail. The hetman's archer was floundering not far from me, but the hetman himself (still, I was delighted to see, gripping

Terminus Est), Pia, and the others were clinging to what remained of the bow, and thanks to the buoyancy of the reeds it yet floated, though the lower end was awash. I tore at the cords on my wrists with my teeth until two of the islanders helped me climb into their craft, and one of them cut me free.

XXXI

The People of the Lake

PIA AND I spent the night on one of the floating islands, where I, who had entered Thecla so often when she was unchained but a prisoner, now entered Pia when she was still chained but free. She lay upon my chest afterward and wept for joy—not so much the joy she had of me, I think, but the joy of her freedom, though her kinsmen the islanders, who have no metal but that they trade or loot from the people of the shore, had no smith to strike off her shackles.

I have heard it said by men who have known many women that at last they come to see resemblances in love between certain ones, and now for the first time I found this to be true in my own experience, for Pia with her hungry mouth and supple body recalled Dorcas. But it was false too in some degree; Dorcas and Pia were alike in love as the faces of sisters are sometimes alike, but I would never have confused one with the other.

I had been too exhausted when we reached the island to fully appreciate the wonder of it, and night had been nearly upon us. Even now, all I recall is dragging the little boat to shore and going into a hut where one of our rescuers kindled a tiny blaze of driftwood, and I oiled *Terminus Est*, which the islanders had taken from the captured hetman and returned to me. But when Urth turned her face to the sun again, it was a wondrous thing to stand with one hand on the willow's graceful trunk and feel the whole of the island rock beneath me!

Our hosts cooked fish for our breakfast; before we had finished them, a boat arrived bearing two more islanders with more fish and root vegetables of a kind I had never tasted before. We roasted these in the ashes and ate them hot. The flavor was more like a chestnut's than anything else I can think of. Three more boats came, then an island with four trees and bellying, square sails rigged in the branches of each, so that when I saw it from a distance I thought it a flotilla. The captain was an elderly man, the closest thing the islanders had to a chief. His name was Llibio. When Pia introduced me to him, he embraced me as fathers do their sons, something no one had ever done to me previously.

After we separated, all the others, Pia included, drew far enough away to permit us to speak privately if we kept our voices low—some men going into the hut, and the rest (there were now about ten in all) to the farther side of the island.

"I have heard that you are a great fighter, and a slayer of men," Llibio began.

I told him that I was indeed a slayer of men, but not great.

"That is so. Every man fights backward—to kill others. Yet his victory comes not in the killing of others but in the killing of certain parts of himself."

To show that I understood him, I said, "You must have killed all the worst parts of your own being. Your people love you."

"That is also not to be trusted." He paused, looking out over the water. "We are poor and few, and had the people listened to another in these years . . ." He shook his head.

"I have traveled far, and I have observed that poor people usually have more wit and more virtue than rich ones."

He smiled at that. "You are kind. But our people have so much wit and virtue now that they may die. We have never possessed great numbers, and many perished in the winter just past, when much water froze."

"I had not thought how difficult winter must be for your people, without wool or furs. But I can see, now that you have pointed it out to me, that it must be hard indeed."

The old man shook his head. "We grease ourselves, which does much, and the seals give us finer cloaks than the shore people have. But when the ice comes, our islands cannot move, and the shore people need no boats to reach them, and so can come against us with all their force. Each summer we fight them when they come to take our fish. But each winter they kill us, coming across the ice for slaves."

I thought then of the Claw, which the hetman had taken from me and sent to the castle, and I said, "The land people obey the master of the castle. Perhaps if you made peace with him, he would stop them from attacking you."

"Once, when I was a young man, these quarrels took two or three lives in a year. Then the builder of the castle came. Do you know the tale?"

I shook my head.

"He came from the south, whence, as I am told, you come as well. He had many things the shore people wanted, such as cloth, and silver, and many well-forged tools. Under his direction they built his castle. Those were the fathers and grandfathers of those who are the shore people now. They used the tools for him, and as he had promised, he permitted them to keep them when the work was done, and he gave them many other things. My mother's father went to them while they labored, and asked if they did not see that they were setting up a ruler over themselves, since the builder of the castle could do as he chose with them, then retire behind the strong walls they had built for him where no one could reach him. They laughed at my mother's father and said they were many, which was true, and the builder of the castle only one, which was also true."

I asked if he had ever seen the builder, and if so what he looked like.

"Once. He stood on a rock talking to shore people while I passed in my boat. I can tell you he was a little man, a man who would not, had you been there, have reached higher than your shoulder. Not such a man as inspires fear." Llibio paused again, his dim eyes seeing not the waters of his lake but times long past. "Still, fear came. The outer wall was complete, and the shore people returned to their hunting, their weirs and their herds. Then their greatest man came to us and said we had stolen beasts and children, and that they would destroy us if we did not return them."

Llibio stared into my face and gripped my hand with his own, which was as hard as wood. Seeing him then, I saw the vanished years as well. They must have seemed grim enough at the time, though the future they had spawned—the future in which I sat with him, my sword across my lap, hearing his story—was grimmer than he could have known at the time. Yet there was joy in those years for him; he had been a strong young man, and though he was not, perhaps, thinking of that, his eyes remembered.

"We told them we did not devour children and had no need of slaves to fish for us, nor any pasturage for beasts. Even then, they must have known it was not we, because they did not come in war against us. But when our islands neared the shore, we heard their women wailing through the night.

"In those times, each day after the full moon was a trading day, when those of us who wished came to the shore for salt and knives. When the next trading day came, we saw that the shore people knew where their children had gone, and their beasts, and whispered it among themselves.. Then we asked why they did not go to the castle and carry it by storm, for they were many. But they took our children instead, and men and women of all ages, and chained them outside their doors so that their own people might not be taken—or even marched them to the gates and bound them there."

I ventured to ask how long this had gone on.

"For many years—since I was a young man, as I told you. Sometimes the shore people fought. More often, they did not. Twice warriors came from the south, sent by the proud people of the tall houses of the southern shore. While they were here, the fighting stopped, but what was said in the castle I do not know. The builder, of whom I told you, was seen by no one once his castle was complete."

He waited for me to speak. I had the feeling, which I have often had when talking with old people, that the words he said and the words I heard were quite different, that there was in his speech a hoard of hints, clues, and implications as invisible to me as his breath, as though Time were a species of white spirit who stood between us and with his trailing sleeves wiped away before I had heard it the greater part of all that was said. At last I ventured, "Perhaps he is dead."

"An evil giant dwells there now, but no one has seen him."

I could hardly repress a smile. "Still, I would think his presence must do a great deal to prevent the shore people from attacking the place."

"Five years past, and they swarmed over it by night like the fingerlings that crowd a dead man. They burned the castle, and slew those they found there."

"Do you continue to make war on you by habit, then?"

Llibio shook his head. "After the melting of the ice this year, the people of the castle returned. Their hands were full of gifts—riches, and the strange weapons you turned against the shore people. There are others who come there too, but whether as servants or masters, we of the lake do not know."

"From the north or the south?"

"From the sky," he said, and pointed up to where the faint stars hung dimmed by the majesty of the sun; but I thought he meant only that the visitors had come in fliers, and inquired no further.

All day the lake dwellers arrived. Many were in such boats as had followed the hetman's; but others chose to sail their islands to join Llibio's, until we were in the midst of a floating continent. I was never asked directly to lead them against the castle. Yet as the day wore on, I came to realize that they wished it, and they to understand that I would so lead them. In books, I think, these things are conventionally done with fiery speeches; reality is sometimes otherwise. They admired my height and my sword, and Pia told them I was the representative of the Autarch, and that I had been sent to free them. Llibio said, "Though it is we who suffer most, the shore people were able to make the castle their own. They are stronger in war than we, but not all they burned has been rebuilt, and they had no leader from the south." I questioned him and others about the lands near the castle, and told them we should not attack until night made it difficult for sentries on the walls to see our approach. Though I did not say so, I also wanted to wait for darkness to make good shooting impossible; if the master of the castle had given the bullets of power to the hetman, it seemed probable that he had kept much more effective weapons for himself.

When we sailed, I was at the head of about one hundred warriors, though most of them had only spears pointed with the shoulder bones of seals, pachos, or knives. It would swell my self-esteem now to write that I had consented to lead this little army out of a feeling of responsibility and concern for their plight, but it would not be true. Neither did I go because I feared what might be done to me if I refused, though I suspected that unless I did so diplomatically, feigning to delay or to see some benefit to the islanders in not fighting, it might have gone hard with me.

The truth was that I felt a coercion stronger than theirs.

Llibio had worn a fish carved from a tooth about his neck; and when I had asked him what it was, he had said that it was Oannes, and covered it with his hand so that my eyes could not profane it, for he knew that I did not believe in Oannes, who must surely be the fish-god of these people.

I did not, yet I felt I knew everything about Oannes that mattered. I knew that he must live in the darkest deeps of the lake, but that he was seen leaping among the waves in storms. I knew he was the shepherd of the deep, who filled the nets of the islanders, and that murderers could not go on the water without fear, lest Oannes appear alongside, with his eyes as big as moons, and overturn the boat.

I did not believe in Oannes or fear him. But I knew, I thought, whence he came—I knew that there is an all-pervasive power in the universe of which every other is the shadow. I knew that in the last analysis my conception of that power was as laughable (and as serious) as Oannes. I knew that the Claw was his, and I felt it was only of the Claw that I knew that, only of the Claw among all the altars and vestments of the world. I had held it in my hand many times, I had lifted it above my head in the Vincula, I had touched the Autarch's uhlan with it, and the sick girl in the jacal in Thrax. I had possessed infinity, and I had wielded its power; I was no longer certain I could turn it over tamely to the Pelerines, if I ever found them, but I knew with certainty that I would not lose it tamely to anyone else.

Moreover, it seemed to me that I had somehow been chosen to hold—if only for a brief time—that power. It had been lost to the Pelerines through my irresponsibility in allowing Agia to goad our driver into a race; and so it had been my duty to care for it, and use it, and perhaps return it, and surely my duty to rescue it from the hands, monstrous hands by all accounts, into which it had now fallen through my carelessness.

I had not thought, when I began this record of my life, to reveal any of the secrets of our guild that were imparted to me by Master Palaemon and Master Gurloes just before I was elevated, at the feast of Holy Katharine, to the rank of journeyman. But I will tell one now, because what I did that night on Lake Diuturna cannot be understood without understanding it. And the secret is only that we torturers obey. In all the lofty order of the body politic, the pyramid of lives that is immensely taller than any material tower, taller than the Bell

Keep, taller than the Wall of Nessus, taller than Mount Ty-phon, the pyramid that stretches from the Autarch on the Phoenix Throne to the most humble clerk grubbing for the most dishonorable trader—a creature lower than the lowest beggar—we are the only sound stone. No one truly obeys un-less he will do the unthinkable in obedience; no one will do the unthinkable save we.

How could I refuse to the Increate what I had willingly given the Autarch when I struck off Katharine's head?

XXXII

To the Castle

THE REMAINING ISLANDS were separated now, and though the boats moved among them and sails were bent to every limb, I could not but feel that we were stationary under the streaming clouds, our motion only the last delusion of a drowning land.

Many of the floating islands I had seen earlier that day had been left behind as refuges for women and children. Half a dozen remained, and I stood upon the highest of Llibio's, the largest of the six. Besides the old man and me, it carried seven fighters. The other islands bore four or five apiece. In addition to the islands we had about thirty boats, each crewed by two or three.

I did not deceive myself into thinking that our hundred men, with their knives and fish spears, constituted a formidable force; a handful of Abdiesus's dimarchi would have scattered them like chaff. But they were my followers, and to lead men into battle is a feeling like no other.

Not a glimmer showed upon the waters of the lake, save for the green, reflected light that fell from the myriad leaves of the Forest of Lune, fifty thousand leagues away. Those waters made me think of steel, polished and oiled. The faint wind brought no white foam, though it moved them in long swells like hills of metal.

After a time a cloud obscured the moon, and I wondered briefly whether the lake people would lose their bearings in the dark. It might have been broad noon, however, from the way they handled their vessels, and though boats and islands were often close together, I never in all that voyage saw two that were in the slightest danger of fouling each other.

To be conveyed as I was, by starlight and in darkness, in the midst of my own archipelago, with no sound but the whisper of the wind and the dipping of paddles that rose and fell as regularly as the ticking of a clock, with no motion that could be felt beyond the gentle swelling of the waves, might have been calming and even soporific, for I was tired, though I had slept a little before we set out; but the chill of the night air and the thought of what we were going to do kept me awake.

Neither Llibio nor any of the other islanders had been able to give me more than the vaguest information about the interior of the castle we were to storm. There was a principal building and a wall. Whether or not the principal building was a true keep—that is, a fortified tower high enough to look down upon the wall—I had no idea. Nor did I know whether there were other buildings in addition to the principal one (a barbican, for example), or whether the wall was strengthened with towers or turrets, or how many defenders it might have. The castle had been built in the space of two or three years with native labor; so it could not be as formidable as, say, Acies Castle; but a place a quarter of its strength would be impregnable to us.

I was acutely conscious of how little fitted I was to lead such an expedition. I had never so much as seen a battle, much less taken part in one. My knowledge of military architecture came from my upbringing in the Citadel and some casual sightseeing among the fortifications of Thrax, and what I knew—or thought I knew—of tactics had been gleaned from equally casual reading. I remembered how I had played in the necropolis as a boy, fighting mock skirmishes with wooden swords, and the thought made me almost physically ill. Not because I feared much for my own life, but because I knew that an error of mine might result in the deaths of most of these innocent and ignorant men, who looked to me for leadership.

Briefly the moon shone again, crossed by the black silhouettes of a flight of storks. I could see the shoreline as a band of denser night on the horizon. A new mass of cloud cut off the light, and a drop of water struck my face. It made me feel suddenly cheerful without knowing why—no doubt the reason was that I unconsciously recalled the rain outside on the night when I stood off the alzabo. Perhaps I was thinking too of the icy waters that spewed from the mouth of the mine of the man-apes.

Yet leaving aside all these chance associations, the rain might be a blessing indeed. We had no bows, and if it wet our opponents' bowstrings, so much the better. Certainly it would be impossible to use the bullets of power the hetman's archer had fired. Besides, rain would favor an attack by stealth, and I had long ago decided that it was only by stealth that our attack could hope to succeed.

I was deep in plans when the cloud broke again, and I saw that we were on a course parallel to the shore, which rose in cliffs to our right. Ahead, a peninsula of rock higher still jutted into the lake, and I walked to the point of the island to ask the man stationed there if the castle was situated on it. He shook his head and said, "We will go about."

So we did. The clews of all the sails were loosed, and retied on new limbs. Leeboards weighted with stones were lowered into the water on one side of the island while three men strained at the tiller bar to bring the rudder around. I was struck by the thought that Llibio must have ordered our present landfall, wisely enough, to escape the notice of any lookouts who might keep watch over the waters of the lake. If that were the case, we would still be in danger of being seen when we no longer had the peninsula between the castle and our little fleet. It also occurred to me that since the builder of the castle had not chosen to put it on the high spur of rock we were skirting now, which looked very nearly invulnerable, it was perhaps because he had found a place yet more secure.

Then we rounded the point and sighted our destination no more than four chains down the coast—an outthrust of rock higher still and more abrupt, with a wall at its summit and a keep that seemed to have the impossible shape of an immense toadstool.

I could not believe my eyes. From the great, tapering central column, which I had no doubt was a round tower of native stone, spread a lens-shaped structure of metal ten times its diameter and apparently as solid as the tower itself.

All about our island, the men in the boats and on the other islands were whispering to one another and pointing. It seemed that this incredible sight was as novel to them as to me.

The misty light of the moon, the younger sister's kiss upon the face of her dying elder, shone on the upper surface of that huge disk. Beneath it, in its thick shadow, gleamed sparks of orange light. They moved, gliding up or down, though their movement was so slow that I had watched them for some time before I was conscious of it. Eventually, one rose until it appeared to be immediately under the disk and vanished, and just before we came to shore, two more appeared in the same spot.

A tiny beach lay in the shadow of the cliff. Llibio's island ran aground before we reached it, however; I had to jump into the water once more, this time holding *Terminus Est* above my head. Fortunately there was no surf, and though rain still threatened, it had not yet come. I helped some of the lake men drag their boats onto the shingle while others moored islands to boulders with sinew hawsers.

After my trip through the mountains, the narrow, treacherous path would have been easy if I had not had to climb it in the dark. As it was, I would rather have made the descent past the buried city to Casdoe's house, though that had been five times farther.

When we reached the top we were still some distance from the wall, which was screened from us by a grove of straggling firs. I gathered the islanders about me and asked—a rhetorical question—if they knew from where the sky ship above the castle had come. And when they assured me they did not, I explained that I did (and so I did, Dorcas having warned me of them, though I had never seen such a thing before), and that because of its presence here it would be better if I were to reconnoiter the situation before we proceeded with the assault.

No one spoke, but I could sense their feeling of helplessness. They had believed they had found a hero to lead them, and now they were going to lose him before the battle was joined.

"I am going inside if I can," I told them. "I will come back to you if that is possible, and I will leave such doors as I may open for you."

Llibio asked, "But suppose you cannot come back. How shall we know when the moment to draw our knives has come?"

"I will make some signal," I said, and strained my wits to think what signal I might make if I were pent in that black tower. "They must have fires on such a night as this. I'll show a brand at a window, and drop it if I can so that you'll see the streak of fire. If I make no signal and cannot return to you, you may assume they have taken me prisoner—attack when the first light touches the mountains."

A short time later I stood at the gate of the castle, banging a great iron knocker shaped (so far as I could determine with my fingers) like the head of a man against a plate of the same metal set in oak.

There was no response. After I had waited for the space of a score of breaths, I knocked again. I could hear the echoes waked inside, an empty reverberation like the throbbing of a heart, but there was no sound of voices. The hideous faces I had glimpsed in the Autarch's garden filled my mind and I waited in dread for the noise of a shot, though I knew that if the Hierodules chose to shoot me—and all energy weapons came ultimately from them—I would probably never hear it. The air was so still it seemed the atmosphere waited with me. Thunder rolled to the east.

At last there were footsteps, so quick and light I could have thought them the steps of a child. A vaguely familiar voice called, "Who's there? What do you want?"

And I answered, "Master Severian of the Order of the Seekers for Truth and Penitence—I come as the arm of the Autarch, whose justice is the bread of his subjects."

"Do you indeed!" exclaimed Dr. Talos, and threw open the gate.

For a moment I could only stare at him.

"Tell me, what does the Autarch want with us? The last time I saw you, you were on your way to the City of Crooked Knives. Did you ever get there?"

"The Autarch wanted to know why your vassals laid hold of one of his servants," I said. "That is to say, myself. This puts a slightly different light on the matter."

"It does! It does! From our point of view too, you understand. I didn't know you were the mysterious visitor at Murene. And I'm sure poor old Baldanders didn't either. Come in and we'll talk about it."

I stepped through the gateway in the wall, and the doctor pushed the heavy gate closed behind me and fitted an iron bar into place.

I said, "There really isn't much to talk about, but we might begin with a valuable gem that was taken from me by force, and as I have been informed, sent to you."

Even while I spoke, however, my attention was drawn from the words I pronounced to the vast bulk of the ship of the Hierodules, which was directly overhead now that I was past the wall. Staring up at it gave me the same feeling of dislocation I have sometimes had on looking down through the double curve of a magnifying glass; the convex underside of that ship had the look of something alien not only to the world of human beings, but to all the visible world.

"Oh, yes," Dr. Talos said. "Baldanders has your trinket, I believe. Or rather, he had it and has stuck it away somewhere. I'm sure he'll give it back to you."

From inside the round tower that appeared (though it could not possibly have done so) to support the ship, there came faintly a lonely and terrible sound that might have been the howling of a wolf. I had heard nothing like it since I had left our own Matachin Tower; but I knew what it was, and I said to Dr. Talos, "You have prisoners here."

He nodded. "Yes. I'm afraid I've been too busy to feed the poor creatures today, what with everything." He waved vaguely toward the ship overhead. "You don't object to meeting cacogens, I hope, Severian? If you want to go in and ask Baldanders for your jewel, I'm afraid you'll have to. He's in there talking to them."

I said I had no objection, though I am afraid I shuddered inwardly as I said it.

The doctor smiled, showing above his red beard the line of sharp, bright teeth I recalled so well. "That's wonderful. You were always a wonderfully unprejudiced person. If I may say so, I suppose your training has taught you to take every being as he comes."

XXXIII

Ossipago, Barbatus, and Famulimus

AS IS COMMON in such pele towers, there was no entrance at ground level. A straight stair, narrow, steep, and without railings, led to an equally narrow door some ten cubits above the pavement of the courtyard. This door stood open already, and I was delighted to see that Dr. Talos did not close it after us. We went through a short corridor that was, no doubt, no more than the thickness of the tower wall and emerged into a room that appeared (like all the rooms I saw within that tower) to occupy the whole of the area available at its level. It was filled with machines that seemed to be at least as ancient as those we had in the Matachin Tower at home, but whose uses were beyond my conjecture. At one side of this room another narrow stair ascended to the floor above, and at the opposite side a dark stairwell gave access to whatever place it was in which the howling prisoner was confined, for I heard his voice floating from its black mouth.

"He has gone mad," I said, and inclined my head toward the sound.

Dr. Talos nodded. "Most of them are. At least, most of those I've examined. I administer decoctions of hellebore, but I can't say they seem to do much good."

"We had clients like that in the third level of our oubliette, because we were forced to retain them by the legalities; they had been turned over to us, you see, and no one in authority would authorize their release."

The doctor was leading me toward the ascending stair. "I sympathize with your predicament."

"In time they died," I continued doggedly. "Either by the aftereffects of their excruciations or from other causes. No real purpose was served by confining them."

"I suppose not. Watch out for that gadget with the hook. It's trying to catch hold of your cloak."

"Then why do you keep him? You aren't a legal repository in the sense we were, surely."

"For parts, I suppose. That's what Baldanders has most of this rubbish for." With one foot on the first step, Dr. Talos turned to look back at me. "You remember to be on your good behavior now. They don't like to be called cacogens, you know. Address them as whatever it is they say their names are this time, and don't refer to slime. In fact, don't talk of anything unpleasant. Poor Baldanders has worked so hard to patch things up with them after he lost his head at the House Absolute. He'll be crushed if you spoil everything just before they leave."

I promised to be as diplomatic as I could.

Because the ship was poised above the tower, I had supposed that Baldanders and its commanders would be in the uppermost room. I was wrong. I heard the murmur of voices as we ascended to the next floor, then the deep tones of the giant, sounding, as they so often had when I was traveling with him, like the collapse of some ruinous wall far off.

This room held machines too. But these, though they might have been as old as those below, gave the impression of being in working order; and moreover, of standing in some logical though impenetrable relation to one another, like the devices in Typhon's hall. Baldanders and his guests were at the farther end of the chamber, where his head, three times the size of any ordinary man's, reared above the clutter of metal and crystal like that of a tyrannosaur over the topmost leaves of a forest. As I walked toward them, I saw what remained of a young woman who might have been a sister of Pia's lying beneath a shimmering bell jar. Her abdomen had been opened with a sharp blade and certain of her viscera removed and positioned around her body. It appeared to be in the early stages of decay, though her lips moved. Her eyes opened as I passed her, then closed again.

"Company!" Dr. Talos called. "You won't guess who."

The giant's head swung slowly around, but he regarded me, I thought, with as little comprehension as he had when Dr. Talos had awakened him that first morning in Nessus.

"Baldanders you know," the doctor continued to me, "but I must introduce you to our guests."

Three men, or what appeared to be men, rose graciously. One, if he had been truly a human being, would have been short and stout. The other two were a good head taller than I, as tall as exultants. The masks all three wore gave them the faces of refined men of middle age, thoughtful and poised; but I was aware that the eyes that looked out through the slits in the masks of the two taller figures were larger than human eyes, and that the shorter figure had no eyes at all, so that only darkness was visible there. All three were robed in white.

"Your Worships! Here's a great friend of ours, Master Severian of the torturers. Master Severian, let me present the honorable Hierodules Ossipago, Barbatus, and Famulimus. It's the labor of these noble personages to inculcate wisdom in the human race—here represented by Baldanders, and now, yourself."

The being Dr. Talos had introduced as Famulimus spoke. His voice might have been wholly human save that it was more resonant and more musical than any truly human voice I have ever heard, so that I felt I might have been listening to the speech of some stringed instrument called to life. "Welcome," it sang. "There is no greater joy for us, than greeting you, Severian. You bow to us in courtesy, but we to you will bend our knees." And he did briefly kneel, as did both the others.

Nothing he could possibly have said or done could have astounded me more, and I was too much taken by surprise to offer any reply.

The other tall cacogen, Barbatus, spoke as a courtier might to fill the silence of an otherwise embarrassing gap in the conversation. His voice was deeper than Famulimus's, and seemed to have something soldierly in it. "You are welcome here—very welcome, as my dear friend has said, and all of us have tried to indicate. But your own friends must remain outside as long as we are here. You know that, of course. I mention it only as a matter of form."

The third cacogen, in a tone so deep that one felt rather than heard it, muttered, "It doesn't matter," and as though he feared I might see the empty eye slits of his mask, turned and made a show of staring out the narrow window behind him.

"Perhaps it doesn't, then," Barbatus said. "Ossipago knows best, after all."

"You have friends here then?" Dr. Talos whispered. It was a peculiarity of his that he seldom spoke to a group as most people do, but either addressed a single individual in it almost as though he and the other were alone, or else orated as if to an assembly of thousands.

"Some of the islanders gave me an escort," I said, trying to put the best face I could on things. "You must know of them. They live on the floating masses of reeds in the lake."

"They are rising against you!" Dr. Talos told the giant. "I warned you this would happen." He rushed to the window through which the being called Ossipago seemed to look, shouldering him to one side, and stared out into the night. Then, turning toward the cacogen, he knelt, seized his hand, and kissed it. This hand was quite plainly a glove of some flexible material painted to resemble flesh, with something in it that was not a hand.

"You will help us, Worship, will you not? You have fantassins aboard your ship, surely. Once line the walls with horrors, and we will be safe for a century."

In his slow voice, Baldanders said, "Severian will be the victor. Else why did they kneel to him? Though he may die, and we may not. You know their ways, Doctor. The looting may disseminate knowledge."

Dr. Talos turned upon him furiously. "Did it before? I ask you!"

"Who can say, Doctor?"

"You know it did not. They are the same ignorant, superstitious brutes they have always been!" He whirled again. "Noble Hierodules, answer me. You must know, if anyone does."

Famulimus gestured, and I was never more aware of the truth behind his mask than I was at that moment, for no human arm could have made the motion his did, and it was a meaningless motion, conveying neither agreement nor disagreement, neither irritation nor consolation.

THE SWORD OF THE LICTOR

"I will not speak of all the things you know," he said. "That those you fear have learned to overcome you. It may be true that they are simple still; still, something carried home may make them wise."

He was addressing the doctor, but I could contain myself no longer and said, "May I ask what you're talking about, sieur?"

"I speak of you, of all of you, Severian. It cannot harm you now, that I should speak."

Barbatus interjected, "Only if you don't do it too freely."

"There is a mark they use upon some world, where sometimes our worn ship finds rest at last. It is a snake with heads at either end. One head is dead—the other gnaws at it."

Without turning from the window, Ossipago said, "That is this world, I think."

"No doubt Camoena could reveal its home. But then, it doesn't matter if you know it. You will understand me the more clearly. The living head stands for destruction. The head that does not live, for building. The former feeds upon the latter; and feeding, nourishes its food. A boy might think that if the first should die, the dead, constructive thing would triumph, making his twin now like himself. The truth is both would soon decay."

Barbatus said, "As so often, my good friend is less than clear. Are you following him?"

"I am not!" Dr. Talos announced angrily. He turned away as if in disgust and hurried down the stair.

"That does not matter," Barbatus told me, "since his master does."

He paused as though waiting for Baldanders to contradict him, then continued, still addressing me. "Our desire, you see, is to advance your race, not to indoctrinate it."

"Advance the shore people?" I asked.

All this time, the waters of the lake were murmuring their night-grief through the window. Ossipago's voice seemed to blend with it as he said, "All of you . . ."

"It is true then! What so many sages have suspected. We are being guided. You watch over us, and in the ages of our history, which must seem no more than days to you, you have raised us from savagery." In my enthusiasm, I drew out the brown book, still somewhat damp from the wetting I had given it earlier in the day, despite its wrappings of oiled silk. "Here, let me show you what this says: 'Man, who is not wise, is yet the object of wisdom. If wisdom finds him a fit object, is it wise in him to make light of his folly?' Something like that."

"You are mistaken," Barbatus told me. "Ages are aeons to us. My friend and I have dealt with your race for less than your own lifetime."

Baldanders said, "These things live only a score of years, like dogs." His tone told me more than is written here, for each word fell like a stone dropped down some deep cistern.

I said, "That cannot be."

"You are the work for which we live," Famulimus explained. "That man you call Baldanders lives to learn. We see that he hoards up past lore—hard facts like seeds to give him power. In time he'll die by hands that do not store, but die with some slight gain for all of you. Think of a tree that splits a rock. It gathers water, the sun's life-bringing heat . . . and all the stuff of life for its own use. In time it dies and rots to dress the earth, that its own roots have made from stone. Its shadow gone, fresh seeds spring up; in time a forest flourishes where it stood."

Dr. Talos emerged again from the stairwell, clapping slowly and derisively.

I asked, "You have left them these machines, then?" I was acutely conscious, as I spoke, of the eviscerated woman mumbling beneath her glass somewhere behind me, a thing that once would not have bothered the torturer Severian in the least.

Barbatus said, "No. Those he found, or constructed for himself. Famulimus said that he wished to learn, and that we saw to it that he did, not that we taught him. We teach no one anything, and only trade such devices as are too complex for your people to duplicate."

Dr. Talos said, "These monsters, these horrors, do nothing for us. You've seen them—you know what they are. When my poor patient ran wild through them in the theater of the House Absolute, they nearly killed him with their pistols."

The giant shifted in his great chair. "You need not feign sympathy, Doctor. It suits you badly. Playing the fool while they looked on . . ." His immense shoulders rose and fell. "I shouldn't have let it overcome me. They've agreed now to forget."

Barbatus said, "We could have killed your creator easily that night, as you know. We burned him only enough to turn aside his charges."

I recalled then what the giant had told me when we parted

in the forest beyond the Autarch's gardens—that he was the doctor's master. Now, before I had time to consider what I was doing, I seized the doctor's hand. Its skin seemed as warm and living as my own, though curiously dry. After a moment he jerked away.

"What are you?" I demanded, and when he did not answer, I turned to the beings who called themselves Famulimus and Barbatus. "Once, sieurs, I knew a man who was only partly human flesh . . ."

They looked toward the giant instead of replying, and though I knew their faces were only masks, I felt the force of their demand.

"A homunculus," Baldanders rumbled.

XXXIV

Masks

THE RAIN CAME as he spoke, a cold rain that struck the rude, gray stones of the castle with a million icy fists. I sat down, clamping *Terminus Est* between my knees to keep them from shaking.

"I had already concluded," I said with as much self-possession as I could summon, "that when the islanders told me of a small man who paid for the building of this place, they were speaking of the doctor. But they said that you, the giant, had come afterward."

"I was the small man. The doctor came afterward."

A cacogen showed a dripping, nightmare face at the window, then vanished. Possibly he had conveyed some message to Ossipago, though I heard nothing. Ossipago spoke without turning. "Growth has its disadvantages, though for your species it is the only method by which youth can be reinstated."

Dr. Talos sprang to his feet. "We will overcome them! He has put himself in my hands."

Baldanders said, "I was forced to. There was no one else. I created my own physician."

I was still attempting to regain my mental balance as I looked from one to the other; there was no change in the appearance or manner of either. "But he beats you," I said. "I have seen him."

"Once I overheard you while you confided in the smaller

woman. You destroyed another woman, whom you loved. Yet you were her slave."

Dr. Talos said, "I must get him up, you see. He must exercise, and it is a part of what I do for him. I'm told that the Autarch—whose health is the happiness of his subjects—has an isochronon in his sleeping chamber, a gift from another autarch from beyond the edge of the world. Perhaps it is the master of these gentlemen here. I don't know. Anyway, he fears a dagger at his throat and will let no one near him when he sleeps, so this device tells the watches of his night. When dawn comes, it rouses him. How then should he, the master of the Commonwealth, permit his sleep to be disturbed by a mere machine? Baldanders created me as his physician, as he told you. Severian, you've known me some time. Would you say I was much afflicted with the infamous vice of false modesty?"

I managed a smile as I shook my head.

"Then I must tell you that I am not responsible for my virtues, such as they are. Baldanders wisely made me all that he is not, so that I might counterweight his deficiencies. I am not fond of money, for example. That's an excellent thing for the patient, in a personal physician. And I am loyal to my friends, because he is the first of them."

"Still," I said, "I have always been astounded that he did not slay you." It was so cold in the room that I drew my cloak closer about me, though I felt sure that the present deceptive calm could not long endure.

The giant said, "You must know why I keep my temper in check. You have seen me lose it. To have them sitting there, watching me, as though I were a bear on a chain—"

Dr. Talos touched his hand; there was something womanly in the gesture. "It's his glands, Severian. The endocrine system and the thyroid. Everything must be managed so carefully, otherwise he would grow too fast. And then I must see that his weight doesn't break his bones, and a thousand other things."

"The brain," the giant rumbled. "The brain is the worst of all, and the best."

I said, "Did the Claw help you? If not, perhaps it will, in my hands. It has performed more for me in a short time than it did for the Pelerines in many years."

When Baldanders's face showed no sign of comprehension, Dr. Talos said, "He means the gem the fishermen sent. It is supposed to perform miraculous cures."

At that Ossipago turned to face us at last. "How interesting. You have it here? May we see it?"

The doctor looked anxiously from the cacogen's expressionless mask to Baldanders's face and back again as he said, "Please, Your Worships, it is nothing. A fragment of corundum."

In all the time since I had entered this level of the tower, none of the cacogens had shifted his place by more than a cubit; now Ossipago crossed to my chair with short, waddling steps. I must have recoiled from him, for he said, "You need not fear me, though we do your kind much hurt. I want to hear about this Claw, which the homunculus tells us is only a mineral specimen."

When I heard him say that, I was afraid that he and his companions would take the Claw from Baldanders and carry it to their own home beyond the void, but I reasoned that they could not do so unless they forced him to produce it, and that if they did that, it might be possible for me to gain possession of it, which I might fail to do otherwise. So I told Ossipago all the things the Claw had accomplished while it had been in my keeping—about the uhlan on the highway, and the man-apes, and all the other instances of its power that I have already recorded here. As I spoke, the giant's face grew harder, and the doctor's, I thought, more anxious.

When I had finished, Ossipago said, "And now we must see the wonder itself. Bring it out, please," and Baldanders rose and stalked across the wide room, making all his machines appear mere toys by his size, and at last pulled out the drawer of a little, white-topped table and took out the gem. It was more dull in his hand than I had ever seen it; it might have been a bit of blue glass.

The cacogen took it from him and held it up in his painted glove, though he did not turn up his face to look at it as a man would. There it seemed to catch the light from the yellow lamps that sprouted downward from above, and in that light it flashed a clear azure. "Very beautiful," he said. "And most interesting, though it cannot have performed the feats ascribed to it."

"Obviously," Famulimus sang, and made another of those gestures that so recalled to me the statues in the gardens of the Autarch.

"It is mine," I told them. "The shore people took it from me by force. May I have it back?"

"If it is yours," Barbatus said, "where did you get it?"

I began the task of describing my meeting with Agia and the destruction of the altar of the Pelerines, but he cut me short.

"All this is speculation. You did not see this jewel upon the altar, nor did you feel the woman's hand when she gave it to you, if in fact she did. *Where did you get it?*"

"I found it in a compartment of my sabretache." It seemed that there was nothing else to say.

Barbatus turned away as though disappointed. "And you . . ." He looked toward Baldanders. "Ossipago has the jewel now, and he got it from you. Where did you get it?"

Baldanders rumbled, "You saw me. From the drawer of that table."

The cacogen nodded by moving his mask with his hands. "You see then, Severian, his claim has become as good as yours."

"But the gem is mine and not his."

"It is not our task to judge between you; you must settle that when we are gone. But out of curiosity, which torments even such strange creatures as you believe us to be—Baldanders, will you keep it?"

The giant shook his head. "I would not have such a monument to superstition in my laboratory."

"Then there should be little difficulty in effecting a settlement," Barbatus declared. "Severian, would you like to watch our craft rise? Baldanders always comes to see us off, and though he is not the type to rhapsodize over views artificial or natural, I should think myself that it must be worth seeing." He turned away, adjusting his white robes.

"Worshipful Hierodules," I said, "I would very much like to, but I want to ask you something before you go. When I arrived, you said you had no greater joy than seeing me, and you knelt. Did you mean what you said, or anything like it? Were you confusing me with someone else?"

Baldanders and Dr. Talos had risen to their feet when the cacogen first mentioned his departure. Now, though Famulimus remained to listen to my questions, the others had already begun to move away; Barbatus was mounting the stair that led to the level above, with Ossipago, still carrying the Claw, not far behind him.

I began to walk too, because I feared to be separated from it, and Famulimus walked with me. "Though you did not now pass our test, I meant no less than what I said to you." His voice was like the music of some wonderful bird, bridging the abyss from a wood unattainable. "How often we have taken counsel, Liege. How often we have done each other's will. You know the water women, I believe. Are Ossipago, brave Barbatus, I, to be so much less sapient than they?"

I drew a deep breath. "I don't know what you mean. But somehow I feel that though you and your kind are hideous, you are good. And that the undines are not, though they are so lovely, as well as so monstrous, that I can scarcely look at them."

"Is all the world a war of good and bad? Have you not thought it might be something more?"

I had not, and could only stare.

"And you will kindly tolerate my looks. Without offense may I remove this mask? We both know it for one and it is hot. Baldanders is ahead and will not see."

"If you wish, Worship," I said. "But won't you tell—"

With a quick flick of one hand, as though with relief, Famulimus stripped away the disguise. The face revealed was no face, only eyes in a sheet of putrescence. Then the hand moved again as before, and that too fell away. Beneath it was the strange, calm beauty I had seen carved in the faces of the moving statues in the gardens of the House Absolute, but differing from that as the face of a living woman differs from her own life mask.

"Did you not ever think, Severian," she said, "that he who wore a mask might wear another? But I who wore the two do not wear three. No more untruths divide us now, I swear. Touch, Liege—your fingers on my face."

I was afraid, but she took my hand and lifted it to her cheek. It felt cool and yet living, the very opposite of the dry heat of the doctor's skin.

"All of the monstrous masks you've seen us wear are but your fellow citizens of Urth. An insect, lamprey, now a dying leper. All are your brothers, though you may recoil."

We were already close to the uppermost level of the tower, treading charred wood at times—the ruin left by the conflagration that had driven forth Baldanders and his physician. When I took my hand away, Famulimus put on her mask again. "Why do you do this?" I asked.

"So that your folk will hate and fear us all. How long, Severian, if we did not, would common men abide a reign not ours? We would not rob your race of your own rule; by sheltering your kind from us, does not your Autarch keep the Phoenix Throne?"

I felt as I sometimes had in the mountains on waking from a dream, when I sat up wondering, looked about and saw the green moon pinned to the sky with a pine, and the frowning, solemn faces of the mountains beneath their broken diadems instead of the dreamed-of walls of Master Palaemon's study, or our refectory, or the corridor of cells where I sat at the guard table outside Thecla's door. I managed to say, "Then why did you show me?"

And she answered, "Though you see us, we will not see you more. Our friendship here begins and ends, I fear. Call it a gift of welcome from departing friends."

Then the doctor, ahead of us, threw open a door, and the drumming of the rain became a roaring, and I felt the cold, deathlike air of the tower invaded by icy but living air from outside. Baldanders had to stoop and turn his shoulders to pass the doorway, and I was struck by the realization that in time he would be unable to do so, whatever care he received from Dr. Talos—the door would have to be widened, and the stairs too, perhaps, for if he fell he would surely perish. Then I understood what had puzzled me before: the reason for the huge rooms and high ceilings of this, his tower. And I wondered what the vaults in the rock were like, where he confined his starving prisoners.

XXXV

The Signal

THE SHIP, WHICH from below had appeared to rest upon the structure of the tower itself, did not. Rather it seemed to float half a chain or more above us—too high to provide much shelter from the lashing rain that made the smooth curve of its hull gleam like black nacre. As I stared up at it, I could not help but speculate on the sails such a vessel might spread to catch the winds that blow between the worlds; and then, just as I was wondering if the crew did not ever peer down to see us, the mermen, the strange, uncouth beings who for a time walked the bottom below their hull, one of them indeed came down, head foremost like a squirrel, wreathed in orange light and clinging to the hull with hands and feet, though it was wet as any stone in a river and polished like the blade of *Terminus Est*. He wore such a mask as I have often described, but I now knew it to be one. When he saw Ossipago, Barbatus, and Famulimus below, he descended no farther, and in a moment a slender line, glowing orange too so that it seemed a thread of light, was cast down from somewhere above.

"Now we must go," Ossipago told Baldanders, and he handed him the Claw. "Think well on all the things we have not told you, and remember what you have not been shown."

"I will," Baldanders said, his voice as grim as I was ever to hear it.

Then Ossipago caught the line and slid up it until it bent

around the curve of the hull and he disappeared from sight. But it somehow seemed that he did not in fact slide up, but down, as if that ship were a world itself and drew everything belonging to it to itself with a blind hunger, as Urth does; or perhaps it was only that he was become lighter than our air, like a sailor who dives from his ship into the sea, and rose as I had risen after I leaped from the hetman's boat.

However that may be, Barbatus and Famulimus followed him. Famulimus waved just as the swell of the hull blocked her from view; no doubt the doctor and Baldanders thought she bade them farewell; but I knew she had waved to me. A sheet of rain struck my face, blinding my eyes despite my hood.

Slowly at first, then faster and faster, the ship lifted and receded, vanishing not upwards or to the north or the south or the east or west, but dwindling into a direction to which I could no longer point when it was gone.

Baldanders turned to me. "You heard them."

I did not understand, and said, "I spoke with them, yes. Dr. Talos invited me to when he opened the door in the wall for me."

"They told me nothing. They have shown me nothing."

"To have seen their ship," I said, "and to have spoken to them—surely those things are not nothing."

"They are driving me forward. Always forward. They drive me as an ox to slaughter."

He went to the battlement and stared out over the vast expanse of the lake, whose rain-churned waters made it seem a sea of milk. The merlons were several spans higher than my head, but he put his hands on them as upon a railing, and I saw the blue gleam of the Claw in one closed fist. Dr. Talos pulled at my cloak, murmuring that it would be better if we were to go inside out of the storm, but I would not leave.

"It began long before you were born. At first they helped me, though it was only by suggesting thoughts, asking questions. Now they only hint. Now they only let slip enough to tell me a certain thing may be done. Tonight there was not even that."

Wanting to urge that he no longer take the islanders for his experiments, but without knowing how to do so, I said that I had seen his explosive bullets, which were surely very wonderful, a very great achievement.

"Natrium," he said, and turned to face me, his huge head

lifted to the dark sky. "You know nothing. Natrium is a mere elemental substance spawned by the sea in endless profusion. Do you think I'd have given it to the fishermen if it were more than a toy? No, I am my own great work. And I am my only great work!"

Dr. Talos whispered, "Look about you—don't you recognize this? It is just as he says!"

"What do you mean?" I whispered in return.

"The castle? The monster? The man of learning? I only just thought of it. Surely you know that just as the momentous events of the past cast their shadows down the ages, so now, when the sun is drawing toward the dark, our own shadows race into the past to trouble mankind's dreams."

"You're mad," I said. "Or joking."

"Mad?" Baldanders rumbled. "*You* are mad. You with your fantasies of theurgy. How they must be laughing at us. They think all of us barbarians . . . I, who have labored three lifetimes."

He extended his arm and opened his hand. The Claw blazed for him now. I reached for it, and with a sudden motion he threw it. How it flashed in the rain-swept dark! It was as if bright Skuld herself had fallen from the night sky.

I heard the yell, then, of the lake people who waited outside the wall. I had given them no signal; yet the signal had been given by the only act, save perhaps for an attack on my person, that could have induced me to give it. *Terminus Est* left her sheath while the wind still carried their battle cry. I lifted her to strike, but before I could close with the giant, Dr. Talos sprang between us. I thought the weapon he raised to parry was only his cane; if my heart had not been torn by the loss of the Claw, I would have laughed as I hewed it. My blade rang on steel, and though it drove his own back upon himself he was able to contain the blow. Baldanders rushed past me before I could recover and dashed me against the parapet.

I could not dodge the doctor's thrust, but he was deceived, I think, by my fuligin cloak, and though his point grazed my ribs, it rattled on stone. I clubbed him with the hilt and sent him reeling.

Baldanders was nowhere to be seen. After a moment I realized that his headlong charge must have been for the door behind me, and the blow he had given me no more than an afterthought, as a man intent on other things may snuff a candle before he leaves the room.

The doctor sprawled on the stone pavement that was the roof of the tower—stones that were, perhaps, merely gray in sunlight, but now appeared a rain-drowned black. His red hair and beard were visible still, permitting me to see that he lay belly down, his head twisted to one side. It had not seemed to me that I had struck him so hard, though it may be I am stronger than I know, as others have sometimes said. Still I felt that beneath all his cocksure strutting Dr. Talos had been weaker than any of us except Baldanders would have guessed. I could have slain him easily then, swinging *Terminus Est* so the corner of her blade would bury itself in his skull.

Instead I picked up his weapon, the faint line of silver that had fallen from his hand. It was a single-edged blade about as wide as my forefinger, very sharp—as befitted a surgeon's sword. After a moment I realized that the grip was only the handle of his walking stick, which I had seen so often; it was a sword cane, like the sword Vodalus had drawn in our necropolis once, and I smiled there in the rain to think of the doctor carrying his sword thus for so many leagues, unknown to me, who had labored along with my own slung over my back. The tip had shattered on the stones when he thrust at me; I flung the broken blade over the parapet, as Baldanders had flung the Claw, and went down into his tower to kill him.

When we had climbed the stair, I had been too deep in conversation with Famulimus to pay much heed to the rooms through which we passed. The uppermost I recalled only as a place where it seemed that everything was draped in scarlet cloth. Now I saw red globes, lamps that burned without a flame like the silver flowers that sprouted from the ceiling of the wide room where I had met the three beings I could no longer call cacogens. These globes stood on ivory pedestals that seemed as light and slender as the bones of birds, rising from a floor that was no floor but only a sea of fabrics, all red, but of varying shades and textures. Over this room stretched a canopy supported by atlantes. It was scarlet, but sewn with a thousand plates of silver, so well polished that they were mirrors nearly as perfect as the armor of the Autarch's praetorians.

I had nearly descended the height of the stair before I understood that what I saw was no more than the giant's bedchamber, the bed itself, five times the expanse of a normal one, being sunk level with the floor, and its cerise and carmine coverings scattered about upon the crimson carpet. Just then, I saw a face among these twisted bedclothes. I lifted my sword and the face vanished, but I left the stair to drag away one of the downy cloths. The catamite beneath (if catamite he was) rose and faced me with the boldness small children sometimes show. Indeed he was a small child, though he stood nearly as tall as I, a naked boy so fat his distended paunch obscured his tiny generative organs. His arms were like pink pillows bound with cords of gold, and his ears had been pierced for golden hoops strung with tiny bells. His hair was golden too, and curled; beneath it he looked at me with the wide, blue eyes of an infant.

Large though he was, I have never been able to believe that Baldanders practiced pederasty as that term is usually understood, though it may well be that he had hoped to do so when the boy grew larger still. Certainly it must have been that just as he held his own growth in check, permitting only as much as needed to save his mountainous body from the ravages of the years, so he had accelerated the growth of this poor boy in so far as was possible to his anthroposophic knowledge. I say that because it seemed certain that he had not had him under his control until some time after he and Dr. Talos had parted from Dorcas and me.

(I left this boy where I had found him, and to this day I have no notion of what may have become of him. It is likely enough that he perished; but it is possible also that the lake men may have preserved and nourished him, or that the hetman and his people finding him at a somewhat later time, did so.)

I had no sooner descended to the floor below than what I saw there wiped all thought of the boy from my mind. This room was as wreathed in mist (which I am certain had not been present when I had passed through before) as the other had been in red cloth; it was a living vapor that seethed as I might have imagined the logos to writhe as it left the mouth of the Pancreator. While I watched it, a man of fog, white as a grave worm, rose before me brandishing a barbed spear. Before I realized he was a mere phantom, the blade of my sword went through his wrist as it might have penetrated a column of smoke. At once he began to shrink, the fog seeming to fall in upon itself, until he stood hardly higher than my waist.

I went forward, down more steps, until I stood in the cold, roiling whiteness. Then there came bounding across its surface a hideous creature formed, like the man, of the fog itself. In dwarfs I have seen, the head and torso are of normal size or larger, but the limbs, however muscled, remain childlike; this was the reverse of such a dwarf, with arms and legs larger than my own issuing from a twisted, stunted body.

The anti-dwarf brandished an estoc, and opening its mouth in a soundless cry, it thrust its weapon into the man's neck, utterly heedless of his spear, which was plunged into its own chest.

I heard a laugh then, and though I had seldom heard him merry, I knew whose laugh it was.

"Baldanders!" I called.

His head rose from the mist, just as I have seen the mountaintops lifted above it at dawn.

XXXVI

The Fight in the Bailey

"HERE IS A real enemy," I said. "With a real weapon." I walked down into the mist, groping ahead of me with my sword blade.

"You see in my cloud chamber real enemies too," Baldanders rumbled, his voice quite calm. "Save that they are outside, in the bailey. The first was one of your friends, the second one of my foes."

As he spoke, the mist dispersed, and I saw him near the center of the room, sitting in a massive chair. When I turned toward him, he rose from it and seizing it by the back sent it hurtling toward me as easily as he might have thrown a basket. It missed me by no more than a span.

"Now you will attempt to kill me," he said. "And all for a foolish charm. I ought to have killed you, that night when you slept in my bed."

I could have said the same thing, but I did not bother to reply. It was clear that by feigning helplessness he was hoping to lure me into a careless attack, and though he appeared to be without a weapon, he was still twice my height and, as I had reason to believe, of four times or more my strength. Then too I was conscious, as I drew nearer him, that we were reenacting here the performance of the marionettes I had seen in a dream on the night of which he had reminded me, and in that dream, the wooden giant had been armed with a bludgeon. He retreated from me step by step as I advanced; yet he seemed always ready to come to grips.

Quite suddenly, when we were perhaps three quarters across the room from the stair, he turned and ran. It was astonishing, like seeing a tree run.

It was also very quick. Ungainly though he was, he covered two paces with every step, and he reached the wall—where there was just such a slit of window as Ossipago had stared from—long before me.

For an instant I could not think what he meant to do. The window was far too narrow for him to climb through. He thrust both his great hands into it, and I heard the grinding of stone upon stone.

Just in time I guessed, and managed a few steps back. A moment later he held a block of stone wrenched from the wall itself. He lifted it above his head and hurled it at me.

As I leaped aside, he tore free another, and then another. At the third I had to roll desperately, still clutching my sword, to avoid the fourth, the stones coming quicker and quicker as the lack of those already torn away weakened the structure of the wall. By the purest chance, that roll brought me close to a casket, a thing no bigger than a modest housewife might have for her rings, lying on the floor.

It was ornamented with little knobs, and something in their form recalled to me those Master Gurloes had adjusted at Thecla's excruciation. Before Baldanders could pry out another stone, I scooped the casket up and twisted one of its knobs. At once the vanished mist came boiling out of the floor again, quickly reaching the level of my head, so that I was blinded in its sea of white.

"You have found it," Baldanders said in his deep, slow tones. "I should have turned it off. Now I cannot see you, but you cannot see me."

I kept silent because I knew he was standing with a block of stone poised to throw, waiting for the sound of my voice. After I had drawn perhaps two dozen breaths, I began to edge toward him as silently as I could. I was certain that despite all his cunning he could not walk without my hearing him. When I had taken four steps, the stone crashed on the floor behind me, and there was the noise of another being torn from the wall.

It was one stone too many; there came a deafening roar, and I knew a whole section of the wall above the window must have gone crashing down. Briefly I dared to hope it had killed him; but the mist began to thin at once, pouring through the rent in the wall and out into the night and the rain outside, and I saw him still standing beside the gaping hole.

He must have dropped the stone he had wrenched loose when the wall fell; he was empty-handed. I dashed toward him hoping to attack him before he realized I was upon him. Once again he was too quick. I saw him grasp the wall that remained and swing himself out, and by the time I had reached the opening he was some distance below. What he had done seemed impossible; but when I looked more carefully at that part of the tower illuminated by the lights of the room in which I stood, I saw that the stones were roughly cut and laid without mortar, so there were often sizable crevices between them, and that the wall sloped inward as it rose.

I was tempted to sheathe *Terminus Est* and follow him, but I would have been utterly vulnerable if I had done so, since Baldanders would be certain to reach the ground before me. I flung the casket at him and soon lost sight of him in the rain. With no other choice left to me, I groped my way back to the stair and descended to the level I had seen when I first entered the castle.

It had been silent then, uninhabited save by its ancient mechanisms. Now it was pandemonium. Over and under and through the machines swarmed scores of hideous beings akin to the ghostly thing whose phantom I had seen in the room Baldanders called his chamber of clouds. Like Typhon, some wore two heads; some had four arms; many were cursed with disproportionate limbs—legs twice the length of their bodies, arms thicker than their thighs. All had weapons, and so far as I could judge, were mad, for they struck at one another as freely as at the islanders who fought with them. I remembered then what Baldanders had told me: that the courtyard below was filled with my friends and his foes. He had surely been correct; these creatures would have attacked him on sight, just as they attacked each other.

I cut down three before I reached the door, and I was able to rally the lake men who had entered the tower to me as I went, telling them that the enemy we sought was outside. When I saw how much they dreaded the lunatic monsters who leaped still from the dark stairwell (and whom they failed to recognize for what they undoubtedly were—the ruins of their brothers and their children) I was surprised they had dared to enter the castle at all. It was wonderful, however, to see how my presence stiffened them; they let me take the lead, but by the look of their eyes I knew that wherever I led they would follow. That was the first time, I think, that I truly understood the pleasure his position must have given Master Gurloes, which until then I had supposed must have consisted merely in a celebration of his ability to impose his will on others. I understood too why so many of the young men at court forsook their fiancees, my friends in the life I had as Thecla, to accept commissions in obscure regiments.

The rain had slackened, though it still fell in silver sheets. Dead men, and many more of the giant's creatures, lay on the steps—I was compelled to kick several over the side for fear I would fall if I tried to walk over them. Below in the bailey there was still much fighting, but none of the creatures there came up to attack us, and the lake men held the stair against those we had left behind in the tower. I saw no sign of Baldanders.

Fighting, I have found, though it is exciting in the sense that it takes one out of oneself, is difficult to describe. And when it is over, what one best remembers—for the mind is too full at the time of struggle to do much recording—is not the cuts and parries but the hiatuses between engagements. In the bailey of Baldanders's castle I traded frantic blows with four of the monsters he had forged, but I cannot now say when I fought well and when badly.

The darkness and the rain favored the style of wild combat forced on me by the design of *Terminus Est*. Not only formal fencing but any sword or spear play that resembles it requires a good light, since each antagonist must see the other's weapon. Here there was hardly light at all. Furthermore, Baldanders's creatures possessed a suicidal courage that served them badly. They tried to leap over or duck under the cuts I made at them, and for the most part they were caught by the backhand that followed. In each of these piecemeal fights, the warriors of the islands took some part, and in one case actually dispatched my opponent for me. In the others, they distracted him, or had wounded him before I engaged him. None of these encounters was satisfactory in the sense that a well-performed execution is.

After the fourth there were no more, though their dead and

dying lay everywhere. I gathered the islanders about me. We were all in that euphoric state that rides with victory, and they were willing enough to attack any giant, no matter how huge; but even those who had been in the bailey when the stones fell swore they had seen none. Just as I was beginning to think they were blind, and they were no doubt ready to believe I was mad, we were saved by the moon.

How strange it is. Everyone looks for knowledge in the sky, whether in studying the influence of the constellations upon events, or like Baldanders in seeking to wrest it from those the ignorant call cacogens, or only, in the case of farmers, fishermen, and the like, in searching for weather signs; yet no one looks for immediate help there, though we often receive it, as I did that night.

It was no more than a break in the clouds. The rain, which had already grown fitful, did not truly cease; but for a very short time the light of the waning moon (high overhead and, though hardly more than half full, very bright) fell upon the giant's courtyard just as the light from one of the largest luminaries in the odeum in the oneiric level of the House Absolute used to fall upon the stage. Beneath it the smooth, wet stones of the pavement shone like pools of still, dark water; and in them I saw reflected a sight so fantastic that I wonder now that I was able to do more than stare at it until I perished—which would not have been long.

For Baldanders was falling upon us; but he was falling slowly.

XXXVII

Terminus Est

THERE ARE PICTURES in the brown book of angels swooping down upon Urth in just that posture, the head thrown back, the body inclined so that the face and the upper part of the chest are at the same level. I can imagine the wonder and horror of beholding that great being I glimpsed in the book in the Second House descending in that way; yet I do not think it could be more frightful. When I recall Baldanders now, it is thus that I think of him first. His face was set, and he held upraised a mace tipped with a phosphorescent sphere.

We scattered as the sparrows do when an owl drops among them at twilight. I felt the wind of his blow at my back and turned in time to see him alight, catching himself with his free hand and bounding from it upright as I have watched street acrobats do; he wore a belt I had not noticed before, a thick affair of linked metal prisms. I never found out, however, how he had contrived to reenter his tower to get the mace and the belt while I thought him descending the wall; perhaps there was a window somewhere larger than those I saw, or even a door that had provided access to some structure that the burning of the castle by the shore people had destroyed. It is even possible that he only reached through some window with one arm.

But, oh, the silence as he came floating down, the grace as he, who was large as the huts of so many poor folk, caught himself on that hand and turned upright. The best way to describe silence is to say nothing—but what grace!

I whirled then with my cloak wind-whipped behind me and my sword, as I had so often held it, lifted for the stroke; and I knew then what I had never troubled to think upon before— why my destiny had sent me wandering half across the continent, facing dangers from fire and the depths of Urth, from water and now from air, armed with this weapon, so huge, so heavy that fighting any ordinary man with it was like cutting lilies with an ax. Baldanders saw me and raised his mace, its head shining yellow-white; I think it was a kind of salute.

Five or six of the lake men hedged him about with spears and toothed clubs, but they did not close with him. It was as though he were the center of some hermetic circle. As we came together, we two, I discovered the reason: a terror I could neither understand nor control gripped me. It was not that I was afraid of him or of death, but simply that I was *afraid.* I felt the hair of my head moving as if beneath the hand of a ghost, a thing I had heard of but always dismissed as an exaggeration, a figure of speech grown into a lie. My knees were weak and trembled—so much so that I was glad of the dark because they could not be seen. But we closed.

I knew very well from the size of that mace and the size of the arm behind it that I would never survive a blow from it; I could only dodge and jump back. Baldanders, equally, could not endure a stroke from *Terminus Est,* for though he was large and strong enough to wear armor as thick as a destrier's bardings, he had none, and so heavy a blade, with so fine an edge, easily capable of cleaving an ordinary man to the waist, could deal him his death wound with a single cut.

This he knew, and so we fenced much as players do upon a stage, with sweeping blows but without actually coming to grips. All that time the terror held me, so that it seemed that if I did not run my heart would burst. There was a singing in my ears, and as I watched the mace-head, whose pale nimbus made it, indeed, too easy to watch, I became aware that it was from there that the singing came. The weapon itself hummed with that high, unchanging note, like a wineglass struck with a knife and immobilized in crystalline time.

No doubt the discovery distracted me, even though it was only for a moment. Instead of a quartering stroke, the mace drove downward like a mallet hammering a tent peg. I moved to one side just in time, and the singing, shimmering head flashed past my face and crashed into the stone at my feet, which cracked and flew to pieces like a clay pot. One of its shards laid open a corner of my forehead, and I felt my blood streaming down.

Baldanders saw it, and his dull eyes lit with triumph. From that time forward he struck a stone at every stroke, and at every stroke stone shattered. I had to back away, and back away again, and soon I found myself with the curtain wall at my back. As I retreated along it, the giant used his weapon to greater advantage than ever, swinging it horizontally and striking the wall again and again. Often the stone shards, as sharp as flints, missed me; but often too they did not, and soon blood was running into my eyes, and my chest and arms were crimson.

As I leaped away from the mace for perhaps the hundredth time, something struck my heel and I nearly fell. It was the lowest step of a flight that climbed the wall. I went up, gaining a bit of advantage from the height but not enough to let me halt my retreat. There was a narrow walkway along the top of the wall. I was driven backward along it step by step. Now indeed I would have turned to run if I had dared, but I recalled how quickly the giant had moved when I surprised him in the chamber of clouds, and I knew that he would be upon me in a leap, just as I had, as a boy, overtaken the rats in the oubliette below our tower, breaking their spines with a stick.

But not every circumstance favored Baldanders. Something white flashed between us, then there was a bone-tipped spear thrust into one huge arm, like an ylespil's quill in the neck of a bull. The lake men were now far enough from the singing mace that the terror it waked no longer prevented them from throwing their weapons. Baldanders hesitated for a moment, stepping back to pull the spear out. Another struck him, grazing his face.

Then I knew hope and leaped forward, and in leaping lost my footing on a broken, rain-slick stone. I nearly went over the edge, but at the last instant caught hold of the parapet—in time to see the luminous head of the giant's mace descending. Instinctively I raised *Terminus Est* to ward off the blow.

There was such a scream as might have been made if all the specters of all the men and women she had slain were gathered on the wall—then a deafening explosion.

I lay stunned for a moment. But Baldanders was stunned as well, and the lake men, with the spell of the mace broken, were swarming along the walkway toward him from either side. Perhaps the steel of her blade, which had its own natural frequency and, as I had often observed, chimed with miraculous sweetness if tapped with a finger, was too much for whatever mechanism lent its strange powers to the giant's mace. Perhaps it was only that her edge, sharper than a surgeon's knife and as hard as obsidian, had penetrated the mace-head. Whatever had occurred, the mace was gone, and I held in my hands only the sword's hilt, from which protruded less than a cubit of shattered metal. The hydrargyrum that had labored so long in the darkness there ran from it now in silver tears.

Before I could rise, the lake men were springing over me. A spear plunged into the giant's chest, and a thrown club struck him in the face. At a sweep of his arm, two of the lake warriors tumbled screaming from the wall. Others were upon him at once, but he shook them off. I struggled to my feet, still only half comprehending what had taken place.

For an instant, Baldanders stood poised upon the parapet; then he leaped. No doubt he received great aid from the belt he wore, but the strength of his legs must have been enormous. Slowly, heavily, he arched out and out, down and down. Three who had clung to him too long fell to their deaths on the rocks of the promontory.

At last he fell too, hugely, as if he were—alone and in himself—some species of flying ship out of control. White as milk, the lake erupted, then closed over him. Something that writhed like a serpent and sometimes caught the light rose from the water and into the sky, until at last it vanished among the sullen clouds; no doubt it was the belt. But though the islanders stood with spears poised, his head never showed above the waves.

XXXVIII

The Claw

THAT NIGHT THE lake men ransacked the castle; I did not join them, nor did I sleep inside its walls. In the center of the grove of pines where we had held our council, I found a spot so sheltered by the boughs that its carpet of fallen needles was still dry. There, when my wounds had been washed and bandaged, I lay down. The hilt of the sword that had been mine, and Master Palaemon's before me, lay beside me, so that I felt I slept with a dead thing; but it brought me no dreams.

I woke with the fragrance of the pines in my nostrils. Urth had turned almost her full face to the sun. My body was sore, and the cuts I had received from the flying shards of stone smarted and burned, but it was the warmest day I had experienced since I had left Thrax and mounted into the high lands. I walked out of the grove and saw Lake Diuturna sparkling in the sun and fresh grass growing between the stones.

I sat down on a projecting rock, with the wall of Baldander's castle rising behind me and the blue lake spread at my feet, and for the last time removed the tang of the ruined blade that had been *Terminus Est* from the lovely hilt of silver and onyx. It is the blade that is the sword, and *Terminus Est* is no more; but I carried that hilt with me for the rest of my journey, though I burned the manskin sheath. The hilt will hold another blade someday, even if it cannot be as perfect and will not be mine.

What remained of my blade I kissed and cast into the water.

Then I began my search among the rocks. I had only a vague idea of the direction in which Baldanders had hurled the Claw, but I knew his throw had been toward the lake, and though I had seen the gem clear the top of the wall, I felt that even such an arm as his might have failed to send so small an object far from shore.

I soon found, however, that if it had gone into the lake at all, it was lost utterly, for the water was many ells deep everywhere. Yet it still seemed possible that it had not reached the lake and was lodged in a crevice where its radiance was invisible.

And so I searched, afraid to ask the lake men to assist me, and afraid also to give up the search to rest or eat for fear someone else would take it up. Night came, and the cry of the loon at the dying of the light, and the lake men offered to take me to their islands, but I refused. They feared that shore people would come, or that they were already organizing an attack that would revenge Baldanders (I did not dare to tell them that I suspected he was not dead, but remained alive beneath the waters of the lake), and so at last, at my urging they left me alone, still crawling among the sharp-cornered rocks of the promontory.

Eventually I grew too weary to hunt more in the dark and settled myself upon a shelving slab to wait for day. From time to time it seemed that I saw azure gleaming from some crack near where I lay or from the waters below; but always when I stretched out my hand to grasp it or tried to stand to walk to the edge of the slab to look down at it, I woke with a start and found I had been dreaming.

A hundred times I wondered if someone else had not found the gem while I slept under the pine, which I cursed myself for doing. A hundred times, also, I reminded myself how much better it would be for it to be found by anyone than for it to be lost forever.

Just as summer-killed meat draws flies, so the court draws spurious sages, philosophists, and acosmists who remain there as long as their purses and their wits will maintain them, in the hope (at first) of an appointment from the Autarch and (later) of obtaining a tutorial position in some exalted family. At sixteen or so, Thecla was attracted, as I think young women often are, to their lectures on theogony, thodicy, and the like, and I recall one particularly in which a phoebad put forward as an ultimate truth the ancient sophistry of the existence of three Adonai, that of the city (or of the people), that of the poets, and that of the philosophers. Her reasoning was that since the beginning of human consciousness (if such a beginning ever was) there have been vast numbers of persons in the three categories who have endeavored to pierce the secret of the divine. If it does not exist, they should have discovered that long before; if it does, it is not possible that Truth itself should mislead them. Yet the beliefs of the populace, the insights of the rhapsodists, and the theories of the metaphysicians have so far diverged that few of them can so much as comprehend what the others say, and someone who knew nothing of any of their ideas might well believe there was no connection at all between them.

May it not be, she asked (and even now I am not certain I can answer), that instead of traveling, as has always been supposed, down three roads to the same destination, they are actually traveling toward three quite different ones? After all, when in common life we behold three roads issuing from the same crossing, we do not assume they all proceed toward the same goal.

I found (and find) this suggestion as rational as it is repellent, and it represents for me all that monomaniacal fabric of argument, so tightly woven that not even the tiniest objection or spark of light can escape its net, in which human minds become enmeshed whenever the subject is one in which no appeal to fact is possible.

As a fact the Claw was thus an incommensurable. No quantity of money, no piling up of archipelagoes or empires could approach it in value any more than the indefinite multiplication of horizontal distance could be made to equal vertical distance. If it was, as I believed, a thing from outside the universe, then its light, which I had seen shine faintly so often, and a few times brightly, was in some sense the only light we had. If it were destroyed, we were left fumbling in the dark.

I thought I had valued it highly in all the days in which I had carried it, but as I sat there upon that shelving stone overlooking the benighted waters of Lake Diuturna, I realized what a fool I had been to carry it at all, through all my wild scrapes and insane adventures, until I lost it at last. Just before sunrise I vowed to take my own life if I did not find it before the dark came again.

* * *

Whether or not I could have kept that vow I cannot say. I have loved life so long as I can remember. (It was, I believe, that love of life that gave me whatever skill I possessed at my art, because I could not bear to see the flame I cherished extinguished other than perfectly.) Surely I loved my own life, now mingled with Thecla's, as much as others. If I had broken that vow, it would not have been the first.

There was no need to. About mid morning of one of the most pleasant days I have ever experienced, when the sunlight was a warm caress and the lapping of the water below a gentle music, I found the gem—or what remained of it.

It had shattered on the rocks; there were pieces large enough to adorn a tetrarchic ring and flecks no bigger than the bright specks we see in mica, but nothing more. Weeping, I gathered the fragments bit by bit, and when I knew them to be as lifeless as the jewels miners delve up every day, the plundered finery of the long dead, I carried them to the lake and cast them in.

I made three of those climbs down to the water's edge with a tiny heap of bluish chips held in the hollow of one hand, each time returning to the place where I had found the broken gem to search for more; and after the third I found, wedged deep between two stones so that I had, in the end, to return to the pine grove to break twigs with which to free it and fish it up, something that was neither azure nor a gem, but that shone with an intense white light, like a star.

It was with curiosity rather than reverence that I drew it out. It was so unlike the treasure I had sought—or at least, unlike the broken bits of it I had been finding—that it hardly occurred to me until I held it that the two might be related. I cannot say how it is possible for an object in itself black to give light, but this did. It might have been carved in jet, so dark it was and so highly polished; yet it shone, a claw as long as the last joint of my smallest finger, cruelly hooked and needle-pointed, the reality of that dark core at the heart of the gem, which must have been no more than a container for it, a lipsanotheca or pyx.

For a long time I knelt with my back to the castle, looking from this strange, gleaming treasure to the waves and back again while I tried to grasp its significance. Seeing it thus without its case of sapphire, I felt profoundly an effect I had never noticed at all during the days before it had been taken from me in the hetman's house. Whenever I looked at it, it seemed to erase thought. Not as wine and certain drugs do, by rendering the mind unfit for it, but by replacing it with a higher state for which I know no name. Again and again I felt myself enter this state, rising always higher until I feared I should never return to the mode of consciousness I call normality; and again and again I tore myself from it. Each time I emerged, I felt I had gained some inexpressible insight into immense realities.

At last, after a long series of these bold advances and fearful retreats, I came to understand that I should never reach any real knowledge of the tiny thing I held, and with that thought (for it was a thought) came a third state, one of happy obedience to I knew not what, an obedience without reflection because there was no longer anything to reflect upon, and without the least tincture of rebellion. This state endured all that day and a large part of the next, by which time I was already deep into the hills.

Here I pause, having carried you, reader, from fortress to fortress—from the walled city of Thrax, dominating the upper Acis, to the castle of the giant, dominating the northern shore of remote Lake Diuturna. Thrax was for me the gateway to the wild mountains. So too, this lonely tower was to prove a gateway—the very threshold of the war, of which a single far-flung skirmish had taken place here. From that time to this, that war has engaged my attention almost without cease.

Here I pause. If you have no desire to plunge into the struggle beside me, reader, I do not condemn you. It is no easy one.

Appendix

A Note on Provincial Administration

SEVERIAN'S BRIEF RECORD of his career in Thrax is the best (though not the only) evidence we have concerning the business of government in the age of the Commonwealth, as it is carried out beyond the shining corridors of the House Absolute and the teeming streets of Nessus. Clearly, our own distinctions between the legislative, executive, and judicial branches do not apply—no doubt administrators like Abdiesus would laugh at our notion that laws should be made by one set of people, put into effect by a second, and judged by a third. They would consider such a system unworkable, as indeed it is proving to be.

At the period of the manuscripts, archons and tetrarchs are appointed by the Autarch, who as the representative of the people has all power in his hands. (See, however, Famulimus's remark on this topic to Severian.) These officials are expected to enforce the commands of the Autarch and to administer justice in accordance with the received usages of the populations they govern. They are also empowered to make local laws—valid only over the area governed by the lawmaker and only during his term of office—and to enforce them with the threat of death. In Thrax, as well as in the House Absolute and the Citadel, imprisonment for a fixed term—our own most common punishment—seems unknown. Prisoners in the Vincula are held awaiting torture or execution, or as hostages for the good behavior of their friends and relatives.

As the manuscript clearly shows, the supervision of the Vincula ("the house of chains") is only one of the duties of the lictor ("he who binds"). This officer is the chief subordinate of the archon involved with the administration of criminal justice. On certain ceremonial occasions he walks before his master bearing a naked sword, a potent reminder of the archon's authority. During sessions of the archon's court (as Severian complains) he is required to stand at the left of the bench. Executions and other major acts of judicial punishment are personally performed by him, and he supervises the activities of the clavigers ("those with keys").

These clavigers are not only the guards of the Vincula; they act also as a detective police, a function made easier by their opportunities for extorting information from their prisoners. The keys they bear seem sufficiently large to be used as bludgeons, and are thus their weapons as well as their tools and their emblems of authority.

The dimarchi ("those who fight in two ways") are the archon's uniformed police as well as his troops. However, their title does not appear to refer to this dual function, but to equipment and training that permits them to act as cavalry or infantry as the need arises. Their ranks appear to be filled by professional soldiers, veterans of the campaigns in the north and nonnatives of the area.

Thrax itself is clearly a fortress city. Such a place could scarcely be expected to stand for more than a day at most against the Ascian enemy—rather, it seems designed to fend off raids by brigands and rebellions by the local exultants and armigers. (Cyriaca's husband, who would have been a person almost beneath notice in the House Absolute, is clearly of some importance, and even some danger, in the neighborhood of Thrax.) Although the exultants and armigers seem to be forbidden private armies, there appears little doubt that many of their followers, though called huntsmen, stewards, and the like, are fundamentally fighting men. They are presumably essential to protect the villas from marauders and to collect rents, but in the event of civil unrest they would be a potent source of danger to such as Abdiesus. The fortified city straddling the headwaters of the river would give him an almost irresistible advantage in any such conflict.

The route chosen by Severian for his escape indicates how

closely egress from the city could be controlled. The archon's own fortress, Acies Castle ("the armed camp of the point"), guards the northern end of the valley. It appears to be entirely separate from his palace in the city proper. The southern end is closed by the Capulus ("the sword haft"), apparently an elaborate fortified wall, a scaled-down imitation of the Wall of Nessus. Even the cliff tops are protected by forts linked by walls. Possessing, as it does, an inexhaustible supply of fresh water, the city appears capable of withstanding a protracted siege by any force not provided with heavy armament.

G.W.

About the Author

Gene Wolfe was born in New York City and raised in Houston, Texas. He spent two and a half years at Texas A&M, then dropped out and was drafted. As a private in the Seventh Division during the Korean War, he was awarded the Combat Infantry Badge. The GI Bill permitted him to attend the University of Houston after the war, where he earned a degree in Mechanical Engineering. He is currently a senior editor on the staff of *Plant Engineering Magazine*.

Although he has written a "mainstream" novel, a young-adult novel, and many magazine articles, Wolfe is best known as a science-fiction writer, the author of over a hundred science-fiction short stories and of *The Fifth Head of Cerberus*. In 1973 his *The Death of Doctor Island* won the Nebula (given by the Science Fiction Writers of America) for the best science-fiction novella of the year. His novel *Peace* won the Chicago Foundation for Literature Award in 1977; and his "The Computer Iterates the Greater Trumps" has been awarded the Rhysling for science-fiction poetry.

The fourth and final volume of *The Book of the New Sun*, *The Citadel of the Autarch*, has just appeared in hardcover.

285

84